DESERT
REFUGE

DESERT REFUGE

CHERYL D. MURPHY

authorHOUSE®

AuthorHouse™
1663 Liberty Drive
Bloomington, IN 47403
www.authorhouse.com
Phone: 1-800-839-8640

Published by AuthorHouse 12/09/2013

ISBN: 978-1-4918-0862-7 (sc)
ISBN: 978-1-4918-0861-0 (hc)
ISBN: 978-1-4918-0863-4 (e)

Library of Congress Control Number: 2013914499

With heartfelt love and thanks
to my wonderful husband, John,
daughter, Mary,
my sisters, Carol and Martha, and mom, Veronica,
for all their care, understanding, and patient support;
and
With deep gratitude and love for the constant
encouragement, guidance, and friendship
of Sam and Pat Colenzo

Contents

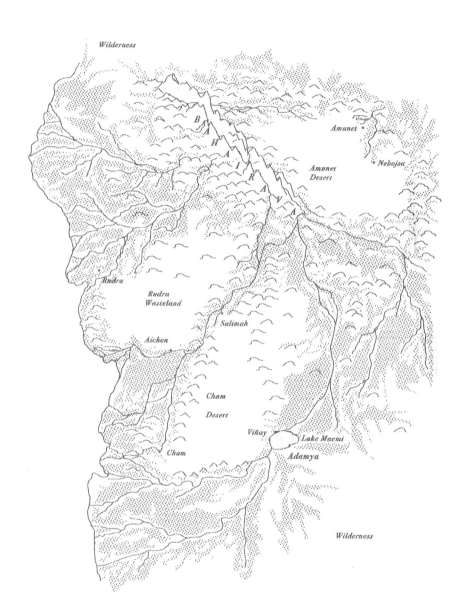

*"The spirit-souls of our beloved hover over Hidaya,
blessing and encouraging all who walk her pathways.
None are lost or forgotten even from eons past."*
~ *First Book of Instruction*

CHAPTER 1

❖

DESERT CALLING

Rawiya, the caravan storyteller, casually glanced at the novice retreatants scheduled to cross the Cham Desert with her this season. She mused wryly that they were swirling around her more than necessary probably enjoying the way their new robes billowed out. They all wore coarsely woven, voluminous, ankle-length desert robes for comfort and protection, which differed so much from the narrower robes or simple trousers of city and agricultural folk. The bleached, rough fiber of their robes would soften with desert wear and tighten to a soft, supple finish with repeated washing at the oases and daily use; at the end of their journey the robes would feel light and comfortably cozy, and would merely be loose-fitting, softly flowing garments. This was standard garb for someone on a pilgrimage on the planet Hidaya.

The travel agent's prattle, back at the crossroads city of Viñay, truly had inspired these pilgrims not just with visions of personal renewal, but with misleading descriptions of exciting adventures and breathtaking sights they were now anticipating to be revealed just beyond every thorny desert bush. Yet, even though the travel agent's promises were blatantly excessive, since not all crossings of the Cham were adventurous excursions into beauty or spiritual renewal, he had

1

successfully extracted money, waivers, contracts, and time from an eclectic number of individuals who had randomly tarried in Viñay.

As frantic late arrivals rushed to join the already chaotic assembly, Rawiya deliberately absented herself from amidst the organizational frenzy. She moved beside the restive travel beasts standing in a rough, impatient line calming them with crooned encouragement while observing the frenetic excitement from a safe distance.

Names were checked off, supplies, personal bedrolls and backpacks were tagged and given to runners who stowed the bundles on specified travel beasts by securing them in expandable leather packs slung behind the cushioned blankets upon which the travelers would sit for their rides between oases. Only when all belongings had been stowed properly were the pilgrims shown their assigned shaggy travel beasts. They were carefully given instructions on how to identify and treat the enormous animals; and finally the enthusiastic retreatants were directed towards public sanitary facilities for a last-minute comfort break.

Meanwhile, Rawiya had crooned and calmed her way along the travel beasts' ragged queue until she stood beside the last one. Cid, Rawiya's favorite travel beast, woofed warm air out at her through his large, hairy nostrils before nuzzling her shoulder. She caressed his velvety nose affectionately, and held her hand out flatly to him offering a sweet grain-roll, which his thick, sticky tongue immediately curled around, pulling it back into position for his stained molars to crunch and grind into a mushy, palatable paste.

"Don't roll your big, brown eyes at me as if you were surprised, you furry lunk! I know you've smelled this treat all across the city when the supply arrived yesterday. What you don't know is that it's doctored with herbs to limit *your* fragrance. Aha! If it works we may have to call you something else, you nasty monster."

The service-attendants were thankful that Cid was Rawiya's first choice of travel beasts though she ritually pretended to do them the favor of reluctantly choosing Cid for their benefit; but truly Cid's gait was one of the smoothest and most comfortable of any travel beast she had ever ridden, and that was a definite draw when traveling for several weeks. His name, unfortunately, had been justifiably earned because Cid — the abbreviated name for Rancid — tended to develop a sour stomach after several days of traveling. The foul fermentation subtly permeated his breath, flesh, and fur, and was distinctly released through his hide as well as through his flatulence. It wasn't strong enough to cause nausea or choking, but travelers tended to hold their breath and move away rapidly when near Cid. It was Rawiya's luck that she had a poor sense of smell and a hedonistic need for traveling comforts, including extra time to cleanse herself after riding Cid. That hygienic necessity often eliminated her from the tedious chores of unpacking at a new campsite for if she didn't carefully complete washing up after riding Cid she was sure to be avoided by the other travelers who found her as repulsive as her mount. For now, though, Rawiya scratched Cid behind his nervous, swiveling ears before turning back to idly observe the gradually quieting crowd of travelers.

Even though most guides, attendants and pilgrims by now were standing expectantly beside their travel beasts, there were still some spontaneously enthusiastic puppy-like yelps and hurried errands. Almost everyone had gathered shapeless hoods or swaths of veiling around their heads in the pre-dawn chill so their faces were hidden in deep shadows even though the overhead energy panels lighting the plaza glowed gently above; but there were also a few overly-thoughtful novices who wore woven, wide-brimmed, shading hats for the daytime anticipating that they would need the protection when Bozidara, the day star, had risen and had begun to shine warmly on them all.

"Thrilling. Just thrilling," Rawiya mumbled grumpily to herself looking at these mobile cocoons. "Where are the fashion consultants when you need them?" But she shrewdly felt her belt to be sure her own shade-hat was securely attached, and then also pulled up her hood.

Nurtured with a raw sense of adventure fed by exhilarating naiveté, neither even remotely touching upon reality – at least not the reality Rawiya lived – the unlikely pilgrims listened with guides and service attendants for one last check-off before departing as the scheduled caravan retreat into the soon-to-be-springtime desert. Dawn was still a distantly gentle prospect when they mounted their travel beasts and hustled away from the sheltering gates of Viñay to disappear beyond a scuffed-up dusty cloud into the darkness.

Rawiya muttered to herself as she pulled her own well-worn robes around her ample form more securely and settled into Cid's furred padding. Now that they were free from the township's confinement, her own shadowed visage resentfully stared impatiently at the backs of her charges as they strung themselves irregularly in front of her. The grape-seed oil she had excessively rubbed over herself after the last herbal bath she would have for several weeks made Rawiya's umber-hued skin glossy in smooth richness. Her wiry, black tresses were securely coiled into a tightly braided knot at the back of her head. Simple ear-lobe rings of silver and a tiny, antique silver medallion hanging from a black cord around her neck were her only ornamentations. With a broad forehead now furrowed with last-minute concerns, and her usually full, up-turned lips distractedly pinched into a thin, flat line, Rawiya shifted her attention from the riders themselves to the rear ends of the lumbering travel beasts as they all became distorted with her emotions. Rawiya's large, brown eyes were over-bright with tears anxious to be shed, but were hurriedly blinked into submission by her long, curved eyelashes. Some personal concerns had been left unresolved back in Viñay.

The irony of being part of this renewing retreat event was that Rawiya had counted on the cancellation of this season's caravan hoping for several weeks to herself for her own personal needs; but the skillful travel agent had, in the end at the last moment, earned his commissions, and here they all were together facing several hours of dark, star-guided journeying before full daylight and rest were gifted.

As the initial exuberant whoops and chatter heralding their departure quieted, the monotonous motion of the travel beasts rocked the riders back into the dreams they had quit abruptly to reach the departure gate on time. Later, even the dawn's rosy, golden rays and tentative warmth didn't waken them.

When the caravan arrived at the first oasis by mid-morning, the experienced attendants quickly dismounted and began to set up the campsite. Most of the pilgrims revealed their inexperience with travel beasts; their stretched, sore muscles cramped up from the unfamiliar strain and exercise, and the majority of the novices dismounted merely by falling clumsily to the uncushioned ground. Rawiya turned away to hide her snickers at their inadvertent comedic antics. She grimaced realizing that as usual with so many tenderfoot pilgrims on this journey the schedule would require adjustment.

Recovery for these desert neophytes would take the remainder of the day at the very least, but Rawiya wanted to impatiently hurry through the entire retreat and have it be done with completely. Those temporarily suppressed personal issues of hers gnawed quietly at the back of her consciousness. Taking care of the retreatants's needs would distract her for a while, but those issues would eventually need to be addressed. The postponement could be considered either a regrettable delay or a blessed detour for the time being. Since patience was not a strong point, Rawiya merely sighed deeply and patted her thanks to Cid before handing the reins to the waiting service attendant.

She chose a site at the far edge of the clustering tent village now efficiently being erected by focused attendants and jocular retreatants. After skillfully setting up her own tent, Rawiya feigned deep concentration while repeatedly organizing her supplies and checking off items on useless lists, ignoring the chaos around her with a distracted expression crowning her face. If she appeared busy she could possibly avoid nonsensical small talk or worse, being tagged by senior guides or supervising attendants for loathsome tasks since she had not yet washed the dust from the journey. There was a definite bit of rebellious sloth in her attitude. When it looked as if most of the chores were completed, Rawiya slipped off to cleanse herself before a mid-day meal was called for.

Meanwhile, unable to dodge their own responsibilities, attendants led the travel beasts to a large pool shaded by heat-tolerant palms and 25 meter nurse trees providing a protective canopy for the other various trees and shrubs beneath. The travel beasts would not be fed until their body temperatures had cooled sufficiently, and though they were used to that delay, that didn't stop their obvious begging with indignant bellows demanding food. Until then they were watered and tethered in a rough curve so they could visit or grumble amongst themselves until their food was served.

Another pool of gently bubbling spring water on the western edge of the oasis was set aside for the exclusive use of the bipedal travelers. Several attendants split the retreatants into more manageable groupings to help unload personal baggage and settle them into their tents. Then guides gathered any idly loitering pilgrims into small classes teaching oasis etiquette, basic safety procedures, desert biome facts, and introducing the majority of plants and animals they might encounter at this oasis. Of course, most of the pilgrims were primarily interested in personal comfort – latrines, food, water, cleansing, and rest – but after a generous period of respite, the attendants patiently repeated their teachings and presented new information to more interested and attentive participants.

The first spring rains hadn't arrived yet, and most trees were still barren silver-green trunks and stems with nothing of interest to gawk at. Other trees shone as if polished as the daystar reflected off their waxy trunks and sparsely-leafed branches. Raggedly torn, dry-thatched bark swaddled the squat brittle tree trunks, shelving-bark woof trees, and spiceberry trees spread heat-scorched, dry leaves on shaggy branches stretching to Bozidara's golden light. A few gray-green spikes pushed through the sand, and various succulents and cacti claimed space between small-leafed, fragrant spindle-bushes and thorny scabbed shrubs. The outwardly dry appearance of most of the oasis plant life still created the overall impression that an immensely, unlikely crystalline emerald stopper of flora floated above a hidden, natural cistern of living spring water in the midst of harshly baked bleakness. The boundary between actual desert and this oasis appeared abrupt and unnatural.

Even here in this lush oasis the desert's spring blooming was a mere expectation in this mild pre-season. The higher, almost intolerable temperatures usually started after the brief springtime, but in the meanwhile, the evenings were definitely expected to be chilly. The nights could produce skimpy frosts and stiffened morning joints from the cold; but by afternoon the heat varied from merely uncomfortable to oppressively life threatening.

Already many tired and discouraged tourists regretted their impulsive choice of presence here after a cursory survey of the oasis boundaries, but they were too uncomfortable and weary to complain. The afternoon heat of the day boldly claimed the world from horizon to horizon, and so after a hurried and simple mid-day mean and quick wash up, all the travelers spent the silent afternoon in mercifully shaded, exhausted sleep.

When all the hustle of unpacking, rearranging, and settling-in subsided into muted, rhythmic, somnolent breathing patterns, curious dust-lizards emerged from behind camouflaging fronds and foliage. They crept closer to examine the newcomers, and gazed motionlessly at the pilgrims from within scant centimeters, scrutinizing faces inquisitively and intensively. Soon the tiny dust-lizards were joined by flamboyantly iridescent mock-scorpions. These more agitated newcomers twittered haughtily at the lizards conversationally and were answered by muted, rasped comments gurgled from deeply within the lizards' elongated throats. Silent glass beetles, dirt burrowers, sand spiders and silken fliers peeked around tent flaps shyly, and then scurried or flitted away in giddy merriment to spy on other pilgrims.

The pompous mock-scorpions scuttled around pallets, pillows, bundles, and bags, examining the contents by folding back coverings with their enlarged pincers and peering intently into packs, before loquaciously disclosing their discoveries with high pitched, self-important twitters to anything near. Meanwhile, the dust-lizards stared statically for many long minutes, seldom blinking as they studied the sleepers. Their lateral ear-pans vibrated rhythmically as they took in the information relayed by the garrulous mock-scorpions, eventually giving guttural acknowledgement they had heard. Finally, their curious examinations concluded, the dust-lizards darted off to report to the patient, emerald carapaced cockroaches that maintained the oasis. When the dust-lizards had shared their last morsel of information, added onto by other little intrusive beasties, they retired into the virescent shade for the remainder of the long afternoon until twilight, leaving indistinct footprints in the dirt as the only evidence of their presence.

A spectacularly brilliant setting of Bozidara graced the retreatants' awakenings. Refreshed by their naps, they ambled about idly enjoying re-energized attitudes. As nightfall deepened, they were surprised at the efficiency with which the first evening meal was prepared while the deep universe unfurled its starry banner overhead. Ishwa, the teacher, gathered them together when Cook sent a messenger advising him that the meal would be served shortly.

When the pilgrims had seated themselves around the campfire, Ishwa gave a brief welcome and overview of their retreat. He encouraged them to get to know each other, and to respect the uniqueness of them all, and then after a moment of silence thanking the Compassionate One for blessings received, he announced that their supper was in the final phase of preparation. Then, sauntering over to introduce himself to an elderly couple, Ishwa began conversing. His lighthearted laughter soon wafted over to Rawiya on the night air.

She had quietly slipped into a gap in the informal circle of talkative pilgrims waiting for supper. The volume of the tumultuous banter around her pulsed erratically, rising and falling chaotically in contrast to the steady, self-restrained stillness of the oasis behind and around them. Rawiya winced as the retreatants brayed and bellowed trying to conquer the wilderness quiet by slaying it with obtrusive garrulity. "I forgot how annoying some novices can be," she breathed in frustration.

Two thin youths on her right leaned over her — ignoring the discomfort and disrespect given to her as they traded greetings with three shapely girls on her left, sharing enthusiastic tales of what friends back home had seen on their own desert retreat last season: awesome scenery, exotically gross travel beasts, unbelievable insects and fauna, and the incredible variety of plants encountered. Rawiya made a sound at the back of her throat that resembled a crude gag reflex, and the youths straightened up abruptly. "Uh, 'scuse me. 'You all right?" One of them inquired as he leaned back into his place.

"Why, yes, thank you. I take it that this is your first retreat. The first for all of you?" Rawiya asked gesturing inclusively at the girls. There were head-bobbing assents, and then Rawiya led the conversation in a polite manner more suitable to her mood than the bouncing, bounding energetics of the young. Still, even while adeptly fulfilling her role as hostess, her eyes wandered to skim the rest of the circle.

The white-robed travelers sat upon thick, fibrous mats that kept the granular dirt temporarily out of their food and clothing. The campfire, fueled by dried dung, was bright enough to discourage marauding predators from bothering them should there by any, but as the desert chill began settling after dusk, the firelight also flickered like a gentle caress across faces and fabric with its yellow-orange warmth and gave wavering form to what almost seemed to be restless, encircling spirits.

Soon attendants processed towards the campfire from the cook-tent bearing steaming bowls of tempting vegetables, stew, and grains. There was enough food with variety to overcome prudent guidelines, and satisfied sighs echoed around the camp circle. The meal pleasantly proceeded with some high-spirited mischief committed, and then the lads and lasses decided to escort each other to the latrines before returning to the campfire. Rawiya watched them stumble to rise and then grab at each other for support before they giggled and wandered off. She nodded directively to perceptive veteran attendants who caught up with the youths to make sure they got to their destination and back safely without detouring assignations. Meanwhile, Rawiya gathered up her supper bowls for the assistants to collect.

Set apart in the campfire circle, now, no longer rubbing shoulders with elbow-nudging diners, Rawiya again pulled her own white robe protectively around her in a characteristic gesture. Her long-held impatience with the rude comments and habits of the exuberantly unaware youths escaped in a half-hearted grumble to herself – a rare insult for her. "Thoughtless tourists."

One of the passing veteran assistants distributing after dinner cleansing towels overheard Rawiya, paused with a frown, and then smiled encouragingly; misunderstanding her mood.

"It's always like this at the beginning," he whispered close to her ear. "You know that!"

"Yes, but I always forget," Rawiya sighed back to her companion, letting his misperception of the cause of her foul temper pass without correction. "Starting out is the hardest part because all I have to work with at the beginning is hope."

"Ahh, yet hope is always a good starting point. It's all about hope! Why complain about having to start again especially when we are surrounded by hopefulness? And where would we be if we didn't do this for a living?" he queried mostly to himself with a self-satisfied chuckle. Rawiya knew that even before she had become part of caravan life this attendant himself had been one of the white-robed novices. As a result of his own desert experience he had chosen to join the caravan as a permanently hired attendant. He remembered his retreat in great detail, a blessing few retreatants could boast of because the intensity of the retreat often caused the memories to be erased, though the benefits continued. That probably accounted for the wildly unreal accounts of their adventures once they returned home.

"Blind trust has led these travelers to a place of growth and healing. They will be renewed and given wisdom in the Cham. Let these novices have the experience," he admonished gently before moving on to continue his care-giving and comforting attentiveness. Rawiya glared foully at his back and enjoyed momentary sulkiness before lapsing into the peaceful relaxation one slips into when well fed, comfortable, and fully sated. She found herself idly and amusedly watching the conversation and movement around her without feeling the need to participate as hostess.

Many guests were running their tongues over their teeth trying to work out pieces of stringy, tough vegetable threads. From the pained expressions, some were also already silently suffering from gas caused by that same fibrous feast. They probably would be the ones who would soon leave to visit the camp latrines she wickedly mused, absently betting with herself on the time needed before she was called on to fulfill her job tonight.

Since this tour had been advertised as an "Inspirational Desert Retreat," and these travelers expected guidance through the magnificent sites and legendary, mystical experiences that were part of the Cham Desert's history and intrigue, the plan was that as their little caravan trekked steadily across the sparse landscape towards the township of Cham on the other side of the desert, the guide, teacher, and healer, Ishwa, would lead them across seemingly death-touched wastelands that were strategically dotted with awesome rock formations, unexpected canyons, and vibrant oases. They would spend two weeks traveling across the Cham to greet the first spring rains and to witness the incredible jewelling of the desert with wildflowers when one week was more than sufficient for travel. But then, these were pilgrim retreatants who needed ample time to explore and discover, rather than hurriedly and expediently rush across the desert like panicking, sandstorm-driven granules on a fierce schedule to find rest.

There were to be daily inspiring conferences and individual counseling by calm and perceptive Ishwa during their layovers at the oasis refuges, environmentally educational workshops would be given by their assigned attendants throughout the day, and in the evenings Rawiya would tell the traditional history of the planet for the evening's entertainment.

All travelers knew the history Rawiya told, but they listened to it with fresh ears for many facts were not described as they might be in a textbook. This was her gift to them.

Here, right now, they walked, ate, rested, and defecated along the same path trod by revered heroes. They would soon see the same painted canyons reverenced and awed ancestors had seen, step over the same scorched sand dunes and hard dirt *they* had, and would see the desert bloom overnight with a plethora of brilliant, short-lived wildflowers before the desert returned to its seemingly unimaginative self with no visible evidence of their passing just as *they* had. And perhaps, some of the rarely revealed, mysterious charisma of the Cham Desert would be gifted to their perceptions.

Already the glazed, far-away looks of some of the relaxing pilgrims revealed they were lost beyond the glow of the present campfire, imagining themselves to be part of an ancient camp encirclement wherein sat the noble and the brave, instead of – *themselves!*

"Actually," Rawiya sighed begrudgingly to herself, surreptitiously scanning the chatting travelers; "Actually, they are doing better than most groups at the end of their first day." It was difficult to maintain a critical attitude when so many possibilities and mysteries were imminent. The enticing invitation of the Cham wheedled itself past her negative barricades until she gradually capitulated to be completely united with the flow of life around her without realizing she had done so.

It was almost time for the storytelling, but the signal had not yet been given to her to start. Rawiya popped another nutty morsel from the remains of her dinner into her mouth, and crunched on it loudly, before drinking expertly from the water skin at her side, swishing the water over-noisily around her mouth, and gulping it down with a deliberately rude, glugging sound. If the sound alone didn't exasperate many watchers, their envious lack of coordination with their own water skins did; their clumsy handling of the water skins caused precious water to dribble down onto their chests instead of into their parched mouths. She knew that by the end of the retreat they would be proud experts at this skill, but in the meantime this hand-to-mouth frustration annoyed her guests causing her great satisfaction as she scanned their mutinous expressions.

Ishwa interrupted her droll thoughts by slowly brushing leftover crumbs from his chest and sleeves. Short of stature, leathery skinned, almost stringy in appearance- except for that slight hint of a paunch – Ishwa strolled slowly around this expectant group joking and distracting the daydreamers back to the present with queries of comfort. His slight limp was hardly noticeable, but Rawiya knew that any movement involving his right hip caused pain. Ishwa pointedly ignored the pain by blessing it away as an intentional offering for those Hidayans in need. His "walk of welcome," as he called it, was Rawiya's cue to begin soon.

She indulged her perversity by allowing the listeners to wait long enough so they had become slightly more than impatient, the degree determined by the number of reshifted derrières and over loud sighs trying to non-verbally inform her that they had paid for this journey, they were uncomfortably bored waiting, and so now, because of their personal wants, she should accommodate their expectations and get on with the program. Even the youths who had returned and sat down within the circled lowered their voices with anticipation.

At that precise juncture, while pretending indifference to their non-verbal cues, but noting that Ishwa had melted into the shadows beyond the camp fire circle, Rawiya deliberately rearranged her own robes so she could focus on the story without distraction while extracting as much pleasure from their unsettled attitudes as possible beforehand. Her resettling was her non-verbal cue to them that they needed to calm down even more and get themselves comfortable.

Now, Rawiya deliberately suppressed any distracting thoughts with modestly downcast eyes and measured breathing, and then serenely looked up intently searching every face, every eye for some unknown, and yet unfound recognition before spinning the legend.

The First Night:

"We are all Hidayans living under the light of Bozidara and our three sister moons. There are some similarities among us because we are all Hidayans, but we each value life in our own individual and remarkable ways. Why? Why are there so many contrasting ways to perceive life? 'Others' lives, our own lives, plants, animals, word, actions, and events? Why are there so many contradictions in perception, direction, respect, and response?

"As Ishwa hinted this evening before our meal, everything we perceive about life is individual. How we live life is partly shaped by the words and examples given to us by others. Those guiding experiences are all as divergent as are our own responses. And yet, despite all those differences, there is something else that is both the same and dissimilar: the Compassionate One knows us completely as we truly are, and gifts us with the freedom to be true to our selves if we choose.

"In ritual and prayer we call the Merciful One by extraordinary names and use uncommon descriptions that reflect the distinctive values in our own homes and cultures, but we are known to the Understanding One as individuals with the same true name.

"To the Knowing One, we are all called Beloved. To the Compassionate One, we are loved and lovable. All of us without exception are found worthy of life, for to the Understanding One we are precious, wanted, and welcomed forever. Even if our choices and actions are dark and unloving, we each are still unconditionally loved.

But that is not always how we perceived ourselves on Hidaya. It may not even be how you have learned to perceive yourself or others now.

"Insects may frighten us and often are killed because they may be neither wanted nor welcomed. Animals may not be wanted or welcomed in our homes or in the countryside around us. Some people may not be wanted or welcomed into our homes and neighborhoods, either.

"Hidaya's history includes many unwelcomed peoples, but to Hidayans ten of these unwelcome individuals are personally important to us; we all have chosen to cross the Cham Desert this season because they crossed it. Because of these ten unwanted persons we are here where we can remember that we are always wanted and welcomed. Tonight we will start that story in Aichen."

"Ah!" The collective inhaling of breath rewarded Rawiya. Her listeners knew the importance of this town in Hidaya's history.

Aichen's protective walls were crumbling. Over the decades the Aichenites had not repaired or even spot-patched the mud plaster that should have smoothed the gaps between the inner rocks and rubble that formed the wall. Households that abutted the wall often increased their storage space by gouging out shelves and niches, leaving cavities as weaknesses in the main enclosing walls. Weathering wore away the mud plaster naturally; complacent citizens idly noted the resultant mounds of gravel, rocks, and sifted dirt that fell below chinks, slots and holes. The base of the wall within and without was lined with these piles of accumulated detritus, but passersby's chose to avoid personal responsibility to mend the breaches, as did the city governors. Because of this, the walls encircling Aichen appeared to be concave, accidental structures, and the town seemed to be thrown together without plan. The town looked like litter thoughtlessly discarded at the side of the road, reflecting the attitude of the people within its boundaries.

Aichen's dirt-dusty town streets wound without plan like a maze. However, if travelers kept mostly to the right after entering the main southern facing gateway, making sure to keep the deteriorating walls within sight as often as possible, turning repeatedly away from the niched shrines to various divinities, they would come to the eastern gateway that welcomed gaming and rough sport of all sorts. It was here that the cock arena could be found. This day an insignificant servant of that arena again frustrated his manager as he had every day since he had been casually hired.

"Bankim! Ya worthless piece o' scum! Get over here an' pick up dat pile of feather an' bones!"

Bankim skittered breathlessly into the cock arena and scooped up the loser of the fight when its owner abandoned it angrily. It fluttered feebly and died in Bankim's arms trying to peck and scratch with its final, brief rally, but Bankim with all his eight years of life was experienced. He held the cock by its stretched neck facing away from himself. This fowl didn't require the effort, but had it had more fight in him, Bankim would have twisted its neck automatically. Often, losing fowl would be given by their owners to the nearby street cooks for a last meal before returning home the poorer after paying debts.

Bankim was short, scrawny, and dressed in impossibly filthy rags. Though his thin legs bowed a bit, he was quick. Bankim didn't bother to answer the arena master just like he didn't respond verbally to anything directed at him by anyone else. Most aficionados of game cocking thought he was mute because he just followed directions. That was one of the ways Bankim held onto his job. He saw and heard much, but shared nothing.

Bankim's employers liked to call their fighting ring, "clean" even though blood, shredded feathers, droppings, spittle and other litter mixed with the sawdust-covered ground within the arena. It was "clean" because bets were promptly paid and enforcers protected bettors from their own greed, cheapness, and from the adrenalin enriched testosterone flooding their blood-sport focused bodies.

Already the gamblers were placing their bets on the next cockfight while others were collecting their winnings or paying their debts. Bankim ran off and hunkered down behind several broken fence boards under the bleachers in a natural cave out of sight of the arena. A small, rusty fire-burner warmed a dented, metal pot filled with idly moving, greasy, yellowish gray water. Another steaming pot settled in a scooped out nest next to the weak fire-burner to gather cast off heat for its debris crusted water. Into this pot Bankim pushed the now dead cock so that the heated water would make the feathers easier to pluck. The smell of wet feathers gagged him, but before long the naked fowl would be floating in the other pot.

"Damn ya, Bankim! Get out here! If ya don't start watchin' when da bouts are done, I'm gonna get another runner. That's right1 Ya better move yer little butt faster! Oh, ho! Look out!"

Bankim erupted from his cave and scuttled into the arena to grab up the latest loser which neither the owner nor his attendant were willing to claim. But this losing cock had more life in him than the last, and rose up unexpectedly and valiantly to scratch blindly at anything to survive. Deep wounds and gashes opened up on Bankim's forearms, thighs, and chest, the cock's talons bypassing Bankim's skillful defense maneuvers, and causing him to step back stunned, dropping the defiant bird. His shocked distraction had kept him from wringing the fowl's neck.

It was another boy avidly watching the sport beside his father who dashed around the arena fence to help. He snatched up the protesting fowl before Bankim could respond, and twisted its neck all in one motion. The rooster's head lolled to the side. The new boy stood in the arena grinning arrogantly with the limp cock held up triumphantly in both his hands. Laughter and cheers were his reward.

"Bankim, yer done. Git outta here fer good. Ya, boy, ya wanna job? Will yer pa 'ere let ya work?" The father, his argumentative attendant, and the arena master huddled together while the boy and Bankim stared blankly at each other for long moments. Bankim looked down eventually at the blood dripping from his now-stinging slashes, and shrugged before turning and stumbling across the sawdust towards his cave. In his hidey-hole he tipped over first one and then the other pot of steaming water, though keeping the fowl's body floating in a bit of it own thin fluids in the latter pot. He wrapped torn cloth scraps around the hot handles so he could hold onto them, and kicked dirt over the fire to smother it. Carting his load in shaking hands he headed for home. Though dismissed, he still had successfully provided another meal for his pa.

Outside of all of Aichen's arched gates squalid squatters' camps had existed long before the walls had even been completed. The rough huts, shacks, and lean-tos were made of whatever unwanted and mislaid materials could be scrounged, scavenged, or stolen from other building sites and refuse heaps. Cleansing rain may have run off the buckling and sagging roofs, but it puddled and spilled into open sewers criss-crossing the camp. The unclean stench was nauseating.

Bankim deftly trotted through this maze of squatters' hovels and shallow trenches, balancing himself on rough boards and large rocks that served as sidewalks. Abruptly he stopped behind one shack and listened. His pa wouldn't be expecting him home at this time, and it was always safer to get the feel of the place before stepping into unnecessary difficulties.

His pa's scratchy voice was haggling with someone. "Heeza good worker. 'Fas', too. 'Don't talk ta much cuz 'e's a bit stupid, but if 'e does talk, jus' hit 'im ta shut 'im up. Dat way ya don' hafta 'ear dumb talk dat muddles yer mind. But 'e's worth ever' coin yer givin' me." There was an assenting grunt and a clinking sound as coins were passed into his pa's hands. "'E's da pit boy at da cock ring. Yull fin' 'im der. If 'e's not out in da front, look in da back unner da bleachers. 'E's gotta place der set up ta rest in 'tween da fights." There was a long silence while Bankim waited in shock trying to figure out what to do while his pa squinted after the men leaving the squatters' camp on their way to the cockfight arena.

"Ya bes' come 'round 'ere, boy. I knows yer der."

Bankim slunk around to the front of the shack with a shiver while still clutching his pots. His father looked at him from his dirty mat, and smiled benignly showing brown, pitted teeth within his dribbling mouth. Apparently forgetting what the deal he had just made meant to Bankim, he jingled the tin coins in his rough, swollen hands with delight. His puffy, red face had been pushed in twice by nature to make room for watery, bagged eyes that shifted back and forth nervously before focusing on Bankim.

"Go ta Still Water an' get me a jug of 'is bes'. Take dis one coin fer pay."

His pa hadn't even asked him why he was home early nor had he commented on the clotting crimson stripes drying on Bankim's stained arms, legs, and dirty, thin torso. Bankim slowly put the pots down in front of his father and stood with uncertainty. Was it life as usual with him bringing back whatever kills he could so there would be food, or had his father betrayed him? His thoughts fogged over increasingly.

"Take it!" his father hawked as he threw a coin into the dirt. "Get movin' or yull learn ta move when I tell ya wit' da back of m'hand!"

Bankim snatched up the coin from the dry dirt and ran in and out of the rough shelters in the general direction of Still Water's business. There was always a market for a product that fogged the memories of so many lost in disappointing lives, but Still Water brewed a quality drink in comparison to what often caused a retching death. Often it was the more prosperous citizens inside the wall who sought out his jugs.

Slowing to a walk, Bankim finally warily sidled up next to the gurgling still. The owner himself, Still Water, sat where he was usually seated, but today his hemp mat was not only exceptionally clean, but decorated with parallel wavering green lines. He was not alone either, for Bankim could see him formally serving a cup of his best brew to an unknown elder. If the vendor had just rearranged the mat or merely had shaken off the dirt then this person would be important, Bankim thought. That Still Water had cleaned and adorned the mat and now offered formal hospitality to this Hidayan meant that he was extraordinarily important. Bankim gaped at the elder in awe and curiosity.

The vendor snapped his fingers sharply at Bankim acknowledging that he was aware that Bankim waited at the edge of his "land." The elder meanwhile studied Bankim while concernedly sucking in his lips at the barely clotting blood criss-crossing the boy's body. Stinging wasps hovered nearby barely waiting to feast on the oozing wounds where flies already walked boldly. The vendor gestured for Bankim to come forward and to sit before him at the edge of the clean mat. With merely a nod, and without any words spoken to him, Still Water got up and returned with a gourd of warm water and reasonably clean rags. The elder reached out silently to take one of Bankim's bloody arms and started to tenderly cleanse the deep scratches. Still Water did the same with the other arm. Nothing was said while Bankim's chest, arms and legs, one by one, were sponged clean, salved with an ointment that numbed the burning edges of the wounds, and then wrapped in clean rags. A deep bowl of hot broth was handed to Bankim who by now was slightly feverish and light headed besides being totally confused by the attention.

Still Water and the Hidayan elder continued their conversation in an unfamiliar language. It had to be the universal trade language called Chi'ma and not the local vernacular Bankim idly thought. He only knew the rough, limited guttural vocabulary of Aichen. Carefully placing the now-empty bowl on the mat, he nodded his thanks and stood shakily. He stumbled to the closest open sewer to relieve himself, and afterwards was stymied of where to go now. He shrugged his thin shoulders, and boldly returned to Still Water's mat and sat at its edge. His thinking was fuzzy and unfocused.

The elder paused in the midst of his conversation to look at Bankim shrewdly. His voice lowered to shield his words from neighboring squatters. "I am Lord Che'ikh. What's your name, boy?" He had to ask twice before Bankim realized that the elder was speaking words he understood and really expected an answer.

"I'm Bankim cuz I'm 'alf o' what my pa wanted in life, an' cuz when I started ta walk, I couldn' do it straight. I walked crooked-like wit bendy legs. Pa said I would always be 'alf-priced cuz I was worthless: so I am Bankim"

"So, you believe this now. Do you want to have a different life, Bankim?"

Bankim pondered that question emptily. "I don' know what dat'd be. Pa jus' got paid by some men fer me, and dis 'ere's part o' it fer a jug of yer best pa said." Bankim held out the coin to Still Water, who slowly picked it from Bankim's tiny, now-cleansed, but swollen and swaddled hand.

"I guess I'd like ta 'ave things differen', but I don' know 'ow," Bankim concluded dizzily. His whole body was throbbing with hurt, and his eyelids heavily settled lower. Spittle dripped unchecked from the side of his open mouth. He slumped drowsily to the mat hearing the elder and the vendor talk for a while in hushed voices, and then there was Bankim's pa yelling above him angrily. Still Water said something soothing and offered his pa three jugs for the price of one, and three times as many coins to be exchanged for Bankim. His pa could now repay the men for the price they had given, and his pa would still have extra money. Bankim heard his pa muttering to himself as he left without even saying good-bye, and then he felt the elder, Lord Che'ikh, and Still Water gently prop him up in a slight reclining position.

"Boy, do you really want a different life, something better than this?" the elder asked, gesturing to the clutter, filth, confusion, stench, and unfulfilled hope around them.

Bankim nodded sleepily trying to focus on the faces of the two men. There seemed to be a filmy cloud between them and himself. He nodded again looking up at them as they shuffled around to reposition themselves so their actions would not be spied on by neighbors, and then Bankim gasped in terror.

Both Still Water and the elder, Lord Che'ikh, had raised their hands above him; Bankim shrank and tensed himself for the punishing blows that he expected to fall on him. Instead he uncomprehendingly watched as their synchronized hands lowered to gently touch his disheveled head before rising and tracing the Blessing of Mercy in the air above him. The glowing trail of that sign hovered almost invisibly in the daytime air and Bankim stared at it stupidly. But then Lord Che'ikh and Still Water were signing above him again, and this was the Blessing of Belonging and Acceptance.

"Young one," the elder whispered in his ear, "We are leaving this very night for a better life. You have been found, and have wisely chosen a different life. You have been blessed with mercy, sanctuary, and welcome. Your name in this new life is Dato, Beloved One.

Rawiya covertly surveyed the nodding heads around the campfire. The reflected firelight in Ishwa's half-open eyes belied his actual alertness, though he himself pretended to be as fatigued as the other travelers.

Catching his eye, and imperceptibly nodding in agreement, Rawiya yawned over loudly, before abruptly announcing, "It is time to end. Your beds await you. Visit the latrine now while the firelight guides you there and back. Take no food into your tents, and light the smudge candles at the entrance to discourage the wildlife of the desert. The teacher will now ask for blessings of peace and protection as you sleep."

Grumblings similar to that of sleepy children stubbornly denying their weariness greeted this announcement, but Ishwa's imposing form standing now before the fire with raised hands forestalled a crescendo of protest.

He spoke in a language unknown to the retreatants calling with gratitude upon the Compassionate One for blessings received asking for guidance and courage to accept that guidance. Then his hands of blessing rose higher, and all bowed to humbly and sleepily receive the gift of mercy. Few dared to raise even their eyes until Rawiya and Ishwa's rustling robes passed beyond the campfire circle, but the impatiently quick were rewarded to see spirit-sparks fall downward into the flames; and their surprised gasps alerted others too late to see anything extraordinary. Nevertheless, one by one they all staggered to their feet and towards their various destinations at the end of this first, very long day.

"Knowing one's future does not take the place of risk to take one more breath or one more step to make that future real."

~ *First Book of Instruction*

CHAPTER 2

❖

DESERT INTRODUCTIONS

As Rawiya had anticipated, deciding to stay over an extra day at the first oasis to avoid extreme travel discomfort was announced before Ishwa's morning conference. They would ease into the schedule gradually because many retreatants were not used to riding the travel beasts and limped painfully. Initially this was a pleasantly received decision, but then the attendants insisted that each pilgrim stretch their muscles regularly throughout the day and participate in scientific excursions within and at the edges of the oasis. When an argumentative recalcitrant held up his group's activities defiantly by refusing to exert himself — an unofficial spokesperson for many - the imposition of severe penalties for his entire group was threatened. The altercation was observed and the consequences avoided by the other pilgrims.

"Peer pressure can be a blessing," murmured Ishwa to Rawiya who was also observing when the attendants chastised the mutinous rebel as he attempted to bluster his way out of a stretching exercise. When that didn't alter his willful balking, amenities were withdrawn from his group. "May he soon experience wisdom in their reactionary wrath."

"I thought you were non-violent!" Rawiya mumbled back. "Now I find that you are merely a bloodthirsty throwback to our ancestors.

What did the ancients call it? Ah! Mob justice! You would enjoy the mob turning on him to teach him a lesson as well as to disguise their own agreement with his protests."

"Hardly a mob, but still we are not that far advanced from them," Ishwa soberly judged. His sudden somber attitude surprised Rawiya momentarily before she brushed it away.

"Look," she whispered nodding towards the group. The rebuked rebel complied by stomping along with the rest of the hikers now, but his crinkled brow and outthrust lower lip made him look like a toddler reluctantly distracted from a temper tantrum. "We truly are sometimes made wise by fear of our peers."

Ishwa squinted at her, his wide brimmed, Bozidara-shading hat shadowing his visage. "Have you been sampling the medical supplies? What wisdom do you see there? He could have just as easily been joined in rebellion by the rest of his group, and then the entire purpose of this retreat would have been sabotaged. They might all prefer to be relaxed noodles instead of hiking around in this heat if they could. Peer pressure would mean we continually would have to slow down for all the aches and pains because they wouldn't be ready to travel, and they wouldn't know what to do just to keep themselves alive unless they were babied along."

"Phst, make up your mind about social pressure, and save your contrariness for someone else," was Rawiya's dismissal before she ticked off her points on her fingers. "We all need the rest, but we also need to be fit enough to continue this journey. We all need the stretching and we all need the information for our survival. Private coaches and tutors are not always available when we feel like it. And when we feel like it, it may be too late. In the meantime, this defiant "child" won't test his group again without thought. He has learned that though he is respected as a person, he is not so important than all the others around him should be burdened unnecessarily by the consequences of his uncooperative choices. He has learned that sometimes he must do things that are good for himself even when he doesn't want to. And because he is marked as a rogue and a trouble-maker, when he tries even just to relieve himself there will probably be someone to monitor him so he won't slink off back to his tent."

"Your logic is flawed," Ishwa whispered back in hushed argument. "He is complying out of fear of the consequences, as are most of his courteous fellow-travelers. His wisdom, if you can call it that, is primitive. When he chooses to participate for his own benefit because he wants to and not because he *should*, then we can start talking about wisdom. In the meantime he is as wise as a child who won't steal a candy only because he knows his hand will be swatted and he will be embarrassed."

"And *your* pessimistic viewpoint, Ishwa, is flawed because even though he acts as if he has made a wise choice while fuming because he was prodded into going along with someone else's decision when he would rather go his own way, the acting "as if" will lead to deeper thought and belonging. It is one way he can save face in front of the others."

"It's a trade off. It would be convenient if we all agreed, but sometimes a wise choice means to rebel, and sometimes it means to conform."

"Ishwa, when you argue both sides of any issue, I am frustrated."

They paused to refocus themselves and the silence between them stretched into calmness.

"What was your morning conference about today?"

"We spoke about healing energy that touches the body and the soul and constantly embraces and encircles us. We discussed how no one can limit or divide the compassion of the One. We closed with acknowledging that compassion and wisdom involve relationships. This is an active group that shared rather openly, even their disagreements and personal examples were not held back."

"The openness usually takes a bit of time. That they shared so quickly is unusual."

"Yes, but it is welcome. They accepted their private meditation homework willingly."

"Do you think they will complete it as some of them are like our friend there who balks and fights directives he doesn't like?"

"Rawiya, do you really wish to continue our previous discussion?"

"No, but you still sometimes confuse me. To keep our relationship balanced I need you to eat something or take a nap. You can do your exercises later since you already know the content of the lessons. Rest and get over your contrariness."

Rawiya's tone of authority momentarily took Ishwa aback, but then he mischievously asked, "And what are you going to do while I separate myself as elite and 'special,' not needing to stretch or include myself in any lessons?"

"I am going to join that group to watch the dynamics unfold. It should be entertaining," Rawiya shot back wickedly.

"I think you have judged me by your own standards. It is you who enjoy blood sport," Ishwa ruefully intoned shaking his head sadly. The playful twinkle in his eyes belied his true feelings.

"If you don't take a break now, you will have proven me just that, and you may become an active participant in a blood sport you weren't expecting," Rawiya threatened with enough vehemence to make Ishwa wince before ambling good humouredly off to his tent. Meanwhile, Rawiya snorted loudly at Ishwa's retreating back, and then turned to join the closest group of pilgrims listening to an attendant describe which plants could not be eaten at this oasis.

The day casually unfolded with fresh discoveries of flora and fauna. "Look here!" was often a tourist's entreaty when a remarkable leaf shape or shiny, metallic-carapaced beetle emerged from the sparse foliage or from underneath the sand itself. Quick-scuttling dust-lizards or ominous looking mock-scorpions with glittering, iridescent scales entertained and mesmerized the Hidayan retreatants more completely than any professional stage drama could possibly attempt. Even the reluctant rebel was seen excitedly pulling another retreatant aside to show off a discovery of his own.

After a light mid-day meal, Bozidara glared more forcefully as if trying to scorch all life, attempting to immolate everything in purifying golden heat. "If this is late winter," complained one pilgrim, "Spring will probably kill us." The enthusiasm to continue making discoveries waned and rest time was observed without exception throughout the caravan. Few of the native reptiles and insects ventured into the camp because the retreatants could now recognize their filigree-like footprints.

A short while before Bozidara dipped behind the distant coastal hills to the west, a curious thrumming sound wafted through the stifling, shimmering air. The travel beasts shuffled with increasing anxiety, and bellowed their angry nervousness. It was that beastly, distressed roaring which startled the travelers awake.

The odd thrumming grew louder until it was heard as a whirring sound. Ishwa and Rawiya, along with the other seasoned attendants, had already awakened in expectancy at the first distant sounding, and now stood side-by-side facing the eastern sky, where an ever-changing cloud of dark fliers neared the oasis.

"Are they locusts?" asked a breathless girl with wide, fearful eyes.

"They are bats!" an elder pilgrim declared with disgust.

"No," Ishwa answered, "But they are some of the gifts of the Cham Desert. Locusts and bats are like us, a mixture of givers and takers. These gifts for us are givers."

"Bats are caretakers," Rawiya added simply. "But these are desert birds. We are gifted this trip; gifted as always."

"Oh! Are they coming here for the night?" By now Ishwa and Rawiya's words had been repeated endlessly with ever-growing excitement like a tidal wave's coursing unstopped across the ocean's surface.

"Yes," Ishwa shortly responded. "The desert fliers have sensed our presence in the Cham – their home – and until we leave they will follow us. And prepare for us."

By now the whirring sound had become the distinct whooshing sound of hundreds of wings rhythmically flapping purposefully towards rest and roost. Curiously, the sound also heralded the enlivenment of the sand itself. Throughout the oasis fingerling sand worms emerged, wriggling free from the granules, and rising up like short candlesticks offering themselves in the evening light. The travel beasts stomped nervously and renewed their distressed, baleful bellowing while cries rose from the pilgrims. "Ugh! Disgusting!" But astonished gasps quickly replaced repugnance. "Oh! Look! The fliers are eating them all!"

They raptly watched as tiny, nondescript, brownish-gray birds swarmed over the oasis from the east to devour the unresisting, self-offering worms. The birdlets' cheeps and chirps were deafening as they foraged voraciously until they were sated, and then soared up to the highest branches of the oasis canopy where they started to obsessively preen themselves. The display was awesome. Then unexpectedly, they all hushed *en masse.*

The dramatic silence of the oasis commenced simultaneously with Bozidara's bright, ochre rim touching the edge of the distant silhouetted hills and gradual sliding beyond sight; unusual luminescence transfigured the sky with white light before dimming to dusky, evening softness. Astonished attentiveness muted all thought and movement in momentary quietude; and just as abruptly, it ended. The chirruping resumed along with the preening, courting, and jostling above. Travelers lowered their astounded examining eyes from the sky to wondrously stare into the eyes of others near them. "It's as if Hidaya itself took a breath and held it for a moment!" gasped a portly matron.

"I never noticed it happening before," countered another desert neophyte. "But then I am a city dweller. Perhaps it is the Breath of the Imminent One as some other travelers have called it. But what about the birds?"

"They are here as always," cryptically repeated an attendant to no one in particular, before starting the preparations for the evening meal.

"Yes, they are here," a more veteran attendant thoughtfully responded to himself. "They are here, but never before in this manner of appearance." Then he shuffled off to calm the still-anxious travel beasts.

Later, even though the excitement caused by the arrival of the desert birds had not waned, other moods related to tiredness, travel, and timing surfaced throughout the day, and were expressed in peevish complaints by dinnertime.

"What that storyteller told last night was not new. I was bored long before she ended," grumbled one traveler to another, deliberately loudly enough so that Rawiya could hear twelve paces away. Apparently the birdlets in the dark branches above could hear and understand, also, for there were responding discomforted rustlings and sleepy cheeps of reproach.

"But I never heard it told that way before. Still, maybe we should go back now before we get too far into the wilderness," the other suggested tentatively. "We can get a refund, I'm sure."

"If we do get a refund," crabbed the first speaker. "I want all of my money back, not some pro-rated percentage for this, this falsely advertised waste of time and money!"

More rustling and soft cheeps came from above.

The pilgrims' low-voiced discontent continued to rumble on while they ate and defiantly eyeballed the other retreatants around the campfire. From their perspective, the others in the caravan all seemed low-class as they all sat uniformly clad in the same dusty, white robes, on the same kind of woven hemp mats eating the same savory stew without consideration of importance, preference, or want. There was accommodation for dietary needs, but those specialized dishes were presented quietly, without singling out that retreatant. This undifferentiated respect and consideration was discomforting to some.

Tonight there was a hearty leguminous stew with a multi-grain side dish to sop up the gravy, and a vegetable that looked suspiciously like the weeds that had grown near the path before they had left Viñay for the wilderness. But even Rawiya wisely didn't question Cook outright.

The stew's legume base probably is what was leftover from last night's dinner, Rawiya judged, and the recipe was actually tasty and satisfying. As for this boorish traveler, Rawiya could, of course, curse him resentfully, confront him openly, think derogatory thoughts about him, or dismiss him as a chronically annoying and unimportant complainer. But that was not her way – at least not now. Now, she preferred to bless; perhaps he was in need of more blessings and inspiration than he was capable of accepting, and thus would accept none openly. She would watch this one more closely and bless him more intently because of his needfulness, and if there was no improvement his apparent joy in complaining would be addressed. The others listening to him could also use some immersion in positive thoughts and beneficial intentions directed towards them, Rawiya thought, for she knew complaining was a contagion.

This night's historical installment would be longer than the first-night introduction, which had been overlong in itself, so Rawiya didn't wait for dinner to end. Her telling began at that one point in the meal when most pilgrims were just starting to relax with fullness, were less inclined to talk, and were ready to be distracted.

The Second Night:

Most Hidayans want to live in peace and safety and happiness. They optimistically elect representatives who will intentionally make decisions providing their people with ways towards achieving basic, life-giving goals, protection, and moral direction honoring all life. But even with these good intentions, pessimism or egocentric perversions arise to dissolve the edges of these humble, honest objectives. Greed, self-centered thoughtlessness, success without effort, and power lusting ruins and corrupts many good intentions. Still, we Hidayans keep trying to gratefully live in peace and safety to enjoy what blessings are around us in spite of challenging difficulties.

In this morning's conference Ishwa reviewed some of those planet-wide difficulties experienced by our ancestors as written in our historical texts, and what they mean to us now; our own personal wisdom advises us that we ourselves will encounter difficulties of our own that challenge us in how we Hidayans will honor others and ourselves.

Centuries past, Hidaya experienced unforeseen natural havoc and planet-wide devastation caused by ravaging natural events and politically manipulated, annihilating global wars. Far reaching lava flows from "dormant" volcanoes, horrific earthquakes and equally frightful aftershocks, oceanic tidal risings and tsunamis demolishing communities far from the shoreline, monstrous hurricanes and tornadoes of immense dimensions all destroyed much of Hidaya's worldwide civilization and livable landmasses.

The shifting of the magnetic pole destroyed communication systems as well as confusing migrating mammals, fish, birds, and insects; extremes in weather killed crops and many people. So much and so many were lost! And then the final political intrigues and grabs for world domination and control of water, mineral and land rights encouraged the use of weapons that obliterated, scorched, and sterilized great stretches of once-populated and fertile land.

The remnant communities of Hidaya deliberately tried to change the surviving world for the better, realizing that even with incredible diversity amongst people petty in-fighting could be minimized and prevented from expanding; there was still the possibility of mutual respect and co-existence. This was their collective hope rising from moral, spiritual, and physical debasement like a Phoenix struggling to find life above its ashen nest. The different Hidayan communities collectively chose to bless all Hidayans inclusively as a means to demonstrate that mutual honoring for the benefit of all life, even if that betterment was merely superficial at times for biases can linger well beneath awareness.

Curses, resentments, threats and violence against others always bounced back to despoil those who initiated them; therefore blessings, good intentions, and prayers of healing would attempt to replace expressions of frustration, bigotry, and exclusive self-importance. Perhaps habits of blessed intentionality would become reality.

Of course, there was contention before that collective Hidayan choice. Doubters of the value of intentionally focused blessings and petitions could and can always recall examples of seemingly unanswered prayers – or answers that were gifted years after they had been uttered. But what could they perceive of a single moment in time when Hidayans, groaning collectively in pain, despair, and well-founded apprehension, longing for a thread of hope to touch and trust, prayed their individual private prayers unknowingly *en masse*, simultaneously placing themselves in covenanted surrender before a deep, cosmic, sentient Intention-of-Healing? Within one concentrated nanosecond of unplanned, unitive request, they had touched and linked with a responding Someone whose essence flowed and linked from within themselves to the deep universe beyond Hidaya's atmosphere.

Presence was immediately felt, inviting fantastic coincidences and incredible possibilities to appear in personally apparent responsive ways. Yet, Hidayans still felt defeated by their own personally and historically repetitive self-inflicted dysfunctions. They still submitted to bitter temptations of accepting themselves as a despairingly and unchangeably flawed crude species. Could this Presence lead Hidayans through and beyond the defeatism so often referred to as realism, so that when Hidayans stopped perceiving themselves as victims of inevitable genetic, familial, racial, and cultural defects, actual change and abundant blessings could be the reality experienced for all?

Elected officials tried to stretch that altered perception to enlarge on the blessings and the benefits for their constituents. Speech, writing, art, action, and attitude – all were gently and consistently, nudged towards the felt guidance of the Presence, not to homogenize individual and cultural uniqueness, but to harmonize them. Even with guidance from the Compassionate One, that was a tenuous balance, which at times became overburdened one way or the other. If not in fact, at least in ideal, that balance was honored in recovered communities, typically such as Amunet, trying to overcome the developmental limitations imposed by the race's allurement towards self-important hierarchy.

"We know this," resentfully muttered a young girl fresh out of school and bored with the whole re-hashing of academics.

"But did you hear just now? Amunet." her companion hissed.

"She said that? The storyteller said, 'Amunet?' Are you sure? I didn't hear that."

"Who could hear with you sighing and snorting?"

"I was not," the girl harshly hissed back.

"Right. Think! Amunet."

"I know, I know!"

Rawiya heard restless, rustling sounds around her, and glanced upward at the stars. Their brilliant sparkles had not completed even a quarter of their sweep through the heavens, but the story so far had been somewhat dry and academic. "Perhaps I should continue tomorrow night. We can start with Amunet tomorrow evening because it is so late."

An anguished, protesting moan rose up from the circle. They breathed the name, "Amunet," letting it hover in the air like a morning lake mist.

"The telling of Amunet is long. We can continue another night…" Rawiya hinted more strongly, receiving more vehement protests.

"Perhaps a convenience break would be appropriate before our storyteller continues," suggested Ishwa tactfully.

This was accepted, and stretching, water breaks, and latrine visits were enthusiastically accessed. By now, the evening desert air was chilly. When the travelers returned to the campfire, many hugged their knees and huddled closer. Some had slipped into their tents and now wore an extra insulating tunic underneath their white robes. One or two pulled the protective hoods of their robes over their heads while they shivered closer to the firelight. When they were finally safely nestled like chicks under a mother hen's wings, Ishwa barely lowered his eyelids as Rawiya's cue that all were refreshed and ready to continue while the stars twinkled above.

Amunet lay inland, on one of the more fertile continents of Hidaya. The stubbornly clinging out-post city of Amunet had been built upon the rubble of a previous metropolis, as were all recovered cities. Building something new upon ruins was an exercise in hope as well as spiritual necessity for well-being.

Multi-storied dwellings carefully built of both stone and adobe rose within thick, boulder-fitted walls, for those were the materials available within walking distance when Amunet had been newly founded. Now, service businesses – retail merchants selling jewelry, metal work, yarns, textiles, books, finished clothing, leather goods, ceramics and other more expensive items - occupied the street level stores, as well as seamstresses, tailors, plumbers, ferriers, butchers, restaurateurs, and the like, all of which supplemented the large, tumultuous out-door farmers' markets hemmed by arched pavilions which had been built strategically throughout the planned city streets. All citizens had access to all resources it was hoped, and by using Chi'ma, the universal trade language of Hidaya, all citizens of Amunet could be reasonably understood while retaining their own languages and dialects.

Small inns, one-room dwellings, medical and well-being consultants, personal artisan studios, meeting rooms and classrooms took up space in adobe apartments above the foundational street level enjoying breathtaking views over the city walls of rich, fertile fields, darkly lush forests, reflecting lakes, and gurgling streams originating in distant blue hills – all regenerated over the recent decades with incredibly intensive effort. Dusty roads spider-webbed out from the three main city gates of Amunet, providing boring entertainment for idle eyes watching the moderate number of travelers to the somewhat isolated metropolis.

Indeed, life was reasonably stable within the city, but few strangers, or new trader-caravans enjoyed the picturesque journey needed to reach Amunet's cautious residents for travel between cities was naturally hazardous. Those who did come guarded their tongues and diaries, keeping the profitable knowledge of this and other isolated urbana shrewdly to themselves. Those who spoke without discretion often disappeared despite the best intentions of Hidaya's global representatives, for constructive change seldom moved uniformly through towns, societies, or individual hearts.

Below the street level - though the lush view was lost - were more expansive residential dwellings accessed by curving flagstone stairways and long labyrinthine avenues. Arching keystoned supports upheld the rounded, concave roofs of the subterranean corridors which were cleverly constructed using the fitted stone pavements traversed by pedestrians above-ground, thus duplicating the by-way plan above and below.

Batteries and generators built from past technology were stingily shared from municipal resources with the general population, and despite the ideal that all resources should be equally accessible to all citizens, those dwelling in the avenues below ground were often the most likely to be gifted with recovered technology, for they were the more stable residents whose families had occupied the same rooms for a generation or more. Thus, air-circulating fans were more prevalent in the lower levels, and small glowing globes that dispelled most shadows and feelings of weighted claustrophobia gently illumined the corridors and subterranean apartments.

An added benefit to underground housing that often offset the cave-like tightness and windowless security, was that some of the generational inhabitants mined and tunneled stealthily below their flooring for relics and trade artifacts, and discretely replaced displaced foundational supports moved during explorations. That entire enterprise was often overlooked because of the benefits of the discoveries.

"That's how my grandfather's export-import business started," murmured a stout matron to her neighbor. "He was from Amunet in the beginning. It was he who found the machines and energy sources that could read the library disks."

Her companion nodded obligingly, but distractedly trying to simultaneously listen to the storyteller while imaginatively thinking of the complex details involved in moving dirt around so that foundations weren't compromised. "Hush," she unconsciously uttered to her astonished friend.

"But..."

"Hush," the command came from several impatient voices nearby them this time, and the talkative matron subsided temporarily into a resentful silence before being drawn into the story again.

Muffled sounds softly echoed unceasingly through these restricted residential avenues though idle pedestrian traffic was discouraged. Actual residents and service people with specific destinations were anticipated to be the only visitors to these depths. In any section of the city's tunneled residential walkways it was important not to be noticed if one didn't live here or have a legitimate purpose to be present below street level. Municipal servants kept citizens safe from the few inevitably curious itinerants by making frequent tours through the avenues to keep them cleared of unexpected and unacceptable visitors.

Though welcome and respite was formally extended to all Hidayans, it was difficult to practice that welcome when confronted with having to share one's own egocentric inner comfort and convenience. However, the eccentric or socially divergent elements in Amunet *were* officially tolerated though they distracted the self-righteous average citizens; they were included just as one would matter-of-factly accept that one had a virus, an allergy, or a sprained ankle to overcome.

As with many spiritual efforts which don't thrive in ungrateful over-abundance, intentional mindfulness and blessing of others became mere empty ritual in Amunet. Respectable, privileged, short-memoried citizens of Amunet often were indignant when the sounds, smells, and essential obligations to the homeless stranger, orphan, less fortunate, or emotionally or intellectually needful imposed on their own resources. That their ancestors just a few generations past had flourished because they themselves had been welcomed though strangers, orphans, and definitely needful unfortunates, eluded their present grasp of hospitality now that they were comfortable. The repugnant sources of their discomfort were often illegally sent beyond the protective stone walls encircling Amunet, a clear violation of Hidayan life-honoring codes. That the carved statues of Amunet's protective goddess and local representative of the Blessed One, cut into every cornerstone, guarding every doorway and intersection, gazed down upon these severe, immoral dismissals of individual worth was ignored.

Another violation against those codes lay in isolated labyrinths far beneath Amunet's storage caverns. Though travelers thought Amunet's name was originally derived from its out-of-the-way, somewhat hidden location, a more recently developed reason literally lay below the city's foundations which explained the absence of this garrulous lout or that unnecessary tinker, this big-eyed merchant or that prying stranger, this fatherless child or that scandalous irritant. Slavery existed here as a hidden municipal resource newly within the lifeline of the present contented generation. Strangers or citizens could be gathered up legally and declared *sudasi*, or life-servant, because searching for useful artifacts amidst ancient, deeply-buried rubble was profitable, the more so if wages were dispensable. As with the private residents' excursions, municipal leaders shored up hollows created by archeological digging to maintain the stability of the city above, disguising and glossing over the wrongness of imposed life-long servitude by pointing out how smoothly daily life gradually had improved for Amunet's citizens in recent years. Discussing the value and importance of one individual life versus the common good was not encouraged.

Rawiya paused here to raise her water skin for a drink. The pause opened a brief moment for listeners to change position, attempt their own water break, or stand to stretch. A lanky youth sitting next to a stout matron studied his fingernails closely, inspiring the older woman to divert her attention.

"So how did your family start out?" she burbled conversationally.

"My grandparents on both sides were jewelers. They also came to Amunet, but after a few years moved on when my great-uncle disappeared. From what is passed down, he was hard to get along with. He also 'borrowed' some rare jewels from one of his brothers, and lied about it. The next week he disappeared. We think...."

"Oh, don't!" the older woman put her arm protectively on the youth's arm. However, a thin man on the other side had been eavesdropping and gasped, "Oh!" before scooting further over to the other side of his mat.

Ishwa watched this interaction from the shadows beyond the fire-circle. "Despite our best intention, 'I'm better than you!' slips in unless one is on guard constantly," he thought. Ignoring muffled movement in the branches above, he shifted his weight before looking to Rawiya to continue.

Extensive recovered records of past history showing that problems could be alleviated using that historical knowledge were ignored in Amunet. Officially pretending problems were adequately and appropriately addressed but would probably disappear by themselves, or were make-believe stories to manipulate those presently living was commonly accepted, so the symptomatic presence of problems exhibited by chronically unhealthy or homeless persons was quickly erased from view in prosperous Amunet. City servants, enforcing unwritten directives, gathered unwanted or nosy strangers quickly. Over time, citizens welcomed forgetting unpleasant memories of confrontations that really were of such short duration they might have been mere momentary fantasies, unless one became one of those pariahs hustled away. Fear kept most citizens quiet; muck-raking rabble rousers were swiftly swept into oblivion, and elders saw with moist eyes what they had worked hard to achieve undermined by fear, apathy, self-seeking, and self-comforting hedonism. An undercurrent of apprehensive uncertainty and oppressive anxiety pervaded Amunet despite its high ideals and luxury.

Global Hidayan enforcer detachments protecting Hidayan rights often did not have the resources to investigate rumors of violations or to timely intervene when violations were confirmed; eventually, however, the planetary envoys and representatives would rotationally visit all cities and had authority to "clean up." Until that time, Amunet's round up of unwary candidates and routing of reluctant chosen ones who attempted to conceal themselves until they could escape life-long servitude as *sudasi* quietly continued. Few challengers of the injustices, and fewer strangers tried to hide themselves, though, because any efforts to evade capture seemed hopeless from the start.

Yet, in one of the slightly shadowed doorways disturbing the barrenness of a wide stretch of one stony corridor below the street level, a bony, scraggly waif struggled to stifle her shuddering sobs until she merely whimpered imperceptibly. She was well aware that finding shelter where she was unwelcome was tricky and dangerous in itself.

"Ah!" gasped many listeners now. The storytelling touched here upon someone else they knew specifically from their history lessons. But the dry telling of historical facts in textbooks had barely alluded to personal details. Even the retreatants whose thoughts had wandered far afield were now brought back abruptly by the audible sucking in of breath by so many around them. All were unconsciously leaning forward in anticipation to hear better what had been glossed over through educational expedience.

The child crouched in as small a space as her small body could enfold itself, breathless, as if waiting for some impending disaster roaming the corridors to seek her out as it had relentlessly done to many of her mouse-pack companions. Listening to the relative silence magnified by withheld breath, she strained to perceive even the slightest scuffling sound, almost suffocating herself in overwhelming terror to hear.

There were other rampaging thoughts, too, for hopeful, trustful, desperately terse requests of the Merciful One for guidance, and despairing, surrendering pleas for death's firm closure, and stoic, rebellious resolve to fight rather than grovel in humiliation swirled in endless confusion. Eventually exhausted, she shut her eyes seeking and securing a safe haven even if it was only within herself momentarily. Her breathing slowed as the minutes gathered her sleepily towards the innermost core of her being where she perceived that her soul was protectively centered. There, in what she called her "heart room," the Compassionate One and the little one met in peaceful, safe Presence.

Softly, and then more urgently, voices intruded on her quiet interlude that bordered somewhere between trance, sleep, and total disassociation. The tiny one's focus faltered and she found herself outside of her "heart room" following the sound and meaning of words just as one might idly follow the progress of a sluggish barge down an equally lethargic river without being aware of one's attention to the movement.

Still hugging herself into smallness, the elfin girl paused, distracted from her internal journey between terror and refuge. Despite the danger that she might be discovered eavesdropping, she listened at the decoratively grooved wooden door beside her, occasionally scratching thoughtlessly at the crawly things in her matted hair. Unlike anything she had heard before, the muffled voices on the other side of the door spoke calmly for surprisingly extended periods, without the thundering belligerence or sharp-edged sarcastic cackling she was used to ruining the halcyon mood; occasionally there was burbling, enthusiastic laughter, but that was not intimidatingly over-loud either.

What the little one was unable to identify, yet was immensely intrigued by, was the unfamiliar attitude of heartfelt mutual respect and trustful reciprocation woven in and out of the overheard conversation – all of which could be sensed, but not named, as no verbal labels for those values existed in her fragmented vocabulary. And there was something else curious in those voices: kind, encouraging acceptance inviting the other participant to be just that – an active, joyful participant. Though huge portions of the muffled conversation were impossible to understand, the tone was always clearly apparent, and as such, was totally foreign to the curious, miniscule listener.

At first confusion overwhelmed her just as heavily as an unanticipated wave might pound down upon the unwary sand-castle digger on the shore, washing all meticulous efforts towards the immensely formless, foaming ocean and simultaneously, momentarily wiping clean any self-awareness with gasping shock. And then, gradually, tenuously, the girl's breathing cautiously stabilized; her tensed, shivering muscles relaxed, and the tiny listener allowed herself to sleep again and deeply dream unusually hopeful, peaceful dreams centered on something incomprehensible.

She awoke long hours later from an overdue, exhausted sleep to find herself loosely curled within the luxurious embrace of a huge armchair upholstered in some sort of deep brown, soft leather that caressed her skin soothingly more like brushed fabric than cured animal hide. The compliant cushion upon which the girl slowly unfolded herself was gently warmed by a low, steady fire centered nearby within an ancient, tiled hearth whose soot-stained depths sucked the twirling, wispy smoke lazily upwards through a hidden flue, allowing it languorous escape from the chuckling flames below. The polished wood floor glowed with smoothly reflected firelight.

Incomprehension of what she perceived upon waking in such lavishness caused the mite of a girl to sit yawning and involuntarily stretching thinking she was still dreaming. But consciousness inevitably bloomed, and the child's muscles twitched before spasmodically tightening in spite of the relaxing warmth of the room. Wit returned to her with fearful suspicion.

Silence – except for the muffled crackling from the flickering glow before her – filled her ears. And then from the center of her being emerged that part of her self which stood in for her when her meager personal resources were challenged: the little one became motionless as the inner strength of her being emerged, leaving her fear-filled identity behind in shadowed, hidden safety. Protectively, her self-defending consciousness smoothly slipped into action to analytically confront the obviously imminent threat of unknowingness surrounding her.

Her brightly bold, hazel eyes cautiously scanned the walls ruled with floor-to-ceiling bookshelves crammed with well-used, leather-bound tomes. A gap here and there was rare, and volumes, reflecting the unsteady firelight, were often stacked sideways over the tops of the shelved books. There were no windows, of course. A partially opened doorway led to bathing and other necessary facilities. There was only one other door to the medium-size rectangular room that she presumed was the exit. If the room was a trap, it was a comfortable one – excessively opulent by her standards. An empty armchair – a twin to the one she occupied – angled towards her showing by its proximity that it had once been host to someone who felt comfortable with whomever had originally sat in her present throne.

The diminutive orphan skillfully reconnoitered the room with widened, astonished eyes, and found it safely empty of others. There was no apparent immediate threat. Looking across at the overly-cushioned arms of the opposing chair, she saw that an unused side table fit perfectly beside it, and that prompted a curious check to discover a similar table beside her own armchair; but upon her table several thickly-sliced pieces of still-warm, buttery toast and a steaming mug of fragrant, herbal tea waited on an clay-ware plate. Unexpected treasure rewarding her thorough reconnaissance overcame the child who wasted no more than a momentary thought on consequences. Any brief, hesitant resistance was sabotaged by gurgling abdominal betrayal; the snatched-up toast was stuffed into an expectant, salivating mouth, buttery fingers were licked clean, and the mug quickly drained. And then stupefied satisfaction borne of unaccustomed fullness dulled her alert reflexes and encouraged a dreamlike fascination with the playful hearth flames warming her, as if a generously filled comforter had been laid upon and tucked around her thin shoulders.

At some point the child shook herself free from her stupor, and stealthily walked around the room, first using the personal facilities for toilet and superficial cleansing, and then trying the main door. She found that it locked from the outside, while allowing exit from within. There was a choice to be made then, comparing and weighing alternatives with anxious looks scouring the seemingly abandoned, gray corridor for movement, and wistfully soft, confused glances back towards to the beckoning hearth.

A decision was made, and quietly the heavy, carved door was released to swing close by itself, and latch securely. Then the waif climbed back onto "her" armchair, and gave in to the unexpected luxury of refuge by drifting contentedly off to sleep.

She was still deeply sleeping when the morning star rose behind distant mountains preceding the dawn by several hours. At this early time, when most citizens slept their soundest, a short, darkly-cloaked woman and a taller, but equally obscured man hurried purposely down the unfriendly, dim corridor, carefully aware of what was seen and unseen, stopping in front of a doorway with deeply grooved designs of great importance only for those who could discern them. The woman waved casually at the key-lock with a weathered hand briefly uncovered from the thick folds of her bulky cloak, and the door swung noiselessly inwards. After they furtively passed the threshold the door swung closed and securely locked itself.

Once inside the room, they paused, and the woman sighed deeply in relief as she looked meaningfully beside her at the hooded man now wiping his damp-sweated forehead. While he momentarily guarded the doorway, vigilant for suspicious city guardians who might be shadowing them, it took the lady seven woman-sized quicksteps to stride across the burnished wooden planks to the side of the sleeping child. It was then that the Lady Ae'sha first looked down at the sprawling assortment of stained rags barely covering an emaciated, scarred, and crawly-infested girl.

Stepping resolutely forward, Lord Z'van glanced quickly at the child in re-appraisal, for he had seen her briefly before. Then, deliberately, both their hands emerged from their enveloping, forest-green folds to compassionately rest as lightly as thistledown on the child's tangle-haired head before rising in unison to encircle the air above with the Blessing of Mercy. The inscribed sign gently and persistently glowed in the air even as the second blessing – the one of Belonging and Acceptance – was begun. At the final moment of the holy ritual, a most unlikely name was bestowed upon the foundling, ensuring her sanctuary and welcome in life: Angharad, Beloved One.

Rawiya let her voice trail off into the silence, noting that her listeners were holding their breath in surprised suspense. She also noted Ishwa had followed the story as closely as the others, though he had heard it countless times.

"What happened to her next, Storyteller?" a voice called out from the circle. A murmur arose letting Rawiya know many more had the same question. Even though they knew the answer, they wheedled for more.

"We will talk more of this tomorrow at the next oasis because it is so late. Remember, take no food into your tents, and light the smudge candles at your tent entrance. The teacher will ask now for blessings of peace and protection as you sleep. We leave this oasis early tomorrow morning."

"But the girl, Angharad, Storyteller! What of the girl?"

But Ishwa's hands were already raised, and many disappointed, protesting eyes refused to look down in reverence or respect. So as Ishwa made his request of the unnamed holy ones and the Compassionate One for blessing on those around him, many saw spirit-sparks condense above them as a cloud might appear made of tiny droplets of water each formed around a speck of dust; but this condensation was not of water, but of light which encircled uncountable unspoken intentions and hopes; they hovered, wavered, then fell gracefully into the glowing coals below, becoming part of the flames. The breaths that were held in awe softly released in sensed loss. Both Rawiya and Ishwa left the circle heading for their own private tents in silence, and no one but the drowsy birds above, the large-eared mice scurrying out of deserted tents, and the motionless dust-lizards listening at the edge of the campfire noted their departure.

CHAPTER 3

❖

WELCOMING ARRIVALS

The morning star glittered like silver crystal in the chilled pre-dawn sky of this third day in the Cham Desert. Stillness permeated the oasis campground, as darkness oozed into all corners like water soaking through thin fabric.

"This group is more attentive than the last," commented Ishwa during the shared breakfast in the cook's tent, confirming Rawiya's prior observation. The revived, gently glowing cinders from the previous evening's cook-fire illumined his face with barely discernable light. "They don't loudly interrupt despite how frustrated they are with your cruel ending times." Ishwa's smirk was all Rawiya needed to know he had been impressed with last night's telling. "Do you know why they were in Viñay?"

"They are mostly tourists and students on holiday from Nebojsa," shrugged Rawiya. "Their families know Amunet well since most arrived in Nebojsa as refugees escaping from being declared *sudasi*, or were expelled as unwanted in past generations."

"So most of these pilgrims are the descendants of Amunet's rubbish," mused Ishwa. "They seem to have done well for themselves for having been discarded by that elite city."

"And some have learned their lessons well. Nebojsa welcomes everyone. It is a city of healing even today."

"Is it… is it a refuge city?" Ishwa whispered now even more vigilantly careful to ensure they were not overheard. Though he had lived for long expanses of time within Viñay, he pointedly did not follow the politics or status of other townships as Rawiya did.

"Not yet," Rawiya murmured back, "But there is enough compassion within Nebojsa's boundaries to be considered for that. Unfortunately, as you have seen, there are still some here who have not learned from Amunet's experience. And then there are a few retreatants from other cities." She paused before asking, "What will you have me do today?"

Ishwa pondered on this question silently, his eyes turned dull and unfocused as he centered his being on knowing the will for this day of the Understanding One who blesses. Rawiya had seen him go into himself often and waited patiently while he meditated. She leisurely finished her breakfast and relaxed over the heat of her steaming tea, unaware that she also had entered a quiet centering of self, open to possibilities encouraged by the Guiding One.

An attendant approached like a silent shadow taking her empty bowl and spoon, and refilling her tepid cup with a warmer herbal brew, receiving a distracted nod of appreciation in return. The chill of the desert night still nipped at the edges of Rawiya's robes, and the clay-ware cup she sipped from was a comfort that helped her focus her meditations. Meanwhile, except for the attendants, Cook and guides soundlessly completing necessary tasks, the rest of the Hidayans in the caravan slept on. The travel beasts dozed, and without their usual waking snorts and shuffling, the silence seemed deeper.

Eventually Ishwa shook himself and stood with determination, signaling by example and a gently placed hand on Rawiya's shoulder that she should stand also. Beside him, she lifted an inquiring eyebrow.

"I want to talk with that elder, today. Perhaps his heart will be persuaded by companionship to be healed of its sadness. Would you ride with Halili today?" the Teacher asked indicating the direction of the young woman's tent. "There is a great fear of some loss facing her she must deal with soon, but not today. Today she needs to find a listening companion so tomorrow she will not stand alone."

"We are never alone," Rawiya responded by rote. "No one stands isolated, though we may not be aware of that."

"True, yet as usual, most of our pilgrims will need an additional advocate before we've traveled even halfway to Cham, but all is well for now," Ishwa commented somberly. "There are healings being worked on that we are not a part of. And others – well, we will know at the moment we are required."

Rawiya's face flashed him a wry smile. "What?" he questioned warily. It was never too early in the day to be a victim of Rawiya's humor. She was never over-awed by him. "What?" he repeated.

"You are not a doctor, nor are you a scab covering a wound so it will be protected while healing. Yet you still practice cryptic medicine. Someday the Hidayan World Guards will come for you and demand that you produce a valid license for all your meddling. We're supposed to be tour guides, remember?" By now Rawiya was soundlessly laughing and a responding muffled chuckle of Ishwa answered her as he recognized her humorous, cajoling enjoyment of the moment, which diverted his seriousness.

"I don't meddle. I just…ah, just…. You think I meddle?" Ishwa asked, hanging his head in playful, dramatic contrition, like a child caught in the act of stealing treats, knowing he would still be indulged. "I have been found out. You wouldn't turn me in, would you? What punishment will you give me if you were to judge?" The corners of his mouth twitched.

"Fake tour guide, tonight you earn your keep."

"You want me to cook dinner?" Ishwa asked in genuine astonishment, now. "Do you want all of us poisoned by my poor skills in the kitchen?"

"No, you dimwit! I want you to tell part of the story tonight. I talked too much last night. I didn't gauge myself, so my throat needs some rest. You tell part of the story tonight."

"I am not a storyteller. But I can bore them just as well as you can." Ishwa's loud guffaws turned heads and woke some pilgrims at the edge of sleep.

"Oomph! We'll see who'll be bored! You will regret that comment!" threatened Rawiya swatting at him.

"Apparently I shall regret a lot today if I have angered you in the first hour of the day. Ah, well. I shall tell something tonight, but I don't know what. Let me think on it. In the meantime, are you going to tell?"

"Which secret don't you want me to tell?" she wheedled slyly.

"All of them you shameless spy! But if you tell anything…." Ishwa threatened with a grin.

"Ach! You know too much about me, also! For now, a truce, especially since you are doing me a favor tonight. But tomorrow is another story. Tour guide, you are safe only for today! But should I start telling your secrets, it will begin with the fruit ball you just stole from Cook when you thought I wasn't looking just now."

Ishwa's chortling followed her as Rawiya danced off to help the attendants roll her sleeping mat into a tiny bundle and unpitch the tent. She had already packed her personal possessions before leaving her tent. When that chore was finished, the attendants began waking the rest of the caravan. Today they would be moving on through the desert for only a short morning trek so they could arrive at the next oasis before the day's heat exhausted them. Once there, Ishwa's abbreviated morning conference would touch on a need for each person to speak the truth in their own way, not copying others' perceptions of truth. To do this he would introduce the mandala as art and as a way for the pilgrims to express who they perceived themselves to be at this point in time. They would be given time in the following days to creatively complete a self-portraying mandala.

Unfortunately, the mid-morning arrival at the next caravan stop was disappointing for all travelers, and the morning conference was deferred to the next day. Veteran guides and attendants tried to hide their revulsion upon arriving at this second oasis, but it was obvious that even Ishwa was concerned with their new surroundings.

Even as they approached the oasis from a distance, a gray dryness of sporadic herb grass offered a foreboding welcome for the usually hardy bushes were dried, brittle skeletons. This second oasis seemed not only desiccated, but also threatening in comparison to the first. Here there were no lush nurse trees, no thriving small-leafed shrubbery, no stoic cacti to offer generous shade and shelter, nor were there any bubbling springs of clear, sparkling water.

There was only one enormously, stagnant pool of mucoid water barely protected from total evaporation by a multitude of thorny, rangy, silver-green bushes whose tortuously twisted branches reached out over the pool like arthritic fingers clutching at the air in pain. The water's sour stench was gaggingly repellant; its thick surface glistened and trembled in the glaring light of Bozidara with the slimy wrigglings of uncountably diverse larval nymphs and predatory pupa. A few broad-leafed plants attempted to offer shade far above, but their efforts were negligible.

Undaunted, the caravan attendants tried to water the travel beasts, but even they refused to drink the befouled water, and eventually were tied in the limited shade the thorny bushes offered. Tents were the only source of shade for the pilgrims who panted with dry throats and swollen tongues relieved only by occasional sips from their water skins. Their drinking water had already been rationed in the morning with a terse warning, so wasteful dribbling or thoughtless glugging of one's only supply of water made the novice-travelers more careful.

"Good grief!" murmured many candidates. "Is this where we're supposed to be? Isn't this a mistake?"

"We are here for a purpose," responded Ishwa carefully. "There may not be a clear purpose elsewhere on Hidaya, but in the Cham there is always a reason we will be made aware of."

Despite the fact that winter was almost over and spring rains were merely days away, the afternoon sizzled on mercilessly and Ishwa, Rawiya and many attendants were called to the side of quite a few pilgrims having difficulty taking one more breath of the thick, hot, motionless air as they rested instead of attending the morning conference. The heat seemed to benefit and encourage only the pond's larvae and slime.

Towards the end of the afternoon, when Bozidara's rays slanted uncaringly upon the sand, tents, and thorns, the embittered pool burbled lethargically for long moments before frantically bubbling and writhing noisily over its banks. Startled pilgrims stumbled to their tent entrances and witnessed the chaotic hatching of glistering nymphlings into adults whose coruscating body lengths often equaled that of an adult Hidayan's thumb. Immediately upon hatching some tenerals rose on delicately luminous wings and hovered expectantly over their slimy birthplaces. Other species shed their opalescent larval shells and rested momentarily on their now-floating exuvia so they could strengthen and pump up their crumpled wings into prismatic clouds of filigreed lace. Within an all-too-brief timing the newly emerged adults joined their earlier cousins as air-borne predators who all quit their foul nursery explosively.

The retreatants hesitated in disbelief facing this unanticipated harsh attack, and then panicked. Some ran and staggered in confusion into thorny bushes that held them captive while the insects overwhelmed them. Some merely closed their eyes and froze in shocked terror and became trembling, shivering monoliths covered by thousands of restless wings. The only bodily areas left uncovered by the insects were the spaces around noses, mouths, eyes and ears; the movement of breathed air apparently bothered them, as well as the fluttering of eyelashes, and the darkness of the ear canal. That avoidance allowed unimpeded breathing as well as observation if one dared.

A few quick-thinking travelers shrewdly sealed themselves inside their tents trusting that the fabric and flaps would protect them. Their sanctuary-creating defense seemed to attract the attention of fliers that managed to negotiate the flaps and enter.

Rawiya had heard the burbling water as she had dozed, and when the violent splashing erupted, stood and swayed groggily in her light, sleeping tunic by the entrance to her tent. Instantly the ravenous swarm covered her with their quivering winged bodies. Underneath this moving, radiant nebula she was startled and terrified, but there was also awe. She breathed quietly to calm herself. Then slowly and deliberately she held her unclothed arms out like branches. Thousands of insects landed and probed her skin leaving tiny irritated bumps behind. Rawiya raptly watched this personal invasion, entranced more by the beauty of the life forms landing on her rather than responding to their violation of her body in terrorized trauma. She would later perceive this moment as watching herself beside herself, viewing the event as something happening to someone else from an emotional distance. Still, she looked on fascinated.

Some insects were a shimmering pastel green with long, oval, gossamer wings, and others were a gentle, soft blue with four tiny, triangular shaped wings moving so rapidly as to appear as a blurry fluff on each side of their sculpted iridescent thoraxes; and still others were pink or lavender-hued with feathery antennae and sticky feet she could feel with each tiny step on her bare skin. None were exactly the same, and the uniqueness enthralled her more than the presence of bumps and droplets of blood over her body where they punctured her skin. There was also a strangely increasing sense of well being as she was blanketed under this rhythmically vibrating mass. Rapture enveloped her so she almost perceived herself floating with the hatchlings on her own set of glistening wings. From the contented facial expressions of nearby travelers she could observe, they also felt peace and bliss as she did now, the trauma transformed into euphoria. Rawiya mused that perhaps the insectoid punctures were made to inject stupefying calmatives or hallucinogens rather than paralyzing toxins.

But her idle peace was interrupted as a familiar thrumming sound intruded on Rawiya's consciousness, becoming a louder whooshing and flapping as the dull, brownish-gray desert birds flocked into sight from the direction of the last oasis and descended upon the insects with obvious delight and relish. They dove into the tumultuous air becoming part of the mêlée as they feasted. What was amazing was that no scream or moan, no squawk or call of any kind was uttered in any of these chaotic moments. The swishing, swooshing, patter of thousands of wings filled the space with overwhelming movement and volume, and when it was finished, the sated desert birds flew to the convoluted branches protecting the already-fouled oasis water to natter amongst themselves in obvious satisfaction.

With the air now still and empty of anything air-borne, the confounded caravan stumbled forward towards the center of the camp, dazed and walking as if in a dream to the edge of the befouled pool. Silent tears trailed down the cheeks of many shocked pilgrims, yet none cried in pain, for they also – though unfairly surprised and invaded – felt a calming, blissful sense of well being and physical health.

Abruptly a singular high note of incredible purity was trilled from the throat of a solitary peasant bird above. Even Ishwa's startled eyes rolled upwards as if to ask, "What now?" Increasingly more and more members of the huge protective flock above included their clearly grateful voices to the one pure tone, while the volume ascended until it was emotionally thrilling to hear such intense gratitude.

In response to the song of thankfulness, the pond's surface capriciously churned to life again without steam, stench, or expulsion of wildlife, and just as suddenly the water's surface smoothed to a flawless, glassy sheen.

Rawiya squinted as blinding, flashing golden rays from Bozidara reflected on the mirroring pond. Evening. The familiar intake and holding of universal breath, and then the sighing with a relief, awe, and peace that seemed to reach from this one clear pond to the far edges of the cosmos. The young schoolgirl, Halili, with whom Rawiya had traveled and counseled with this morning, knelt to smell and examine the quietly reflecting water with astonishment, and then timidly scooped up a mouthful of liquid with her cupped hand while onlookers gagged in nausea.

"But the water is pure!" she cried, "And my skin! It's… it's…!" Sure enough, the bumps from the insect probes were now mere memory. A slight, pleasant tingling over her skin was all that lingered.

One of the youths knelt beside Halili to stare at the changing golden-to-apricot-to-blush-to-rose colored liquid reflecting the progressive twilight sky changing above. Tentatively he bent to sip directly from the pond's surface. His thoughtful appraisal of the water's quality and safety was cut short by his companion's exclamation, "Look! My scar is gone!"

There was a long, silent pause as the significance of both their exclamations made conscious sense to the others. Then, the urge to see for oneself, to taste the water for oneself was overpowering. One tentative step here, another there, and attendants as well as retreatants moved as one towards the pool. It was unclear to Rawiya if the pond water or the insects had caused the apparent healings.

But Ishwa did not join the other travelers, and seemed angrily disturbed. "Clean up for the supper campfire!" he curtly ordered ignoring the pushing crowd focused on getting to the seemingly miraculous water. "Supper will be ready within a few minutes. Attendants, you there, now! Prepare the mats and set the campfire." He watched without expression as his orders led to the appropriate actions despite apparent mass confusion and immense reluctance. Rawiya appeared at his side.

"What was that!" she tersely exclaimed trying desperately to keep her voice low. Lingering euphoria encircled her like billowing mist.

"That was something even I have never witnessed here or anywhere," Ishwa whispered back. "It could have been a spontaneous ritual of sacrifice and purification. Perhaps it was merely a healing event. It may even have been a test. Whatever it was, though, I am also concerned that they have the taste of our blood within them."

"Who? What!"

"The hatchlings probed and drank from us and then the desert birdlets ate them and our blood, and now are filled with our essences. Even if this attack and healing was necessary, for what I have no idea, the unnecessary harshness is uncharacteristic of the Cham. I perceive that the Cham is preparing for us for something I don't know of."

"Preparing for what?" Rawiya asked breathlessly. At any other time she would have been tempted to the edge of genuine fear, but enough ecstasy remained to cushion all her emotions. She still perceived herself wrapped in blissful, relaxed wonder.

"I'm not sure," Ishwa muttered preoccupied with conflicting thoughts and distrustful feelings; he fiercely fought the contentment and inner peace swirling within. "Remember. This is the Cham Desert. This particular retreat may not be what either of us, nor any of our guests was ready for. I was prepared to be surprised by the different life forms present here that changes with every caravan, but I was definitely not prepared for the harsh blood payment required here this afternoon!"

"But look," Rawiya pleaded gesturing towards the travelers. "They are being healed not harmed. We all are! Granted it was an extraordinary, at times frightening yet awesome experience, but I see more healing than harm done today. And there was – for me, at least – a moment of... of grace, you might call it! Maybe it wasn't a 'blood payment!' This was healing, not evil sacrifice! It was as if the One communicated directly with us."

"That may be, but still the blood and fear of this afternoon are not justified in my opinion."

Rawiya stared at Ishwa assessing his state of mind. "You were afraid. So was I. This may not be as it seems because of our emotions. Before we judge we need understanding."

Ishwa did not respond to her comment, but abruptly announced, "I will not be at the campfire tonight. I need to consider these events."

Rawiya watched Ishwa's hunched form hurry from the bustling campsite into the shadowed evening beyond. Though a skeptical thought brushed her mind that this was Ishwa's way of wriggling out of his commitment to her, she realized immediately that this was not his way of escape. She turned to a passing attendant saying, "Please water the travel beasts on the far end of the pool. They have waited patiently enough already. And please bring a freshly filled water-skin to Ishwa's tent." And then she herself hesitantly walked towards the pool to drink its sweetness. Each step felt as if she floated forward in protected caring.

Meanwhile, at Ishwa's original directive, Cook had immediately begun unpacking food supply bundles in preparation of dinner after sending an attendant to fill a water jug for her own use. Some of those bundles looked unfamiliar, however, and it was then that Cook discovered that the cargo placed on one of the travel beasts consisted of delectable tofu steaks sealed in airtight pouches. There were also herbed mashed roots, pod vegetables and sweet fruit compote – all of which merely needed to be steamed or mixed with hot water to be reconstituted. Together there was a complete, unusually easy-to-prepare meal that was extravagant for the circumstances.

"It's a bit too convenient," Cook suspiciously observed to the kitchen attendants with her hands on her wide hips.

"But, you knew they were there," responded the supervising attendant. "You ordered everything."

"Actually, no. I didna' order this. 'Never would 'a' either. I've ordered food for every caravan for the past 7 years. Each oasis provides its own fresh vegetables, fruits, an' roots. Each oasis also provides the necessary protein foods. I buy travel-ready foods that can be made into stews an' thick soups, tea, nuts, dried fruits, an' different kinds of treats. Look at the labels. Here," she said pointing one of her digits at the written label. "We canna' afford this for all these travelers! Either someone slipped in a travel beastie with their own expensive supplies, or we gotta travel beastie that should 'a' been going with some other caravan."

The supervisor tentatively rubbed his stubborn whisker-nubs. His face was both perplexed and thoughtful.

"Donna' say it," Cook said enunciating each sound to add emphasis. "The oasis critters stay here. They donna' go nowhere. They may shape shift or change so that everything is new for each caravan; but they donna' pre-package food and load 'em onto travel beasties. No. Something's been twisted here so we can tonight be the heirs to this… this wealth!"

"But doesn't this mean then that another caravan is eating our food," laughed the attendant. "It may be just a mix up of another kind."

"Or it could 'a' been prepared and arranged for by someone we donna' know about," Cook slowly reflected catching sight of a large dust lizard staring at her with unblinking eyes.

The Third Night:

Serenity overshadowed any lingering emotions from the afternoon's adventure as the caravan gathered for that evening's meal. The mood was light and cordiality extended from each person's depths. Scars, wounds, sores, eczema, fungal infections, and other such surface anomalies had been erased as if they had never existed. Other internal healings were not discernable, but each pilgrim reported feeling unusually healthy and energized.

Ishwa had come and gone like a shadow, and was nowhere within the camp, so the evening's schedule went on, though his presence was noted without worry. All seemed to be well.

Rawiya wiped her hands on a cleansing towel and deeply breathed in the clean air. Glancing leisurely upwards into the universe above to gauge her time, the stars sparkled and reflected back her tranquility. She squirmed around to get into a more comfortable position, and smiled at the encircling group. Curiously, several pilgrims were stroking enigmatic dust lizards that purred with hedonistic contentment.

"We Hidayans try to be honorable people of integrity and kindness, but we know that there is always a pull towards selfishness. We are tempted to feel better than others even though we are aware of the futility of finding satisfaction in that.

We judge others so that our own judgments of ourselves come out better than theirs and we feel special. We hurt others in so many ways on purpose or thoughtlessly, and they hurt us back. We envy others and they are jealous of us. We try to be better while doing exactly the opposite of what we should, but still we try. To accept ourselves as we are is difficult so we fall into the easier temptations rather than to fall into the Accepting One who loves us unconditionally.

Our Hidayan history includes multiple examples of both our failings and successes, but tonight we talk about a search for controlling power that set in motion the beginnings of our healing here on Hidaya."

The upper Rudra Wasteland was clothed in a velvet night so deep that the orange, red and white strata of the ancient hoodoos, fins, and wind-whipped cliffs edging the wasteland were unperceivable. Lady Ansh'mati was a Searcher, but tonight she was hiding from those searching for *her* in the wasteland. Using the shadowed spires and columns around her, the flowing charcoal gray robes she wore hid and warmed her when her apprehension didn't. She walked haltingly careful at times, but even when she hurried forward sure-footedly in the darkness, her progress seldom caused disturbances which would alert any sharp-eared hunters that she was near. She skirted as quickly and closely as she could to the majestic edges of the cliffs that heralded the abrupt southern rising of the Bahairava Mountains. Her night goggles were overlarge, but effective; they had been found in the last cache of food and clothing secreted by other Searchers for just such an emergency. Right now they dangled from a rough rawhide strap around her neck.

Often she paused to catch her breath and to listen to the night sounds. Once horsemen had thundered mere meters from her as she hugged the closest column, becoming part of its shadows and hiding her face and hands in her robe's folds. The farraginous posse thudded past in a noisy, disorderedly mass, sweeping the flatlands all the way to the faint horizon with hostile eyes, but missing what was closest to them.

"When Bozidara rises in a few hours," Lady Ansh'mati thought, "I shall be in plain sight unless I can find another sheltered cache. Salimah is southeast of me by the stars, but I shall be caught in the open if I try to cross now."

Her indecision caused her to pause momentarily, and just that brief silence allowed her to hear a crude scraping sound behind a nearby boulder. She waited frozen with anxiety. It could be only a snake or lizard looking for its dinner, or perhaps one of the desert foxes or rabbits. She would wait in silence while an inner chill impelled her body to shiver instinctively for she would not even risk moving her hand to raise her night goggles in case that movement was heard.

Long moments later a softly sung, incomplete melody was whispered towards her, and Ansh'mati relaxed and grinned in relief. Her lungs sucked in air greedily. She gently hummed the rest of the musical line, pushed the goggles in place, and trotted behind the boulder. Wrapped thickly in similar dusty gray robes, two goggled faces looked up at her. "What brings you here, Lady?" hissed the male closest to her suspiciously from the shadows.

"I come from the north," she whispered back. "I am Ansh'mati. Do you have water?" Silently a travel-gourd was passed to her. Experience had taught her to sip and savor the much-needed water even though she longed to gulp it in. She lowered herself to the ground and propped her back against a small rock. A bowed head of gratitude was the only expression the lady gave for the luxury of releasing tension and ignoring tired muscles after endless hours of desperate escape.

"I'm C'dmon," the taller Hidayan shared, his face close enough across from Ansh'mati so that she could see his haggard expression.

"H'shmand," mumbled the second male. "Are they after you, too, or are these hunters only after us?"

"They are after me for sure," replied Ansh'mati licking her lips between sips of water. "They found me out in Anamya. Two other Searchers were found and killed on the spot. I hid, but my escape was noticed from the city towers, so they have been following me even into the night. And you?"

"Both of us escaped from Rudra," H'shmand explained. "We've been hiding in the mountains and circling the Wasteland trying to lead the posse seeking us away from Salimah."

"They came in the night," sighed C'dmon with what sounded like a muffled sob at the end of his words.

H'shmand reached over to place a steadying hand on his friend's knee. "He saw his whole family slaughtered. Friends and family were herded together and killed. Rudra's guardians supervised the whole thing and said they were shocked, but were really just following orders."

"But they weren't upset carrying out those orders," C'dmon added bitterly.

"Whose orders?" breathed Lady Ansh'mati. Her stillness emphasized the seriousness of the questions.

"I don't know," H'shmand responded staring intently at the Lady. "There is a lot of anger. I heard a rumor that mayors from different cities had met and started talking about some of their citizens mysteriously disappearing. 'A few are missing here, a few there, and no trace of where they had gone. By themselves, the disappearances were just strange, minor curiosities, but when the mayors got to talking together they found a pattern.

"The slaves, the oppressed, the abused, the orphaned, the shunned for whatever reason – the dregs of society were disappearing. And when they started comparing notes more closely, they discovered that there were trading caravans in almost all of the cities at the times of the disappearances."

C'dmon looked up to add his own comments. "The caravans went in different directions, but the rumor had it that every one had a traveler who had arrived alone, but left with at least one additional 'family member.'"

"But they couldn't have identified us as Searchers just on a rumor like that!" exclaimed Ansh'mati in a stage whisper. "They are hunting Searchers down like *conejos*! How…?"

"We have been betrayed by someone who was once saved by us," concluded C'dmon miserably. "Refuge and safety are going to be destroyed."

"You don't know that, friend," H'shmand chided. "There is always hope…."

"No hope, not anymore," C'dmon sobbed shuddering silently. "All is lost." His head drooped despairingly onto to his chest, tears streaming prolifically over his cheeks and dripping down his chin and onto the dirt below. The copious salty drops were covered with fine sand particles until they became multiple spherical globs that were absorbed into the sand below. H'shmand and Ansh'mati looked grimly at C'dmon with genuine concern, but they allowed his grief to spill out for his healing.

Doubt shadowed Lady Ansh'mati's heart for a moment. "Were we wrong to try to change history? Maybe we shouldn't have involved ourselves in this, but just cleaned up one small corner of Hidaya. Maybe our plan was too large for us. Maybe it was too grandiose for such as we. Maybe –"

"Maybe what? What?" the anger in H'shmand's voice was harsh in reprimand, but revealed the depth of his own frustration and apprehension. "We should have let the hurt go on without challenge when it was in our power to do so? We should have saved only ourselves when Hidayan nature is planet-wide? We should not have even offered a prayer when we were powerless by ourselves to change injustice?

"The refuge cities are too small and too temporary compared to the need. Yet just by ourselves each of us is a desperately needed an atom of hope and light in the face of our planet's history! Together we become atoms linked into molecules to face so much hurt and injustice. But we are not like the vengeful vigilantes who return hurt for hurt! Our efforts become the refuge cities, and though they are mere particles in a universe of complex compounds, we are necessary matter." H'shmand hushed himself before affirming mostly to himself, "We matter. We may fail, or become martyrs like some saints in the distant past! But at least we breathe the air of hope so that we may resuscitate others and free them from hopelessness. We need that. I need that. That freedom of soul is wider that this wasteland, even now. Even now."

"Or we might have been called what we are to have attempted this grand plan: crazies!" Ansh'mati's words were laced with bitterness. "To be centered in the Merciful One, in love before being an activist so that mercy would be enduring and not based on charismatic personalities was supposed to make healings and rescues possible and blessed. Have we – have I deluded myself?"

"Ah, Lady! This *is* a grand plan. To seek out wounds and bring those wounds to healers is a loving goal! To create sanctuaries of healing in plain sight; to then send out those who are healed like walking sanctuaries of hope, covering Hidaya like a web, that is loving and is fueled by the intentions of the Compassionate One. Instead of turning our heads pretending our Hidayan tendencies are not trying to control and destroy the souls of others around us with the hurt, fear, anger, threats, slavery, abuse, war, and denigration we struggle with inside our own hearts, something else is offered! It's not about us! It's about loving ourselves and others, responding to the goodness that is real, and protecting it!

"Ansh'mati! Remember our history! Remember what it was like! The world wars for land and power, the so-called religious wars, the deaths, rapes, and tortures! Infants in the wombs killed because neither the lives of the mothers nor their fetuses were valued. The children brought into the world by those who said they valued life, but for false reasons. They couldn't parent or support the children, but used them as pawns to abuse or to puff up their identities. The mothers rented out their bodies as if they were businesses, not persons! The fathers and brothers molested their own daughters or sisters and called it a holy marriage, and after generations, the victims actually believed their abuse was sacred!

All the adjudged useless girl-babies were killed throughout Hidaya, and then many nations of hungry, angry youths sublimated their sexual energy to make war holy! The self-centeredness was endless: 'Look at me! My life, my faith, my nation, my family, my anything is better than anybody else's, and I can do what I want even if the bodies, minds and souls of everybody else is maimed and maligned!' 'Look at me! I can beat up anybody around me and get away with it. I can demean anyone and get my way. I can get drunk, or live drugged out of consciousness forever. I can be incarcerated for life for any crime or insanity or marginalized as a homeless miscreant; it makes no difference. Look at me all tangled in the fabric of life and no one can stop me 'for my name is Legion' – as an ancient holy book said.

"Lady, not to do anything, even if it was a doomed failure from the beginning, would be unfaithful to the Compassionate One who loved us from the first! We would have betrayed ourselves far worse to deny our response to that love. We are pariahs tonight, and may be dead by morning, but we have lived like tiny sparks in a dark night."

C'dmon had been listening and had regained control of himself. He murmured, "In ages past they called them 'sins of omission;' deliberately not doing something good. Withholding what was good." His voice trailed away tiredly.

"Forgive my moment of weakness," Ansh'mati said regretfully. "I am tired, still thirsty and hungry. I fear that Salimah and the other refuge cities on Hidaya are endangered. Even if we can warn them in time, should the different townships unite their local guardians to form an attacking army against the refuge cities, many lives will be lost."

"Eat these," C'dmon responded handing her a packet of nutmeats with shaking hands.

"If we stay here, we will be discovered during the day," persisted Ansh'mati as she opened the packet.

"True. But if we move now we will die of exhaustion. Let us rest and renew ourselves, and then decide before Bozidara rises."

"Perhaps our way will become clearer in the morning," muttered C'dmon wearily.

"The Guiding One is always with us," they whispered in unison.

Silently and solemnly packets and gourds were emptied, and the eyes of the three refugee-Searchers reluctantly closed heavily. By their feet, where C'dmon's tears had fallen, the balls of sand and tears trembled imperceptively.

The stars above moved marking the hours while hidden changes quickened beneath the sand. C'dmon's sand-shrouded spheres of moisture sank into the granular orbs around it; they touched a thick, membranous sac softening it. A shivering microscopic egg animated by the wet tears of desperate sadness was enlivened misinterpreting the wetness for a sign of the rainy season ahead; the patient pupa hatched and ate its moist, discarded casing.

It rested, but even as it paused it changed into a crimson-striped larva wriggling upwards. By the time it had tunneled scant centimeters below the surface eating multitudes of un-germinated seeds on its way, it paused to rest and pupate. The three sister moons of Hidaya briefly rose above the horizon in the pre-dawn of the Rudra Wasteland, and their gravitational influence signaled the insect to metamorphose into an adult.

Like all glass beetles its innards were visible through the hardening black-spotted elytra, and its transparent wings beneath quivered with an "itchiness" to be stretched and used. It dug and crawled upwards by instinct, and then waited on the dirt's surface while its weak eyes took in the three life forms whose soft exoskeletons gently rose and fell breathing.

The beetle listened to Hidaya's vibrations through its six jointed legs and responded. Its ancestors had once been tiny, hand-held beetles often eating tiny parasitic insects, but Hidayan environmental changes had mutated many species, including this rare glass beetle. It crawled into the discarded nutmeat packets and retrieved whatever particles remained; and it grew. It sucked water from the damp rims of the water skins, and it grew. It chomped on tender, silver-budded cacti sheltered under a tiny rock ledge, and grew again. It sucked nutrients from both the night air and sweat in the Hidayans' palms, and when all that moisture there was exhausted, it crept forward with wavering antennae to gather the vapor from the exhalations of the three sleepers, and grew again.

By pre-dawn, the biologically deviant beetle was larger than the boulders that served as pillows for the Hidayan bi-peds. It neatly scooped up the three Searchers to nestle against its awkward elytra, wedging them behind its rounded pronotum. It paused, unfurling its long wings and fanning them first slowly and then more quickly as they strengthened.

Now the Searchers felt gently hugged as the elytra moved with the wings' movement. They slept on feeling as if they were being rocked to sleep in a cramped cradle while the beetle scuttled straight across the Rudra dirt and then swiftly lofted itself to skim across the Rudra Wasteland, not even bothering to detour to one of the isolated oases. When the morning star had almost set the beetle flicked around the low hills dividing the Rudra Wasteland from Salimah.

By the time H'shmand woke, ready to face the challenges of the day, he saw the shadowed walls and towers of Salimah rushing towards him like a swift nightmare confrontation. The first rays of Bozidara were peeking over the hills to the west almost blinding him with their suddenness. H'shmand had no time to think for the next instant he was sliding forwards down a bumpy incline to land on shallowly furrowed ground. His transportation had abruptly stopped, but inertia had carried him forward. C'dmon and Ansh'mati also were roughly and unceremoniously tumbled beside him, and some shiny glass-like mound was scuttling away from him and then launching itself southward in the chilled air so fast that after one or two blinks, it was gone from sight flying low to the ground.

Ansh'mati and C'dmon untangled themselves from their robes and each other, and stood to join H'shmand facing Salimah in astonishment, realization spreading on their faces as fast as Bozidara continued rising beyond the horizon. A group of early farmers with their shouldered field tools stood uncertainly by the seldom-used city gate facing the Cham Desert on their way to a field edging the township's northeastern face. They had observed the manner in which the trio had been transported to Salimah and were in awe. One walked forward, though, bowed respectfully, and invited the refugees to be sheltered within Salimah.

Salimah nestled in the foothills on the western curved edge of the bluestone Bahairava Mountain Range. It was a small-recovered city holding many names, but the most common one, besides its true name, was Refuge. Upon coming to its wide-arched, welcoming, red-hued gateway, one perceived a busy but unhurried community. The architecture was simple and flowing, as the city had been literally carved out of an enormous, ancient limestone outcrop and was decorated with similar strata as that of faraway red-orange cliffs. The city architecture was a visual surprise and delight.

The Compassionate One, acknowledged by most Hidayans, needed no emblems or rooms in which to be honored, and therefore no temples, shrines, chapels, frescoes, totems, charms, sacred carvings, symbolic emblems, statues, monuments, obelisks, banners, flags, or other clues to the underlying values or worship woven into Salimah's cultural tapestry were to be found publicly throughout the city, and often not even within the individual households; personal deities – if honored – mysteriously went un-named. Even though reverence or faith might be the original purpose of such public displays, eventually all these idols and sacred spaces seemed to draw focus away from the deities themselves, and became isolating, superficial distinctions of identity that divisively affected the entire community; often those personal identity practices justified biases and intolerant atrocities or became trite ornaments replacing belief. So the inhabitants of Salimah deliberately shed these items so that nothing could delude them into bisecting their attention between recognition of a divinity and a political ideology, a neighborhood community practice, and monetary or landed gain hierarchy, or any other distraction.

Refugees came to Salimah, of course, with their own preferences learned from family, city, nation, faith, or experience. But if they chose to stay within the city they tried to recognize and accept their biases and do more than just tolerate others so different than themselves. There was always a gap between goal and practice, but the gap was minimal if the Compassionate One was truly honored. And the efforts were genuine, not fanatical!

Salimah citizens extended hospitable courtesy that included gentle reverence for *the-spirit-within* all beings. It was pervasive and deliberate so much so that a stranger could actually feel warmly welcoming inclusion. The only visible, tangibly united cultural expression of commonality was the distinctive, tribal-like costume of its inhabitants, for male and female, young and old, were all dressed in long, comfortable, multi-hued robes. To be sure, some had hooded robes, others had thick leather utility belts, and others had sturdy packs hefted by padded shoulder straps; hair was long, short, curled, straight, styled, disheveled or covered, but all had robes of magnificently varied colors. Visitors often thought they were willingly entrapped within a living rainbow as citizens of Salimah swirled through the streets on their daily business.

Salimah was an enigma on Hidaya – one of many. Itinerant merchants repeatedly were stymied by the native's description of the city, "This is Salimah. Refuge." The persistent or suspicious asked, "Refuge for whom? Refuge from what?" A dismissive shrug, a helpless smile, or an amused shake of the head at the enormity of the response required to adequately express the truth was instead the only response, and one had to be satisfied with that for there was nothing else to be shared without true need.

Had they bothered to learn Pandit, the native dialect of Salimah, no doubt their answers would have been revealed because grammar and vocabulary reliably reveal cultural belief, but no one ventured to expend energy learning this obscure dialect, preferring Chi'ma, the universal trade language of Hidaya, which was truly a divine gift from the Understanding One, allowing clear, unconfused communication between different communities and traders, despite the quaint dialects it embraced. Had they even dallied to listen more persistently to the market musicians or puppeteers teaching the toddlers, they would have uncovered the answers they sought, and more.

The open-air market filled the major public square of Salimah. It was chaos itself with flutes, tambours, harps, bells, shakers, whinnies, grunts, caws, growls, clucks, coos, brays, barks, laughter, squeals, chatter, all layered simultaneously over each other while jugglers, sellers, buyers, dancers, screaming children, exuberant families, hawking farmers, and boisterous friends from within and without the city clamorously completed visitations, errands and purchases.

Fabrics, metalwork, vegetables, fruits, leather, weaving, lacework, ceramics, clayware, spices, perfumes, potions, rare colored glassware, souvenirs, scribes, and more jostled and competed in the huge crowded confines of the main trade center.

Other market plazas connected to the main one by rather narrow neighborhood avenues. It was there that the finer, more delicate, more exquisite, and thus more costly items could be located, as well as the quieter inns one could secure with generous board. Traders, merchant caravans, and occasionally a roving Hidayan detachment from the nearby garrison freely moved about the city, which seamlessly revealed itself as an interesting, but minor, trading site. Salimah was one of the cities of refuge on Hidaya, and the only one that openly declared itself in its very name. Salimah. Refuge.

Deeper within Salimah via a webbed network of streets and alleys, an unexpected city within a city hummed with a life of its own, its daily workings distinct from the public mechanisms beyond its permeable boundaries. It was here, in the true center of Salimah – the actual

Refuge itself – that Angharad slowly opened her eyes without moving any other muscles. Comfortably curling upon herself without the need to tensely clutch protectively into as small a shape as possible, neither for warmth nor for defense, Angharad lingered in the hushed dormitory while distant chimes heralded the time.

Her sleeping space was just as she had left it the night before, as the night before that, and before that and all the weeks before. Hidden light sources softly duplicated the time of day or night in the windowless sleeping hall, with neither garish brilliancy nor fathomless darkness. Rough, thickly woven, bleached curtains hung from wooden hoops looped over long dowels criss-crossing the dormitory's low-beamed ceiling. The curtains barely brushed the stone floor warmed from the kitchen ovens in the story below.

The curtains defined the tiny, private boundaries of Angharad's own personal space within the immense sleeping chamber, as well as those of the other girls and women. She had no bed, but rather, a circular, deeply cushioned nest, which she had pushed against the hard wall at the back of her space. All new arrivals were given this gift of hard wall-space to feel the security of something solid behind them. Angharad, just like others before her, had feared that someone or some un-named threat would surprise her at rest by circling around to attack from an unguarded position.

It truly had taken the many months given to her to finally sleep through the night without startled terror waking her moment to moment. The nest-bed allowed protective boundaries within boundaries to build a sense of safety and security. She was unaware that nighttime protectors had often paused outside of her curtained space should she have called needfully for their presence.

A three-legged stool, a small dresser table with 2 drawers, and the nest-bed in which Angharad now sat surveying her space were the only furniture she called hers; a hand-made brush, new chewing stick, carved comb and 3 handkerchiefs were the only things hidden in the top drawer so far. Dried fruit, nuts and jerky were hidden in the lower drawer – a remnant of the needful insecurity of the past. The only other object within her curtained space was a framed glass with a black fabric backing, which she used as a mirror when she tied back her softly waving, brown hair. Clothing was provided to her and was always the same: a light, comfortably smooth, sleeveless tunic hanging below her knees, other loose-fitting undergarments, and a soft, umber-hued, hooded robe reaching to just above her ankles. Light woven sandals completed the wardrobe. Each morning a clean tunic and robe were provided for her from the laundry. Her used clothing was rolled together and thrown into one of the large wicker hampers at the end of each curtained row. Showers, baths, toilets and other necessaries were in a large room off to the west end of the dormitory.

Angharad confidently rose now that she had assured herself that nothing had changed overnight. She took her chewing stick and comb with her as she walked towards the cleaning room and nearby laundry – a morning ritual that increased her feelings that life could be predictable and good. Finally washed, dried, and dressed, she tossed yesterday's clothing into the hamper and joined other girls and women already on the stairs leading down towards the kitchen and dining hall.

There was a rhythm to life within Salimah's depths. Though there were no rigidly formal rising and eating times, Angharad responded to the rhythms around her and relaxed into their predictability. She was invited to sharing groups for conversation, song, or handwork. At times she was asked to help out in the kitchen or refectory set-up, or within the laundry, or in the gardens or nearby fields, and in each group Angharad learned more words and skills, until she was understanding more than she was capable of speaking and could do more than she could describe; but still, was able to make herself understood.

There were other women and girls who now called her by name and who actually wanted to be with her, and that was a novel experience. It wasn't being needed which made a welcome for her, though; Angharad was welcomed for herself. As she took one tiny step forward at a time beyond her fears, and shared ideas, humor, and personal preferences, Angharad was astounded to discover that she was liked not just because of what she did, but because of who she was as a person! And there were work, play, and sharing groups everywhere to test this out!

Once wandering past the gardens and hearing a low pleasant murmuring down a curving, arched corridor warmed by Bozidara's bright rays, a divide in the corridor confronted Angharad. Both choices looked inviting. Tentatively she took the fork to the right and discovered a veritable honeycomb of rooms wherein small groups met in privacy for sharing, worship, studies, music, or handwork. The curved ceilings and walls of each room, their arched doorways and windows, all were designed to keep sound contained within the rooms, so doors were unnecessary, and curtains sufficed for visual privacy. Several girls waved to her and invited her to join them, but Angharad shook her head. She wanted to explore more.

She turned back retracing herself back to the main corridor and chose the left fork. There were wooden doors on many of the rooms, and written letters which Angharad only touched tracing their shapes with her fingertips. One of the groups she had joined was teaching her how to read and write, but the clustered symbols on these doors were still far beyond her literacy skills.

Some doors were open, and from the color of the forest green robes in sight, she realized that these were the private rooms of Searchers who came and went mostly on their own schedules. Lord Z'van and Lady Ae'sha most likely were sequestered here, unless they had already moved on she thought sadly.

Angharad was still peeking around the corner into one of these rooms when a door further down the corridor abruptly burst open. A cluster of young girls in their umber robes filed out all noisily talking at the same time and laughing at each others' comments. They spoke Pandit so rapidly that Angharad couldn't even grasp one measly word for understanding. They pushed past her nodding recognition and disappeared around the corridor bend, their jocularity melting into the distance. When she turned back from watching them, an elder lady wearing a rich, sienna-hued robe stood quietly observing her. Angharad froze, feeling guilty for probably being where she was not supposed to be.

Wiry gray hairs had escaped from the lady's attempt at an upswept hairdo, and even though she absently tucked them behind her ears, they immediately resumed their original askew placement.

"Were you waiting for someone?"

"N-no," Angharad stuttered in broken Pandit. "I, I was just l-looking around to s-see what w-was h-ere. I-I…"

"Well come on in, and find out then what's *here*. I don't bite, you know."

"C-can I? I m-mean is it all right that I-I'm here. I-I c-could go…."

"You're just fine. Exploring is a good thing to do. Would you like some tea? I'm brewing some now and am desperately thirsty. Would you join me?" the lady smiled in welcome.

Angharad nodded while hesitantly walking towards the lady blocking the doorway who nodded at Angharad's progress and then stepped inside out of sight. When Angharad finally stood under the arched doorway she saw that there were two other persons in the room curiously studying her. They both sat on some of the huge rainbow colored cushions ringing the room's interior. Both looked sunburned and tired, and wore drab gray robes that made the rainbow of cushions call out in splendored vibrancy. Meanwhile, the brown-robed female bent over a stone box in the room's corner. She turned a dial on the side of the box and a ring of fire leaped away from a coil on the box's lid. Upon this coiled fire a heavy teapot was placed.

The lady's back was to Angharad while she adjusted the dial for a higher flame. "Cookie?" she asked tilting her head to listen better.

"Yes, please," Angharad coughed in surprise, still staring at the ring of fire that had appeared magically before her.

"Of course, I'll have one, too," growled the seated gray-robed male closest to the far wall. "I happen to know that you stole an entire baking sheet of them from the kitchen this morning even before they'd cooled, so I know they're fresh. Not like what *you* usually serve." His companion merely grinned at this slight to the lady's cooking skills.

"Uh-huh. You'll get served last then since you know so much. Now, come sit down while the tea warms up," the woman said with a gesture to Angharad. Angharad looked around for a proper chair, but only saw huge overstuffed pillows that seemed more like thrones. She settled on one bright yellow one across the room from both the seated occupants.

"Tea will be ready soon," the lady explained as she now sat on a crimson pillow. "We're all Searchers in this wing of Refuge, but let's put that formal title aside for now. We're on vacation from searching for a while. I'm Ansh'mati, and this is C'dmon. And the grouchy one by the window is H'shmand. We greet you -?"

"Angharad." And she whispered their names to herself to remember them. "What are you searching for?"

"People who need refuge or direction. Some, like you, apparently, come with us Searchers for sanctuary from whatever. Others stay where they are learning to live differently by making different choices. Ah, but here we are now in Salimah.

"Here, take two cookies to start with, pass the bowl to C'dmon, and if old grumpy here doesn't gobble up the rest, then we can try out some more. The tea water is almost ready." She handed a deep bowl of cookies to Angharad who obediently chose two and got up to cautiously pass the bowl to the Searcher on her left. A look of amused longing passed over his face, but he took the restricted two cookies and passed the bowl to H'shmand who didn't bother to count the fistful of cookies he snatched. He winked at Angharad gleefully, as he placed the bowl on the cushion next to him so it would be easier for Ansh'mati to reach for when she sat down. He did not wait for her to join them and immediately began nibbling on the cookie edges making the cookie-wheels smaller and smaller. C'dmon took only one polite bite and waited for his tea.

"Did you find the Beehive in the other corridor?" H'shmand asked between his mouse-bite munching.

"Yes, if that's what it's called. Everyone seemed to be doing so many things! Some were practicing music, some were just talking, and some were sewing or knitting, some were praying, and there was so much going on and all different in each room."

"Are you going to join them?"

"Maybe. I'd have to learn how to sew because I don't know how, and I've never tried singing. But my reading is coming along so if there's a simple group, it might be fun to join. I'm probably not good for much."

"Oh, no, dear," interrupted Ansh'mati handing Angharad the mug of steaming herbal tea she had just brewed. "Every one of us has something special to do. We just have to find out what it is."

"I know what your special talent is Ansh'mati. You irritate everyone who knows you," H'shmand sniped dipping the remnants of a cookie into his tea.

"And you, you old dung ball, are good only for snoring so every animal within meters is scared away. Give me back my cookies."

"I've already eaten them," he responded provocatively licking the crumby fingers that he had just pulled from his mouth. "Are there any left? You surely didn't make them yourself because these *are* rather good."

Ansh'mati smiled despite herself, and automatically passed him the cookie bowl. She turned back to Angharad saying, "We could tell you all the positive differences you make to the people around you here in Salimah, but that won't help you except for a short while. You need to identify your own worth and meaning for yourself, and then when we tell you that we agree with you, you might accept our encouragement."

"Truly," added C'dmon. "Your life is a gift to all of us. That you are here tells me that you've had a rough start, as we all have had, but you also look as if you are thriving here. Can you tell any difference between now and when you first came?"

Angharad thought briefly before responding, while staring at her cookie intensely. "I was always afraid. I had nightmares every night and sometimes in the day. I had no friends before, and now I meet new girls and elders every day that I like. We talk about everything. I've never done that before." She took a deep breath and went on.

"There's always food, and clean clothes, and there's medicine if I'm sick, and there are things to make and do all the time. I don't just sit around waiting. I'm going to classes. And, and – and there's lot to do and places to go, and I feel safe here. I can trust the others here. That's what's different. Oh, that, and there aren't any boys here which is strange."

"They are on the other side of this inner refuge," C'dmon informed her. "The need for safety, trust, and refuge is not limited by gender, or other incidentals. It is extended to all Hidayans. We find it more healing to separate the genders for awhile during recovery."

Then Angharad thought for a moment before popping the cookie into her mouth, crunching on it carelessly, and then picking up her tea mug. She was quiet while she visibly put together a thought. "Why are you here? I mean, you said you were Searchers, but why are you here?"

She caught the quick glances shared among the Searchers, before C'dmon answered, his lips thinned with deep emotions. "Salimah is in danger, as are all refuge cities. Those who view other Hidayans as things to be controlled or manipulated for selfish interests and power have discovered that some of their *property* is being spirited away to be rehabilitated. They recognized that it's happening and are now hunting down and killing Searchers. They say that we are spies and thieves, and they want the return of those who have escaped their control. It's only a matter of time before they discover Salimah is one of the refuge cities where their *property* has found a new life.

"But there is a garrison nearby! They wouldn't dare do anything with protection so close to us!" Angharad called out anxiously. "Are they coming now?"

"If there is enough money, power, and vigilante-minded people involved, a small garrison wouldn't be an obstacle."

"But they have no real proof! They couldn't identify one person out of an entire city! There is no evidence that we are any different than any other township on Hidaya. We look, act, and live like any other city!"

"Ah, well, that's not true. We don't have unpaid servants here," reminded H'shmand. "We have real volunteers who are not coerced to work or help out here."

"We educate everyone irregardless of gender or age," added C'dmon. "That's something valued, but not always honored because learning encourages questions."

"In Salimah there is access to health and well-being consultants," Ansh'mati put in. "You don't need to be important or rich to deserve care, and sometimes lack of hierarchical distinctions is discomforting."

"Our animals are wanted and cared for. They don't breed without control to become strays, or to create a surplus tempting people to misuse them for blood-sport."

"Those who are incapable of caring adequately for their offspring don't reproduce, and those whose biology has been permanently damaged by drugs or other substances don't reproduce either so any genetic abnormality caused by their abusive habits are not passed on to their children. Living has its own challenges without having to pay for your parents' problems."

"Those who cannot be reformed of their unsocial behaviors, don't reproduce either," continued C'dmon. "They are not shunned or placed in isolation from the rest of the population usually, but are given as much healing contact as possible, without exposing citizens to danger. If there is incurable, hurtful insanity or unreformable violent tendencies, there are many hours of attention given to an individual care plan rather than consulting a grand plan that must be applied to everyone."

"A true effort is made so that everyone finds a place of valued belonging in a refuge city like Salimah. You learn to be proud of yourself not just for what you can do or not, but because you are flourishing as yourself."

"Aren't there written guides so everyone is treated fairly?" inquired Angharad.

"There are guides, surely, but they are not laws. Laws become gods on their own. People forget that the laws are there to protect citizens; they are there as our servants, not for us to give up our mercifulness or to give up our freedoms to become enslaved by static laws that don't respond to needs. They are guides that aren't taken lightly or twisted manipulatively with anger to gain revenge. Especially since so many of us were taken from harmful situations we extend as much healing to everyone as possible without demeaning or endangering everyone.

"It is a delicate balance, and there are mistakes," concluded C'dmon, "But it is easier to modify the results of ineffective guides instead of changing entrenched, revered laws."

"It's not perfect, but this is refuge," Ansh'mati added gesturing around her. "All of us have experienced harm in life and are here because of a blessing gifted to us. We are here for another start at life. This is a place to be healed in body and soul and to be surrounding by genuine caring."

"Where are the gods?" Angharad asked with concern, finally able to ask this question of someone who truly knew. "We had a goddess in Amunet. She protected us."

"Did she?" gently prodded C'dmon. "Then why are you here?"

Angharad gaped at him in dismay, unable to answer his blasphemy.

"Didn't your goddess look like a statue? Does plaster, wood, or rock listen to you? No." C'dmon answered himself and went on shocking

Angharad. "No. True gods and goddesses are more powerful than we are and cannot be trapped by wood or rock. They are beyond us and within us. The statues and totems remind us of them, and may encourages us who see and touch those remembrances. They are not holy in themselves except as being created by the One; they remind us that holiness is centered within ourselves."

"Deities don't need rituals or ministers to be real divinities, but they may need those ministers and traditions to call us together in unity. We ourselves need the images and rituals more than they do."

"I can pray to my goddess by myself," insisted Angharad stubbornly.

"Yes, you can," Ansh'mati responded gently. "But C'dmon is talking about strength and focus when we are gathered as a faith community. Haven't you felt more secure here in Salimah? That's because more people are working intently to make that security happen for everyone, not just one person here, or one group there. The goal is that no one is left out because that flaw of omission becomes a weapon to destroy us all. And no one is waiting for someone else to do what their own hands can do with others.

"The intensity and solidity of your safety can be felt in every corridor, room, and field in a refuge city. Even when our opinions on how to create security or abundance differ we can cooperate if the Guiding One is included in our decisions. We do that because those we *do* call our own personal divinities ask that of us."

Angharad looked skeptically around in dismay. These were new ideas that challenged her deepest self. It was time to excuse herself from the confusion of her mind and leave, which she abruptly accomplished. As she whipped out of the room almost colliding with Ansh'mati who held open the door for her, she heard the Lady call out, "You are welcome here. Come when you can."

"She won't come back," muttered H'shmand.

"She will," C'dmon emphatically stated. "She doesn't know it right now, but she will come back."

"I agree," Ansh'mati commented. "She doesn't know yet that she was one of the last girls brought here to the female quarters. The last of the boys is now on his way to the male quarters. It is no longer safe to bring further refugees here. Another refuge city must be found. We have been here for a while, and it is time to move on."

"Are they expecting that we Searchers build this new refuge?" H'shmand grumbled. "I'm too old for that!"

The Lady shook her head slowly. "We are tired. We know how to found a refuge, but using reason, we can only encourage. The physical strength is beyond us, though if it was the will of the Kind One, that strength would be gifted to us. No, someone other than just Searchers must find a new home. And this time, perhaps a different kind of refuge."

C'dmon looked thoughtfully around at his comrades before his words dropped at their feet like rocks. "The Merciful One still guides us. We can keep Salimah safer during an attack than others because of our experience. We know how to negotiate and know when it is time to retreat – whatever that may entail. There have never been so many Searchers in one refuge city as there are now in Salimah. This is no coincidence. We Searchers are gathering here for a purpose, and I believe that ensuring the safety of Salimah is that purpose. The Merciful One will seek out someone else – maybe more than one – who will do what needs to be done and to create a new and different refuge."

"Do you think that that girl is that important?" questioned H'shmand quietly. The silence around him was his only answer.

Angharad ran out of the Searcher's room and found a deserted room in the Beehive. There was one window overlooking the fruitful fields and meandering river. Her thoughts drifted like the clouds gliding in Bozidara's brightness overhead.

She had heard strange beliefs beyond her reasoning today, and grasping them was overwhelming. There was freedom here to disagree if she chose, but there was a reasoning behind those beliefs that her heart of hearts resonated with.

She knew that if she chose to stay in Salimah, responsibilities would come, extensive learning would be provided, chores would be shared, and tasks – often hinted to be more like adventures – would be assigned. Yet, should she choose to leave, food, money, a job, and shelter would still be provided until she decided to make other choices and arrangements. And if she was unable to fit into Salimah's way of life by refusing to try and was "released," there was a great challenge of trust for if the secret of refuge was transmitted to the wrong persons, security was deeply compromised for all refuges.

Right now, Angharad wore the umber-hooded robe of a guest, one still questioning if it was safe to stay or *if* she wanted to stay.

And yet, there was always some older girl or woman nearby, even when she hid in the shadows and corners, someone busy with a task, but ready to comfort should she be invited nearer. Yes, life had changed for her in Salimah. Angharad had not been kidnapped by one of the secret cults of abuse and shame. Free thought and individuality were honored here. She was valued.

One morning soon after meeting the Searchers, Angharad walked into the refectory and noted that though many girls had already gone on to their daily chores, there were still many solitary ones like herself scattered here and there. She noted those whose hoods were used as signals that they wanted privacy or distance, and also recognized one girl who ate with her umber hood hanging welcomingly down her back. Angharad filled her bowl and plate with hot, honey-sweetened cereal, preserves and bread, filled a mug with steaming herbal tea, and hesitantly sat near enough to talk to the girl, but cautiously distant should she be rebuffed.

The girl looked up with deep brown eyes into Angharad's hazel ones, and shyly smiled. "The jam is made from the bant-berries we picked last week. I saw you at the far end of the garden picking them, too."

Angharad smiled back tentatively, and answered back softly in Pandit, the language she was slowly learning, "I saw you, too. You work in the garden a lot – at least, I see you every time I come."

The girl nodded in agreement. "I like gardening because of the flower colors and smells, the feel of the dirt, and getting out to see the sky. I came from farm country. Yesterday, the tall one with us, Anwyl, said if I worked with her today, she would show me which plants were the healing plants that she knew about."

"Anwyl," Angharad repeated hesitantly.

"I'm Kamalei. I've been here for almost a half a year, and I think I'm going to stay. I think it's good here. And besides," she added with a wry chuckle and plucking at her robe, "I'm tired of this dark brown. If I tell anyone here that I want to stay, then I'll get to wear any other colored robe except this color. That means I've chosen to stay."

"Kamalei," Angharad whispered memorizing it in habit. Kamalei chewed thoughtfully on the last chunk of her bread and looking at it intently as if seeing it for the first time. Then she lowered her voice so much that Angharad had to strain to hear. "Anwyl was asked about staying. She's been trying to believe all that Salimah teaches and believes, and has taken it to heart. She trusts life because of Salimah."

By rote Angharad whispered, "What the heart holds true travels to hands and tongue."

Kamalei's brown eyes grew large in her round, ebony-hued face, which reflected the amazement and wonder she felt inside at her own deep thoughts. Her waving hand included so much around her before she slipped the last spoonful of cereal into her mouth. She rose decisively carrying her bowl, plate, spoon and mug towards the kitchen washing room. Taking a few steps farther, Kamalei paused and turned with downcast, shy eyes mumbling questioningly, "See you later in the garden?"

"Uh-huh" smiled Angharad. Now there would be someone else she knew by name who was safe to talk to. As Angharad watched her new friend heading toward the far arched doorway and stairs leading to the gardens above, she whispered the name again for memory, "Kamalei."

Ishwa had not returned from beyond the campfire light, and Rawiya's fretting, nervously restless hands belied her concern. Though the insects and the pond water had healed her sore throat, she decided that ending the evening presentation now was a good decision tonight.

"I am tired," she confessed honestly. "We will stop for tonight. Remember, take no food into your tents, and light the smudge candles at your tent entrance. I will now ask for blessings of peace and protection as you sleep."

"Storyteller?" a voice called out softly from the reclining and slouching pilgrims.

"Yes?" Rawiya responded warily fearing she would be asked to continue the telling.

"Will we stay here tomorrow?"

"Probably, though there might be a good reason to move on I don't know about yet."

"Storyteller?" another voice called out. "Will the birds follow us?"

"Probably. They are part of the mystery of the Cham for this journey. They are gifts, and apparently they are also our protectors."

"Were they here before, at another time for —"

"Yes," interrupted Ishwa unexpectedly from shadows beyond the campfire. He had come back quietly and had listened without being detected. "Yes, they were here before, but not in this form. The Cham Desert itself is a focal point for blessings, and that is why caravan retreats deliberately cross it. There are always blessings and healings here because travelers intentionally seek and welcome them. And there are always mysteries and protectors. On one trip the trees and bushes themselves were the protectors for the caravan. On another trip there were sentient beetles hitching rides with us and whispering guidance. Protection crossing the Cham comes in many forms, but never before have the protectors taken a gift, or an offering from travelers, and definitely never have they taken blood like they took from us today. It has never happened. Never."

"But it has," Rawiya's contradicted hesitantly. Suddenly all eyes focused back on her.

"Ahh! That significant crossing of the Cham so long ago!" exclaimed an elderly scholar. "But... but that wasn't really an offering but a...a...an unfortunate misunderstanding that's really more of a legend or myth. Such a small offering, though important to our origination myth; yet however entertaining, in this context it might as well be worth forgetting about when it comes down to here and now reality,"

"What Life touches is never forgotten, no matter how great or small," spontaneously chanted more than half the caravan travelers for they all had heard that proverb at least once a day since birth.

"But still..." the professor started to argue.

"No," Ishwa interrupted harshly. "Nothing is forgotten from Life. Though our ancestors are not always remembered by name, and their deeds may be incorrectly reported or not, Life still hasn't forgotten them. Even our unspoken needs and intentions are remembered from childhood. No, this crossing is different."

A deep voice questioned, *"Were we required to offer ourselves – willingly or unwillingly?"*

"Was purifying of the water the response of the protecting ones to a blood offering?" a young man called out nervously.

"No. I asked," Ishwa responded without clarifying whom he had asked. *"That purifying gift was from the Healing One who walks Hidaya at the end of the day. There is more than one protector of our small group, so we don't need to be worried or afraid."*

"Could you be wrong? Could you be misinterpreting what is happening?" suggested another voice.

"Perhaps," answered Ishwa. *"That is always a possibility since I am only a servant of this Life, but by the end of the trip the mystery will be made clear to us. For now we need to meditate."*

"Don't you mean we need to pray," grumped the recalcitrant hiker who had intermittently sulked pessimistically throughout the days in frustration.

Ishwa sighed with genuine tiredness, *"Praying means we are talking to Someone. Meditation means we are listening to Someone. We need to meditate. But now, we must rest. Let us be blessed."*

He raised his arms in blessing. Without thought, as if they had always been doing it, each person also raised their arms in blessing. Energy surged around and through them, and though Ishwa spoke the words, the intent of blessing flowed from all pilgrims and attendants. The spirit-sparks hovered just beyond their fingertips daring them to reach out to touch them, and swirled away before any choice to reach out had led to action. They spiraled higher than the gnarly branches above where the desert birds roosted, and then drifted softly, noiselessly back down into the campfire.

"Ahh!" a surprised novice exclaimed.

An attendant held a tray of smoking smudge lights sending their pleasant resinous perfume into the chilling night air. He held the tray as offerings for those passing nearby and responded to the novice's surprise. *"We raise our hands in blessing to acknowledge that we are blessed, and because of that we can share that blessing with others by asking for that gift. Tonight, that's what we have done: used our spiritual birthright expressing heartfelt good intentions for our own benefit and those around us. We have called upon the Compassionate One."*

The attendant scanned the questioning faces around him. *"By blessing those around us, we shared the goodness within our hearts, and the Understanding One acknowledged our good intents with the gift of spirit sparks."*

"But I've never done that before!"

"And I haven't either! I just did it without thinking, and —"

"That's one of the gifts of caring for others and showing those heartfelt caring intentions."

Unexpectedly they all smiled at each other and with palms pressed together bowed to the others. Spirit sparks glowed softly around them in blessing as they sought rest at the end of an amazing day of personal challenge and transformation.

*Discouragement and fear are temptations
that weaken the trust and courage needed to risk
everything to accomplish one's goals. Therefore,
one or more of those goals need to be more
important than fear.*

~ *Searcher's Book of Guidance*

CHAPTER 4

❖

INVITATIONS
OF TRUST

Ishwa held two conferences in the morning about self-perception which included a mandala-making project expressing one's inner self, recognition of compassionate relationship in that mandala, and then he later guided a short, meditative, early-afternoon session focusing on the Compassionate One's presence in life before private consultations and rest. In between those conferences the attendants escorted the Hidayan pilgrims on hikes, scientific activities, and specific searches for bio-diversity unique to this oasis. Already several new, formerly unknown species of insects, lizards and cacti had been identified.

Cook created an exotic marinade for tonight's protein-based bean patties steamed with various tasty herbs that the pilgrims themselves had gathered. With spicy, roasted tubers the meal was more than satisfying.

Rawiya began her storytelling when comfort bespoke for the majority of travelers now resting around her, many still licking the sticky honey balls that had been tonight's dessert. Perched on the shoulders of some of the pilgrims several of the desert birds chirped quietly as if attentively involved in a one-sided conversation; dust lizards nudged other patrons hoping to be petted, and were rewarded.

"What we perceive may not always be an accurate assessment of reality; still, we respond to that misperception as if it were real. If our intentions are hopeful and positive it is possible to bring about the reality we seek. Sometimes the choices of others get in our way and divert our intended goals. Ultimately our attitudes are involved in what happens to us, and changing our attitudes to something more positive than what we start out with can be difficult. But it is not usually insurmountable if we care and are compassionate and forgiving with ourselves and others."

The Fourth Night:

Outside of Salimah's walls the foothills swelled successively towards the wind- honed, craggy Bhairava Mountains rising on their northern and eastern boundaries. The Bhairava Range stretched and strained skyward detaining the abundant mists swirling about its escarpments and ushering the resultant icy trickles of water into larger rivulets and streams that splashed and danced their way through cascades, pools, and riffles on their way to the thirsty irrigated valleys, recovered populated cities, and unknown territories beyond. The sharp-toothed mountains held little soil after eons enduring icy winds, thundering winter storms, and merciless, scorching summer heat from ochre Bozidara.

As soil fertility decreased exponentially the nearer the gently rolling foothills approached their sparse Bhairava big brothers, Salimah gardeners were increasingly challenged to find caches of soil in which to tuck herbs and seedlings. Generations of successful effort, however, had produced a plethora of healing and culinary herbs, several self-sustaining dense forests, and surprising hillside orchards adequately producing an amazing diversity of nuts and fruits for Salimah's slow-growing population.

Closer to the cloistered valley more orderly furrowed fields curved around the yet-to-be forested hills and then creatively meandered towards the city walls. Complicated mechanical planting, irrigating, or reaping machinery did not exist here; but rather, because of many willing hands, such devices were not needed should they be re-invented or should they be found to have survived from previous eras when such mechanisms had been used on huge corporate farms. Since the entire city's population owned the fields and orchards and shared the work as needed, straight rows were deemed boring and unnatural. Therefore, the rows curved artistically, meandering much like a flowing river around Salimah's walls. Even now, teams of workers with lightweight harrows cut slits into the turf so that the rotting debris of last year's crop and the fragile topsoil would not be over-turned excessively. Since the fragility of Hidaya's ecosystems and atmosphere needed adequate protection, tilling only the ground needed for plant growth would not release carbon dioxide stored within the clods of soil harming the atmosphere. Completely overturned and cultivated fields commonly had been done before the Devastation Era, but now that practice was perceived to be a criminal endangerment of all life on Hidaya. The Rudra Wasteland to the south of Salimah hinted at having been destroyed by such unnecessary over-cultivation in the long-ago past. Even those isolated, greedy communes that ignored most of Hidaya's precepts did not ignore this injunction. Surprisingly, the harvests were abundantly more productive and resistant to diseases and pests using this simple method. The produce from these fields kept the population comfortably healthy and satisfied much like an over-sized family garden would beside a farmhouse.

Within the protective walls of Salimah's inner refuge, incredible varieties of heritage flowers and vegetables, once thought lost, flourished here under the postulants' directed attention. These were the fruits of those few, far-seeing gleaners who had saved seeds from hardy native plants, which past civilizations had replaced in favor of genetically engineered or faddishly favored bio-engineered species. These were the kinds of seedlings with which retired professors, backyard enthusiasts and weekend farmers had originally dallied, sharing their unique produce with small circles of friends. These unprofessionally rescued native, hand-pollinated plants continued now as living testimonies to individual curiosity.

For many of the postulants, these were the first plants they had tended. These were also the gardens in which many postulants heard their first requests to care for something of use to the community; these smaller gardens acclimated newcomers to simple chores with directions couched carefully in emotionally neutral requests for most persons in refuge had experienced only brutish commands or curtly barked orders backed up with harsh enforcement. Requests, even gentle directives, had been un-experienced luxuries, and now were heard daily.

Responses to unaccustomed courtesy tested the authenticity of the underlying respect extended through politeness. Who could believe there was a real choice offered where only enforced obedience had been known? Who could believe that polite, calm guidance was directed inclusively when only subservient humiliation and humbling submissiveness had been learned for survival? But in Salimah, in safe surroundings, those once-useful survival patterns were challenged. Tantrums, fearful over-compliance, belligerence, grumbles, retorts, threats, thrashing out, crying fits, cringing confusion, panic in all its forms - all were dealt with as the postulants learned that an honest response to a request was more effective than any previously learned survival reaction. Gently, gradually, the calm gift of consistently respectful example tamed most fears over time. When that fear was too embedded for release, still they were all accepted as is. Belonging in Salimah did not depend upon unattainable perfection. Belonging depended upon accepting that one *did* belong and was welcome in this place; the reciprocal desire to accept others and welcome them was still a huge advance in attitude, but such a maturing step was possible for many.

Angharad walked into the humid greenhouse where she had picked bant-berries before. Partially down the far right, narrow pavement separating the squared, raised growing boxes, Kamalei was hunched over some fuzzy-leafed herbs concentrating on what Anwyl was explaining. Angharad edged cautiously nearer to hear without being overtly detected. Yet, Anwyl unexpectedly tossed the loose hair that had fallen in front of her eyes as she hunched forward, and immediately perceived Angharad's presence.

"Aren't you the girl who can speak Chi'ma? Not many of us can speak it well," Anwyl gently inquired looking sideways, still bent over the plants.

Angharad froze when Anwyl and Kamalei's eyes rested on her with curious anticipation. Trying with all her effort not to tremble under their focus, Angharad nodded slightly.

Now Kamalei enthusiastically straightened and burst out without pause, "Can you really speak Chi'ma? Where did you learn it? Is that why you have an accent?"

"Amunet," Angharad's suddenly dry throat croaked. "I lived in Amunet. That's the only language they spoke that I ever heard. It's close to Pandit, what we speak here."

"But, Amunet's way on the other side of the Bhairava Mountains! Days and days from here!" Anwyl exclaimed. "It's supposed to be almost impossible to cross the Amunet Desert and then the Bhairava Mountains."

"How did you do it?" Kamalei breathlessly asked in awe. "Were you alone?"

Angharad momentarily wanted to shrivel and hide into invisibility because the questioning allowed her wary, self-defensiveness to rise. Against every survival instinct she possessed, opposing all learned shielding responses, some curious, hopeful core of being-ness asserted itself and responded more strongly that the fearfulness. Her foot inched forward revealing her intent to step into the group and answer their questions. Without thought, both Kamalei and Anwyl glided forward to meet her.

"I was found by Lady Ae'sha and Lord Z'van sleeping in one of the visiting rooms of Amunet. There was no way for me to stay in Amunet without being taken by the guards of the city. They wanted to make me *sudasi*, a life-servant. They told my ma that it was the only way I wouldn't be a burden on Amunet's people by my existence."

Angharad's head was now bowed in shame for her birth and in memory of her life in Amunet. Her personal story, hidden for so long, challenged her to tell it so she could be healed. And Angharad shared.

She remembered the disdainful stares of the guards as they had come to her ma's small, illegal apartment behind one of the trade stores, where she had devised her own employment just to survive. The protectors, smelling clean and spicy, strode boldly into this hovel; they were dressed in the official maroon colors of Amunet's municipal guardians. With experienced glances they saw the big and little crawlies, dirt-stained rags, unwashed skin; they smelled the rank sweat, sour filth, putrid remnants of unfinished meals, and the rancid stink of neglected, unloved life. Words were not spoken because protectors were not supposed to judge, but their reviling attitude, thick with acrid condemnation filled the tight space until Angharad almost fainted holding her breath. She knew that protectors walked through Amunet in small contingents searching for persons unbefitting the respect of the general citizenry who could be made useful by becoming *sudasi*. Being declared *sudasi* meant menial slavery until death.

While Angharad's ma resignedly haggled with the protectors for at least some coins for the loss of her child, unaware that she herself was being appraised as *sudasi*, her young daughter wriggled under the piles of hay, rags and papery garbage mattressing towards a thin board that was the hovel's back wall; there was a jagged breach in the board where the wall and flooring did not evenly meet. Once through this emergency exit, Angharad stood in a narrow gap between the back partition of her former home and the stone fortification surrounding Amunet. Given only these scant few inches, Angharad slipped sideways, ignoring painful scratches and scrapes until she reached a side street, where she scampered desperately into the city's maze-like streets and into obscurity. She never saw her ma again.

From there Angharad kept running, hiding, and surviving weeks and months by eating fallen fruits and vegetables, and occasionally begging for food. Whenever the municipal guardians appeared, Angharad melted into nothingness with increasing skill until she was almost invisible both day and night.

That had changed overnight when the streets teemed with outlying visitors and rowdy merchants pushing each other aside roughly during the Spring Festival. Travelers from distant cities meant that even though there were more people to hide behind among crowded, aggressively bunched, argumentative strangers, there were also fewer places to scrunch into without being discovered since more municipal protectors worked those same crowds to keep order.

When there was finally no sanctuary anywhere and exhaustion became her desperate companion, Angharad sneaked behind a temporarily distracted guard barring the entrance to the forbidden, private, lower levels. There were no curious or misdirected pedestrians here. Yet it was a temporary solution until Angharad could emerge and hide in a more acceptable niche. But then, Lord Z'van and Lady Ae'sha had found and doubly blessed her.

Angharad shamefully thought that Kamalei and Anwyl would turn from her now in disgust as she finished sharing this turbulent autobiography, so she simply and succinctly summed it up with, "I wasn't supposed to be where I was, so I hid, but Lady Ae'sha and Lord Z'van found me and brought me here. I don't know how long it took to get here because I slept most of the way, but it took many days. We left with one of the Spring trading caravans, so no one noticed one more girl among all the others. And then we came here."

A moment of awkward thought and silence completed the story, and then both Anwyl and Kamalei performed an astonishing ritual. Each pressed their hands together and bowed towards Angharad. The luminous spirit-energy of blessing hovered around their folded hands before flowing outward to disperse the blessings towards Angharad. The garden around them also glowed with golden energy borrowed from the gifting. Then, as if nothing special had just occurred, Anwyl turned and beckoned to the other girls.

"Now, let me show you an herb that has pleasant smelling flowers, and its seeds not only smell good, but when heated with oil they can heal your skin. It's called lav'ndra." Both Angharad and Kamalei followed her wordlessly.

No one commented on the tears that overflowed from Kamalei's suddenly bright eyes, so she had no need to invent a dissembling explanation of sensitivity to the plant or the brightness of Bozidara's rays through the greenhouse windowing.

Angharad walked without feeling the hard paving stones, and listened without hearing to Anwyl's patiently explaining words. She touched the furred leaves without perceiving their texture, and was overcome by inner calmness and awe at receiving honor and compassionate acceptance for sharing such a tiny bit of herself. Once again, her limited background and vocabulary confounded understanding of what she had just experienced, and yet, even she could perceive that some undefined boundary had been discarded momentarily by her own choice, and an enveloping cushion of comforting peace and safety had replaced the now-empty space in which that dispelled barrier had existed.

"Tonight's story is finished early," Rawiya calmly announced. "But each of us has a story to share and heal. If you are willing, spend some time this evening sharing your past with those around you so you will not be dragging heavy memories and emotions into the present and future as did Angharad. Those of you who choose not to share are still welcome to a second dessert Cook has prepared for the evening. We will remain here for awhile, and then the evening blessing will begin. Relax, and enjoy." And with that Rawiya stood gracefully and headed without distraction towards the first of the attendants carrying mounds of cookie treats still hot from the cook tent. She was not surprised to note that Ishwa was ahead of her.

Sharing was tentative at first, but gathered greater and greater participation. Attendants and pilgrims opened their lives to others' welcome and healing, while they were munching on handfuls of crunchy cookies. Ishwa and Rawiya partnered with many groups as well as hesitant individuals. Taking a break to discuss the journey's destination, they decided that another day of rest at the present oasis was in order. They could always skip one of their scheduled stops and arrive at an oasis with an incredible vista of the desert so they would be precisely where they should be when the spring rains and desert flowering began.

Yet, here at this once-horrific oasis, changes had already begun. New, young shoots around the clean water were already centimeters high, and bud-bumps on smooth stems hinted that the spring rains were immediately imminent and the plants anticipated them. They were ready for growth. The ground almost quivered with the need to burst into bloom. But the caravan relaxed for one more day and night before departing.

*"You are always a worthy and important person.
In your heart you know that truth. Others' evaluations,
your financial success, or personal skills don't change
the reality of your worthiness and importance."*

~ Fifth Book of Instruction

CHAPTER 5

❖

REALITIES REVEALED

During that next day the anticipating air could not be fanned into even a slight breeze once the chill morning breeze had silently ebbed. The heat lay unmoving like a heavy, stifling blanket over the vast, desert bed. Clouds had piled up on the morning horizon and had bravely sailed over the Cham towards the Bahairava Mountains, but they had not survived the complete distance, getting smaller and smaller until they merely had dissolved overhead. If they could have just endured the distance a little farther then the rains would have arrived heralding spring's return and the Cham's blooming would begin. *It was so close!*

Conferences on forgiveness had been today's theme, and Ishwa had finished counseling several retreatants before finally throwing himself onto the mat in his tent spent by the heat and efforts of the day. His eyes had barely closed when he heard a rustling at the tent entrance, and then felt a slight crowding as someone silently sat beside him. Ishwa pretended sleep, but his guest knew his wiles.

"You don't have to open your eyes to listen."

"Thank you, Rawiya," Ishwa intoned patiently.

"I didn't want to be here for this retreat. I needed the time for myself."

"I know."

"How? I didn't tell anyone. I didn't say anything!"

"Your expression. First, you usually are smiling when you bring your camping pack to the first packing and planning meeting. This time you hadn't even packed. You came late to the meeting and sat with a scowl on your face outside of the meeting circle, as if you were an unhappy auditing observer. It wasn't hard to guess that you didn't want to be there."

"But I did come, and I am here now."

"And?"

"Amon would like me to settle down in Viñay and do something less nomadic."

"You haven't told him, yet, of your need to cross the desert every season?"

"No. How do you tell someone that you need to do something just to touch what cannot be touched? How do you tell someone that you need to hear words that aren't spoken, just felt and perceived as clearly as if someone had spoken those words into your ear and heart? How do you tell someone that you will never be satisfied sufficiently with a conventional life? I am not hiding something because it's out in the open, nor am I reluctant to make a commitment to him and am making this up as an excuse."

"But you are hiding something, Rawiya. You are addicted to this desert just as I am. It's not just a long trip from one village to another on opposite sides of the desert; it's not just a job escorting pilgrims from here to there. You are addicted to a Presence you are more receptive to here." Ishwa turned on his side and rested his head on his raised palm now as he looked up at Rawiya. "You are addicted to Presence.

"You and I don't hear words, but we hear the heartbeat of Life here. We don't touch a person or a thing, but we touch what makes us alive and true to ourselves. We don't just counsel or talk to groups or tell stories for entertainment; we perceive and share unchanging Truth the best way we can. And then there are the blessings.

"Some people can get by with a brief desert experience once every few years, or even once in a lifetime. Just that will keep their lives steady and true. Other people can talk to friends and family and feel the aliveness and the center of truth and love and life and be filled to completion and contentment.

"But you and I, no. No. We need to keep touching and hearing and feeling that Compassionate Presence. We need to perceive this reality just to keep focused and centered every day, or we become lost to ourselves and to those we care about." Ishwa let his head drop, and stared at nothing in particular at the top of his tent. Rawiya listened with bowed head nodding in agreement.

"We have a need to pray and meditate every day in order to share and sense the Response which is stronger here than any other place we have on Hidaya. This caravan is not a luxury for us; it's a necessity. We are addicted to the Truth we experience here just as if we were addicted to drugs from the bazaar. You will have to tell Amon this somehow, and maybe share this experience with him so he can understand."

"Are we so weak that we can't live without this contact?" Rawiya's rasping voice was both bitter and resentful as it was filled with so much intense emotion. Her eyes glistened from stoically withheld tears.

"You sound like you are pitying yourself for this gift. Be quiet! It is a gift whether or not you think it is.

"It's not that we are weak — though that may be the truth of the matter. It's that we were made with this need to be receptive to the core of Life itself. Maybe it is a weakness because we are never filled to completion for long, but I prefer to think that it's not an issue of strong or weak, good or bad. It just is." Ishwa sighed deeply in resignation.

"It just is, and we live with it and because of it. It's like a touchstone: we reach out to hold it whenever we can and seldom put it on a shelf. Our souls need it or they are lost. We know that lost feeling well, and the emptiness we feel makes no sense because friends and family surround us, loved ones and abundance of every kind is near, but none of it is any good unless we are close to our touchstones. Everything is dust without that center to our lives."

"Our weakness and our strength, Ishwa," mused Rawiya. "Maybe I don't have the proper words to make Amon understand."

"Maybe not, but I still understand. I know you will find a way. And I also know I am tired," Ishwa drowsily whispered, slurring words in that tiredness.

Rawiya sat silently for a long time. At the edge of Ishwa's consciousness just as he slipped completely from wakefulness into a gentle dream, he heard Rawiya's voice whisper her own personal prayer; "This need is a gift. And I am thankful for it. I thank the Compassionate One for making me as I am. I thank the Merciful One for gifting me with a need that can only be satisfied by opening myself to receive that blessing. I thank the Understanding One for this life as it is, with all it's hurts, frustrations, and goodness.

"I am blessed by Life. And even though I am humbled by the immensity and complexity of it, and stumble through it, I am gifted knowing I am not alone, and am doubly blessed knowing that who and what I need in this life is both within me and without. And my friend understands. May Amon, my beloved, understand, also." Ishwa contentedly sank into deeper sleep even before Rawiya had left his side, leaving a Blessing of Gratitude behind to shimmer softly and disperse above him.

The evening air had that pleasantly tolerable temperature reached only at the end of a scorching day when the shallow exhalations of far-off snowy mountain-crests puff and dip tentatively, caressing distant valleys and plains. Holiday frivolity danced at the edges of camp teasing the pilgrims with enticing, diverting thoughts. Rest and satisfying food around the campfire further lightened the hearts of all travelers who knew each other increasingly well by this time.

A veteran attendant waylaid Rawiya as she returned from successfully begging the cook for more deserts. "Rawiya, have you noticed the health of the travelers?"

Alarmed, Rawiya glanced sharply around her. There were no feverish patrons in sight. Everyone seemed to be accounted for; they mostly idled comfortably around the camp circle. Perhaps the attendant meant the other servant travelers, but no, they were all present, doing their jobs without stressed scurrying to remedy forgotten tasks. Curious now, Rawiya noted quiet, amiable conversation and companionship, punctuated by occasional bursts of laughter and silliness.

Slowly, so as not to miss any possible clue to what the attendant was asking her to perceive, she scanned the pilgrims again, and then focused on the attendant's eyes. "What do you see?"

"They are all healthy. We all are."

"And?"

"Last season, and the season before that and before that, and beyond that, by this time there were strained muscles, back pains, Bozidara-caused skin-burns, allergic reactions, stomach cramps, breathing problems from the heat, and a whole bunch more problems. This trip there is nothing. We started out with aches and pains, but there is nothing now." The importance of the attendant's triumphant proclamation was lost on Rawiya who stared at him dumbly.

"There isn't even a stubbed toe that keeps throbbing to complain about! We are all healthy and almost immune to any malady that naturally would come our way!" Impatience with Rawiya's density clouded the edges of the attendant's eyes. "We are all healthy! Look at yourself!"

Rawiya reflexively looked down at her hands cupped around a pudding bowl. What should she be looking for? And then she abruptly perceived what the attendant had been saying. "I am healthy right down to my fingernails! I should have two broken fingernails from helping to dig the tubers! I should still have those scabbed-over scratches on my arms. I should still have a tender spot on my leg when Cid bumped me. There are no scars or bruises!" She looked up at the attendant dumbfounded. "What about the others?"

"The same," he answered with muted excitement. "They haven't noticed, but then they don't know what to expect. We've been back and forth for many seasons, so we know the usual patterns of aches and complaints and fevers and bruises. There is nothing. Nothing. I think it's the healings because we've stayed at other stops longer before, and we still had sicknesses and pulled muscles or burned mouths or abscessed teeth. I've never seen anything like this, ever. And then, since the healings, we've been healing a lot faster for everything that's happened since. Look there," he said pointing to an elderly woman. "She's the one who fell yesterday and broke her wrist. Today it's as if it never had been broken!"

"Thank you for your perceptions. You did well. When you can, please tell Ishwa," Rawiya distractedly praised the attendant, before finding her place in the campfire circle. She barely had time to finish her extra pudding cup before Ishwa gave her the signal to begin this evening's storytelling.

The Fifth Night:

We are born good. That is our belief as Hidayans. We are good. Yet we don't often believe that especially if those around us poison us with their unfair perceptions or projected self-perceptions of goodness. We don't believe we are good if we fail to forgive ourselves for being imperfect and mortal. We are so judgmental of ourselves and unfairly so.

Tonight we tell of someone just like this who lost and then found the goodness of herself.

"I'll bet she is going to tell us about —"

"Emina!"

"Shush! Let her tell!"

Far beyond Salimah to the south, where the climate was dryer and harsher, but where a satisfying life could still be found, lay the little settlement of Adamya. If abundant living was defined as hard effort in the midst of a tightly supportive community, where no one need sleep with hunger pains while the magnificent starry dome twinkled above, where travelers were welcomed and sheltered and education for all was encouraged, and medical care was available for all, then this rough village was paradise for most inhabitants. For most, but not for all.

In one of the small, tidy hogans, Baya reached into a carved gourd container with her long, brown fingers and felt – nothing! She pushed it away allowing it to clatter on the floor in rejection. She swiftly reached for another, which she shook desperately before discarding that one, also. Nothing! Her deep, ebony-brown eyes scanned the dishes, bowls, lidded cooking pots, and storage vessels thinking, "Where? Where?"

A movement of air behind her alerted her and Baya swung around to see Gamba, her husband, heading purposefully towards the door of their small home. His robes had been carefully arranged as if going to an important appointment, but they still didn't hide his soft, pouching belly, a singular symbol to Baya that even when filled, Gamba always wanted more. His hair had been oiled and cut to show he was meeting someone important, but he still smelled unclean and sourly rank. Baya forced herself to speak, to push the words past the gagging reflex that habitually silenced her when in her husband's presence.

"Husband, the money for Dhakiya, the egg-seller...it was here." Her voice faded as Gamba's dark eyes pinned her arrogantly. Baya involuntarily began to quiver in apprehension. Her shudders often angered Gamba even as they seemed to please him.

"I take what is mine when I want, Baya. Did you think you could hide anything from me? You have no right to keep anything from me! Be quiet!" He was shouting now.

But in her great need Baya persisted. "Husband, she wants her money today. We...I gave my word for the honor of our family that we would finally pay her today. I saved for her. For her life and our honor I must pay her today. We must pay!"

Gamba came closer, almost gliding it seemed to Baya; he seemed to tower over her as far as the ceiling getting taller and swelling with growing anger. Like the spring thunderclouds from the west he appeared always distantly intriguing and peaceful, but whenever he neared, he gathered himself from many sources and became a violent overshadowing storm with flashes of lightning and loud rumbling sounds. And now, being called to account for the missing money his pounding anger came like hard rainfall in words and actions.

Baya couldn't remember many of those words later as she lay on the floor. She had insulted her husband by asking him to give back what he had taken. Now she would have to face the egg-seller, Dhakiya, who had already extended much too much time for the payment owed. Shame and desperation weighted Baya as she pulled herself to a sitting position. Hot tears wet her smooth, ruddy cheeks, and her shoulders shook in silent sobs. If anyone heard her crying, her husband would hear about it, and more punishment for shaming him in front of the community would be his response for the distress. When he left, how long she had lain on the floor, and how long she had sat in fear, hurt, shame and anger was measured in shallow, shuddering, hiccoughing breaths.

Now a shadow fell across the doorway, and after a long pause, a fat arm with short, roly-poly fingers pushed back the Bozidara-shielding fabric so the visitor could enter. Dhakiya stood alertly, centered under the lintel until her light-blinded eyes could see through the dimness inside. She saw everything then, and casually sauntered towards Baya without looking at her. She picked up one of the carved gourds from the floor and thumped her ample bottom on a low stool all in one bent-over motion. Something in the far corner of the room, behind the antique sideboard intrigued her and captured her focus. To that corner she spoke.

"I remember my best friend's daughter, Bahija. How pretty she was. Her smiles delighted everyone. Her laughter was like harp music reaching all the way to my heart. She could have gone on to be a student in the city; there were so many roads she could have walked. But she didn't choose any of them.

"My friend's daughter chose to wait and be married first. She said that there would be time later for learning and adventures. Bahija, girl of beauty and laughter, became the bride. How lovely she was on her wedding day. She renamed her husband as the old traditions ask. She named him Gamba, mighty warrior. He felt proud and his chest, which was bigger than his belly that day, swelled out feeling his importance. I saw Bahija look up shyly smiling into his proud eyes, waiting for her marriage name. Would he call her his loved one? Would he call her his gentle dove? Ah, I saw how hopefully and lovingly she looked up at him. But he had deceived us all with his hidden beingness.

"My friend's daughter was crying in hurt and shame a moment later, for in his pride, to show how much control he had over this woman bound to him in love, he called her his ugly one. He turned her heart inside out and named her Baya. She could have refused then the marriage, but I saw the shock in her eyes, which froze her into silence.

"Now, Baya has become as her husband named her. Her face is lined with worry and fear. Her arms and body are bruised. She walks like an old one, bent and shaking. No one talks to her for fear she will be beaten for speaking without permission to her neighbors. And there are so many debts she has to pay. And where is the money?

"Do I hear a squeak? A whimper like a puppy would make? Ah, that must be the sound of my friend's daughter, for only she would sound so hopeless when Bozidara shines outside and the morning breeze freshens the air. Only Baya, whom I can't see in this gloomy house, would make that sound. She is near, but I can't see her. If I could see her, I would tell her to go now, right now this very morning. I would tell her, late this morning, as it is, go to the beach for the fish market will soon be over.

"A green boat would be the last one on the lake shore. A green batik would be flung on the bottom of the boat, as if forgotten, but it has been waiting for her. The fisherman would not be looking underneath it when he sailed out across Lake Maemi this afternoon to visit his grandmother – a two days' sail north across this great lake we are blessed to live besides. The fisherman would not bring the batik to his grandmother until the last star has come out, and then when he lifted it from the bottom of the boat, nothing would be beneath it."

"How?" mumbled Baya through swollen lips. Confusion filled her puffy, tear-bright eyes. Shivering fear at what was being suggested showed she had heard.

"My friend asked me to watch over her daughter when she died. She asked this of many friends who have watched carefully. They have not interfered because they were not asked to help change what they saw. My friend's daughter chose a life for good when she grew up, but it was an unwise choice. Should she want to choose again, she has only to touch this old, wrinkled hand of mine. My eyes are old, and this room is dark, or I would reach out to help if my friend's daughter were here. Perhaps it is my imagination. Perhaps she has traveled too far on her chosen path so she cannot make a different choice. I need to sit here and think awhile. I am so tired."

A stray breeze wafted the fabric in the doorway. The neighbor's watchdog worried a bone noisily. A newborn squalled its hunger briefly, and then quieted. Baya had not moved since Dhakiya had stopped speaking. She barely saw the well-scrubbed wooden floor beneath her, though she stared at it intently trying to put her thoughts in some reasonable order. This was serious; it was something that was not done.

Was it possible to leave the community and people she loved? Was it possible to make a different choice after so much time?

Her head slowly rose so she could stare now at Dhakiya, who still found something to gaze at behind the sideboard. When the egg-seller had almost given up hope, she felt the sweaty warmth of Baya's hand nestle into her own gnarly palm. Dhakiya had not known she had breathed so shallowly in anticipation until then, and gulped in a huge lungful of air. They sat quietly in the dark interior of the hogan breathing silently and absorbing the golden light of blessing focused around them.

Finally, without a word, Dhakiya stood up, and helped Baya sit down on the stool. Then she went to the back doorway and waved her hand absently as if shooing away a fly. Some females - two childhood friends of Baya, and several widowed elders soon entered. Silently they undressed Baya, helped her to the toilet, bathed her, and re-dressed her in clothes belonging to them all. When Baya stood before them completely clothed in borrowed raiment, they all casually slipped out the back door with Baya in their midst.

Anyone watching later would remember the clothing and think of any female but Baya, who never wore this pattern, or that color; who never owned sandals like this, or held an umbrella like that; they never would think that who was under the veils and dress was not whom they vaguely remembered as a part of a group of chatty females who acted more like laughing, chattering, unruly sisters on an adventure out of their parent's corrective sight for awhile.

As they walked towards the lake other females casually joined them giggling and jostling one another happily. They called to the fishermen who were getting their boats and nets ready for tomorrow, and spontaneously chanted songs and danced with swinging hips and rhythmically stomping feet. One fisherman took out a drum and another revealed a reed flute, and the music flew around joyously. And afterwards, when Bozidara started its descent from its highest point in the blue-gray sky, the females grew tired and told the fishermen to go home to their wives or sail off to night-fish. Their conversation quieted to gentle chatter and they, too, turned towards their homes. The beach was left abandoned.

Gamba came home to find it totally scrupulously clean, dusted, washed, and immaculate; he assumed it was Baya's submissive handiwork. The stove's low fire only heated tea water, as if Baya had anticipated his return and thoughtfully had prepared for him. Gamba waited for her to come and actually brew the tea, but she seemed to be detained somehow. He heard a shuffling outside and a low clearing of the throat to announce someone waited on the threshold. Shoving aside the door fabric, Gamba saw Dhakiya politely waiting with downcast eyes. "What an unfortunate visitor to come here now," thought Gamba, but he only grunted acknowledgment of the egg-seller's presence.

"Ah, Gamba!" Dhakiya exclaimed. "I had hoped to see you or Baya earlier, but I forgot. There was dancing on the beach today, and even though my old bones can't move to keep up the rhythm, my eyes and ears still enjoy the music. So, I was not at the market today." Gamba just stared at her impatiently.

"Ah! Baya bought eggs awhile back, and I had her word that she would pay today. Since I was not at the market, she could not find me to pay me. So on my way home I thought to make it easier for her so she would not have to search for me tomorrow when I go back to my homestead. Is Baya at home?"

A grunted "no" was her answer, because by now Gamba had figured out the end to this conversation and it would embarrass him unless he took control. "She can pay you tomorrow. She takes care of things like that."

"Ah," was the soft response of Dhakiya, but she didn't move. A whispered whistle from between her teeth let Gamba know she was waiting and wouldn't be moving soon. Dhakiya was held in the community's esteem too highly to be disrespectfully dismissed, and Gamba knew that his reputation would be damaged if word got around of any poor behavior.

Grumpily he growled out a lie, "I don't know where she keeps the money for the household."

Still Dhakiya stood waiting, listening patiently, wheezing slightly with each breath until Gamba realized she truly expected him to pay. She almost whooped in laughter when his eyes widened with understanding. He started fumbling through his pockets and finally felt a crinkly roll in his back pocket. Triumphantly he pulled it out and then unfolded it in dismay. It was not money, but a meticulously scribed gambling marker of debt payable to him from his day's activity. Stupidly he stood with it in his hand wondering what to do now. There was no more money at home, and though the marker was for a hefty amount, it was written for far more than he owed the egg-seller.

Dhakiya calmly stood on her tiptoes and peeked at the marker. With deliberate slowness she reached into a heavy pouch at her side and counted out change. She held the money in her left hand flat out, and held her right hand out flat, but empty. Wordlessly Gamba put the marker onto her right hand and then swept the money off her other hand and into his pocket without pausing.

"Ah, thank you, Gamba," Dhakiya murmured respectfully. "May you have a good evening." And then she waited for the polite response by Gamba who wasn't close to feeling courteous at that moment; and afterwards as he watched Dhakiya waddle down the dusty road, he realized that Bozidara had just set and Baya was not home yet. Resentfully he turned and made his own tea. He drank it sullenly while planning how he would teach her for not being here and for making this, so far, a very unpleasant evening. It only got worse for him.

Baya, meanwhile, had deeply dozed under the batik warmed by Bozidara's slanted, ochre rays, and because of the herbal numbing narcotic drink given to her before she had entered the boat, her pains were somewhat eased. She awoke several times to the gentle movement of the skimming fishing boat as it glided over the lake. Lulled by the rocking movement, Baya lost time and repeatedly slipped back into dreamless sleep; but when the fishing boat's hull scraped harshly onto the gritty beach on the opposite side of Lake Maemi, she woke completely. She heard the fisherman shore the oars, lower the sail, and then crunch step by step into the distance. When it was quiet, she pulled aside the batik, and sat up stiffly, gasping at times when bruised muscles and skin were stretched. She had come to this side of the big lake many years ago as a girl, but nothing was familiar now. Looking around Baya saw a light in the distance and thought it must be the grandmother's house of which Dhakiya had spoken. Clumsily she fell out of the boat, scratching her hands and knees on the coarse sand.

She crunched her way towards the house, but because of her disabled distress, sounded like more like ten lumbering camels than one furtive refugee. The low laughter from inside the cottage was pleasant and the muted yet gleeful conversation continued without Baya realizing an entire city could have heard her awkward advance across the beach, and the hilarity of her supposedly unknown arrival had the grandmother and grandson doubled over with tears of laughter despite the desperate situation.

Finally Baya settled down under a young palm tree fanning out its disproportionately huge, pleated fronds. Exhausted and almost numb from tortuous pain, she barely heard the fisher-youth leave, but woke when the grandmother placed her hand gently on her head in blessing. Baya looked up and blurrily saw the hand of the elder gracefully sign above her the Blessing of Mercy. She blinked in surprise for the air around was radiant even after the grandmother's hand paused. And then the grandmother's hand again flowed through the air with deliberate intensity as she signed the Blessing of Belonging and Acceptance. Both rituals silently awed Baya, and only when she heard her now-given name did Emina, beloved one, burst into sobbing, long-held tears.

Rawiya stopped perplexed. She wanted to continue on, but a dust lizard had scuttled in front of her and stared waiting for her attention. Now it barked out a command and dashed out of the camp circle; but Rawiya had heard the intent of the message. She glanced up at Ishwa who merely shrugged at her.

"Apparently we are asked to stop early tonight in preparation for tomorrow. Remember, take no food into your tents, and light the smudge candles at your tent entrance. The teacher will ask now for blessings of peace and protection as you sleep. We leave this oasis tomorrow morning."

All hands were raised in evening prayer and blessing. Tonight some of the younger pilgrims jumped up to playfully capture the elusive spirit sparks. The elder travelers chuckled good-naturedly for they would have like to play with the spirit sparks, also.

Rawiya and Ishwa ambled away from the camp circle with bowed whispering heads.

"This is the strangest crossing we've ever had! Now I'm getting orders from the dust lizards!"

"Well, at least you understood it!"

"What's up with tomorrow? I thought it was another short journey so a mid-morning departure would allow a relaxed breakfast and preparation."

"That's still the plan," muttered Ishwa noticing several silver-stems of new growth alive with softly glowing moths. More moths flittered towards them from the darkened oasis as if called to a gathering of their own. He stopped to point out the phenomenon to Rawiya.

"How lovely!" she whispered. "I haven't seen these before."

"Another surprise of the Cham. Another blessing."

"Do you think they will sing lullabies to us?"

"Go to bed, Rawiya or you will be doing the singing!"

"Oh! But I'm not tired!"

"Go!" and Ishwa left Rawiya to go to his tent.

Rawiya prepared for bed, but sat for a long while in the doorway of her tent watching the moths, admiring the stars, listening to the rustling sounds all around her. She eventually smiled dreamily and snuggled into her bedding at peace with herself and the universe.

"Lost trust can be renewed, but only if the pain and fear involved are shared then left behind. If not, then one's purpose in life will be to be victimized repeatedly by reliving the hurt that destroyed trust. It is best to shed the hurt so life can be fully realized with gratitude and joy."
~ *Senior Book of Searcher Instructions*

CHAPTER 6

❖

CLINGING BURDENS

The morning chill discouraged travel, and sparse clouds on the horizon pointed to spare time progressing toward the ideal oasis encampment to view the desert blooming. Taking advantage of a relaxed schedule, the pilgrims extended their camp out at their present refuge. They listened intently to Ishwa's words at two brief conferences for he spoke of their daily struggles to overcome temptation and low self esteem. He spoke of how this daily struggle taught them to trust and to perceive their original blessings. The pains they experienced in life made them what they were and that maturity was recycled into a life-saving empowering force. Afterwards they spent time in prayer and meditation. It was an incredibly intense morning. Still, they didn't leave.

The mid-day meal was simple, and all were encouraged to relax in the shade or swim in the pools throughout the rest of the day. The oasis seemed to stretch and extend its borders when more space was needed for quiet reflection, and as evening approached, a cozy ambience deflected anxiety and invited more of a holiday mood.

Rawiya had held her own counseling sessions for others that day. Afterwards, she lay secluded in a private pool with her own thoughts. Amon wanted something from her she was not willing to give: her sovereignty and her soul. Must I give up who I am to fit into his expectations? Is there a way we can live in union without lessening either of us? Cooperation and sacrifice for the beloved was understood, but to what degree should that righteously be expected without destroying the spirit? Could she defend her boundaries while allowing Amon's own needs and expectations to flourish? Ideally, both could be accomplished.

Evening coolness eventually brought a shiver to Rawiya reclining in her pool. Examining her water-wrinkled palms, she sighed in resignation and stood to dry off. Well beyond the cover of trees and shrubs surrounding her personal pool, the campfire danced and reflected off the huge fronds overhead. Muffled laughter and conversation were warmly inviting. Even though the oasis canopy was sparse, it seemed as if they had camped in a huge domed house. The savory fragrance of supper wafted from the "kitchen" hearth and brought Rawiya completely back to the present.

She rubbed the sleeve on the robe she had shimmied into. It had never seemed so smooth and silky. This trip was becoming more of a nomadic recreation resort than anything else. "How long are we going to stay at this oasis?" she wondered. Usually they would have been on their way further into the Cham; here they had stopped traveling and were getting too comfortable. But now it was time to eat and tell the history of Hidaya, and perhaps they would be moving on tomorrow. Perhaps.

The Sixth Night:

This morning Ishwa spoke about the difficulties we encounter in this fierce, yet wonderful life. Some of these difficulties come from ourselves, and others come from circumstances and people who cross our life's path. Tonight we continue with Emina's story and her struggles to overcome the physical and emotional pains with which she lived.

Old T'moyo had seen many Bozidara-risings. She had known those who had talked with the founders of the relaxed lakeside community of Viñay. They had had the opportunity to obtain many more luxuries than they had now, but if those luxuries were truly not needed except for showing off and feeling better than others without them, those were not good enough reasons to obtain them.

They had healers, medical doctors and hospitals nearby that were provided by the community for all. They had excellent teachers for the young, and opportunities for life-long learning. They had simple entertainments, and simple lives in comparison to their city cousins, but this was a chosen simplicity. Life choices could be re-chosen if that was wanted, and T'moyo had chosen.

It was a lovely evening with abundant stars guarding over Hidaya. The three sister moons had not yet risen, but Grandmother T'moyo had easily found Emina, blessed her, and hustled her inside the cottage with the help of her grandson. Inside, she briefly rested her hand gently upon Emina's swollen, discolored cheek testing its heat. Then she checked Emina for broken bones or skin that might need surgery, and discovered only one deep cut above Emina's left eyebrow that required stitching, though dark colors and bruising showed almost everywhere. The examination was cursory because she could see that Emina was exhausted. Afterwards, she helped Emina to the cleansing room and then into her own oversized bed that was so soft Emina sank deeply into it. Though she doubted it was necessary, T'moyo urged Emina to drink a slightly bitter tea that would ensure a heavily calming and healing sleep for the rest of that night and most of the following day. As soon as Emina's lashes sank without fluttering, T'moyo plopped herself down into an oversized rocking chair. This rocker was one luxury she was reluctant to leave behind, and perhaps that couldn't be helped, unless it was dismantled T'moyo thought innovatively. That was a possibility, but could it be snugly wrapped well enough for a long journey that would take several difficult weeks? Before her grandson had gone off to sleep, he had told her about Emina's husband; they would have to leave soon if they were to avoid Gamba's reach. A list of absolute necessities and preparations for the trip logically were laid before her consciousness before she herself nodded off.

Weeks later, Emina gasped while changing positions for she was precariously balanced on a sturdy, but bony donkey. She willed her cramped muscles to stillness until she could knead them and force relaxation in a merciless grip, but there was unrelenting, spasmodic pain sitting on the donkey's twisting and rugged back. Yet, Old T'moyo had assured her countless times that the pains would eventually end as her healing progressed. Emina uncomfortably endured the awkward movement beneath her and the hard, contracted muscles until the evening encampment when A'kil, their guide, Grandmother T'moyo, or the Searcher Che'ikh would massage the tissues to sleep. The boy, Dato, who also accompanied them, was good for nothing except annoyance.

They plodded on, one burdened donkey following after another, skirting the rocky cliffs in a parallel course to the mountains until they could turn towards Salimah, their ultimate destination. Emina's mouth screwed up petulantly as she recalled T'moyo's evasive answers of what this place was toward which they had journeyed for weeks already. T'moyo had claimed that she couldn't describe it accurately – one had to experience it. She had said it was a safe place where Gamba would not find her; and even if he did track Emina down to this remote town, she would be protected, always and forever. T'moyo had said that this was the nearest "refuge city," whatever that meant.

A'kil, Che'ikh, and his young friend, Dato, had joined them soon after T'moyo and Emina had left the lakeside area. The male group had already been on the road for days, and their presence lightened up a long, boring trek. Apparently A'kil had also been to Salimah, but his laughing eyes met hers whenever she tried to squeeze more information from him; he would light-heartedly talk about anything except their destination. It often seemed as if A'kil's mouth was turned up at the ends, hinting at humorous thoughts or almost laughing at her or something beyond her, but Emina couldn't be sure because A'kil's beard and mustache hid more than it revealed.

Their seven donkeys walked single file steadily. Two donkeys carried water and other provisions, and five donkeys carried the Hidayan travelers. Except for T'moyo, Emina hadn't known their other three companions until a day's trek from the lakeside town of Viñay, and even after a week of travel, she really didn't know T'moyo that much either, except that she was endlessly kind and patient.

Ahead, A'kil and T'moyo chatted companionably and somewhat secretively Emina thought, for when she or the young boy named Dato kicked their donkey's sides to be part of the conversation, she could tell that A'kil and T'moyo changed subjects to a more inclusive topics. Again, her mouth pinched as if tasting a sour fruit. She resentfully felt left out, and glanced over her shoulder at Che'ikh who liked to follow up at the end and who discouraged company, conversation, and companionship. He was scanning the landscape around them for movement and danger.

They were hours away from finding one of the well-used campsites A'kil was skillful at spotting. Emina would look at the harsh terrain and see nothing but rocks, dirt, scrub, thorny bushes, and silvery-green clumping desert-plants, but A'kil would see a rock behind which was cached water and other resources. Emina would see shimmering, blinding, scorching waves of heat rising from harsh, barren Hidayan dirt stretching to the far horizon, but A'kil would see rocks angled in such a way as to protect them in shadow during the hottest part of the day.

She would complain like a fretful child, or grumble curses at her abandoned husband, and A'kil would patiently divert her anger towards other more satisfying possibilities than endless resentful ranting. A'kil honestly chastised Emina about her cursing because just to hear it hurt his heart, but he also listened tirelessly and sympathetically to her angry, hurt feelings, before directing her to more creative outlets and hope-filling perspectives than vengeful self-pity. Somehow talking with him lessened the whining distress in her voice until she almost enjoyed the journey, though she wouldn't admit it.

T'moyo was less expansive with Emina, but would also listen carefully, and suddenly would drop a pithy observation into Emina's lap based in her own words. Most often these revelations were thought provoking, but sometimes hearing what she had said – or rather what had been heard – caused pain and silent tears. Afterwards, a calmness of heart relaxed Emina who wondered at her own undisturbed spirit while it lasted. Sooner or later, however, Dato's presence or the discomforts of the journey intruded.

Dato was an absolute and complete irritant. This trek was all high adventure to him. He seldom talked about anything disagreeable, and stopping up his mouth was only achieved if food was stuffed in it. Always seeing things, always speculating, always gnawing at Emina's need for quiet – that was Dato – a bigger annoyance than his size merited. The only other thing more annoying than Dato was Che'ikh who was obviously delighted with Dato's chatter, but seldom contributed to any conversation. His silence was more than enough balanced by Dato's verbal noise.

For hours on end Emina's donkey would hear interminable whispered whining and grumbles, "What's wrong with him? Can't he just sit on the damn donkey like the rest of us? Why must he constantly, mindlessly chatter on to torture me? Can't anyone shut him up? If this is what I'd have had to go through if I had had children, I'm glad I never had any! Just look at him gawking at everything around him as if he hadn't seen anything before. And if he eats tonight like a slobbering, starving beast and asks to eat the leftovers one more time, I'll tell him what I think!" Grumbling, mumbling, whining, snarling complaints hovered around Emina until her donkey no longer heard them. He only pricked up its ears when they plodded into a cooler climate. He knew sweet water and abundant food were waiting for him someplace near, and there would be satisfying scratching behind his ears as a reward by someone who was not his rider, for she was unable or unwilling to bestow that pleasure herself.

They traveled northwest, and the horizon now included low foothills sizzling in sweltering heat behind which loomed the impossibly jagged, blue Bahairava Mountains that slashed at the sky like unsheathed claws.

The donkeys seemed to have traveled this way before for their clopping pace perceptively quickened as the mountains captured cooler air, relieving the arid terrain of it's complete desolation. A'kil called them the Bahairava Mountain Range, and they often were surrounded by fluffy puffs of clouds crowding each other onto the western slopes where the driven breezes bunched them. Sometimes gray, square-topped thunderheads majestically rose over the Bahairava Mountains, and sometimes amorphous, foggy swirls shimmied around the distant peaks, before evaporating in the daylight. Emina's pessimistic, skeptical eye looked ahead and saw only blistering heat and discomfort. But what was that jackanapes of a boy talking about now that distracted her?

"I know 'ow ta cook a chicken, and if I hafta, I could kill one, too. I know 'ow ta pluck its feathers an' clean out its innards so da meat don' get bitter, and I know 'ow ta make a soup from da leftover bones dat tastes really good. What 'bout you? Do you know 'ow ta cook chickens? I bet ya do, seeing as 'ow yer a married lady."

I bet ya –"

Emina's eyes widened in terror. "How do you know I am married? I never said anything one way or the other."

"Oh, it's yer hair – 'ow you fix it an' put da shawl over yer 'ead; an' it's 'ow ya do homey stuff ta clean up an' fix t'ings wit'out t'inking 'bout it – t'ings only a married lady might know 'bout. An' den, ya never say anyt'ing really 'bout yer past so I t'ink yer running away from yer husband or a mean family. But den again, ya might –"

"Enough!" Emina shrieked cutting short his speculation. "Be quiet and just leave me alone!"

Up ahead T'moyo and A'kil pulled their donkeys up short and looked back. Emina's startling cry had caused the donkey-line to shy and pull on their guidelines in distress. A'kil's eyebrows raised in inquiry at T'moyo. She nodded and turned her mount back while thumbing at Dato to join A'kil.

Once they started moving again Dato could be heard prattling again, "I don' know what upset 'er. I was only talking 'bout fixin' a chicken fer dinner, if we 'ad a chicken. Dat's probably not going ta 'appen cuz we're in a desert an' chickens don't live in da desert. But I know 'ow ta fix a chicken, an' if we had a chicken…."

Lagging back behind the last pack-donkey, T'moyo rode beside Emina who savagely kicked her donkey in anger. Without raising her voice, T'moyo took the reins from Emina's curled fists and led the donkey as if leading a spoiled child's ride. Che'ikh silently rode past them, ignoring them completely.

"Tell me," T'moyo commanded quietly of Emina.

"He's always talking so there's not a minute's rest. There's no place to be to get away from his constant talking. It's making me crazy listening day in and day out to his stupid nonsense. Can't we go to this place by ourselves? Why do we have to go with them? All Dato does is talk and eat, talk and eat, and I can't take it anymore. I can't take it!" And then fat tears rolled down Emina's cheeks in powerless anger while she spasmodically sobbed.

Patiently T'moyo waited for Emina to reach a calmness that would allow her to listen. "Have you never wondered why Dato speaks so much? Have you never wondered why he is traveling with us to Salimah?"

"No! And I don't care. I just want him to go away, as far away from me as he can go!" Emina cried with a self-pitying, pouting face.

T'moyo waited again quietly before talking to her donkey. "Silly donkey! Stop turning your ears! You can't understand us, so why try? You silly thing! Here, let me scratch that ear. And just to be fair, now, let me scratch the other one. There, that feels better, doesn't it?" The distraction got Emina listening again. She drew in long weepy breaths, but she was listening when T'moyo spoke to her.

"Emina, you are blessed with welcome, belonging and protection. Have you never wondered at Dato's name? Dato also means 'beloved,' just like your name. He is included in welcome and protection."

"I don't care! I don't want him near me!"

"Ah! So you want the blessings just for yourself."

"No! I mean, yes! I mean – you make me sound so selfish! I just want him to stop talking and give me some peace."

"Look at him!" T'moyo commanded. "Dato is just a boy. All his chatter that he was never able to share before now covers up the hurt he has lived with in his short life. Lord Che'ikh says that Dato used to be almost a mute as his own way to protect himself. Look at his eyes when he rattles off his endless nonsense. He watches your face because maybe he just might say something right to you or me or A'kil or Che'ikh – or to even one of the donkeys or even to the rocks! For just that precise second he will feel the peace and blessings he was given, but still can't receive. It's not real for him yet. He hides from both hurt and blessings. But then, so do you. You just do it in a different way."

Was T'moyo looking smug? A raging sneer covered Emina's face. "What do you mean? I have too accepted the blessings! I'm here aren't I?"

"If you had accepted the blessings in your heart, you would share them with yourself and others. Because you still don't trust them, you don't keep them; and because you don't own the blessings for yourself, deep down you really don't believe they belong to you; maybe they were given to you by mistake. Maybe you really don't deserve them." T'moyo's hand steadied both donkeys who momentarily shied away from the path A'kil was leading them on. She ignored Emina's silence and went on. "You don't believe they are your blessings which you deserve. Which everyone deserves.

"The hurt you've experienced is part of you, but eventually it will recede into the past. It will not stay as fresh hurt. However, at some time you will need to let the anger go so the healing can continue.

"Until then, Dato is left out once again. Once again, even on this journey to refuge, he is treated like a leftover: a tiny scrap of something nobody wants – and perhaps never wanted. But here he is, just like you! And you can't change that, Emina, because this is real. You are here, I am here, A'kil is here, Che'ikh is here, and so is Dato. You have been badly and unfairly hurt. Do you now have the right to do the same to Dato?"

T'moyo's frown weighed down Emina's sulky scowl. "I –" began Emina.

"Don't talk! Just think. Be thankful that you are here. And be thankful that there is welcome here and in your future at Salimah. Be thankful that Dato is here, also, for he needs Salimah, too. If you can be thankful for the blessings, the healing will be that much quicker for both of you. For all of us."

"What do you mean?" came a watery question.

"My name, T'moyo, means 'wise one.' Did I become wise because nothing ever happened to me? Wisdom doesn't come to those without experiences. Wisdom comes to those who live life, often with extensive scars to show for that living. My first name, Morna, is just like yours in meaning. Beloved. From being able to accept and give love comes wisdom. But I am tired of your complaining," Grandmother T'moyo sighed decisively.

"Go spew your anger out onto everyone around you! Yes, keep doing that. Then you will have become just like Gamba, and will have reclaimed the name he gave you unfairly. Perhaps that name is more comfortable for you after so many years. Or you can try to let the anger sift like sand between your fingers until most or all of it is gone. You will always remember the gritty feel of the anger, because there was hurt first. You will always remember the heat of the sand, and how afraid you were to walk on it barefoot; but you don't have to keep the sand around you every day for the rest of your life. You don't have to live out here," T'moyo waived her hand around to include the bleak landscape.

"And you don't have to force others to live out here, either," T'moyo's voice faded to a whisper as she spoke these last words. "You have a chance to live in peace, and in blessing. But you need to claim that by wanting it! You do deserve it! And so does Dato. Go think!"

T'moyo gave the reins back to Emina, and then encouraged her donkey to trot forward so that she could join A'kil and Dato, who were now chuckling over a story from Dato's innovative past: how to prepare chicken tail soup. It tasted delicious Dato claimed, and the contracted chicken claws swirling in broth reaching into the air created a visual image that had both A'kil and T'moyo laughing and remembering when they had eaten that treat.

Meanwhile, Che'ikh silently allowed Emina's donkey to overtake his, and then followed behind her as usual.

"The story telling is over for tonight," Rawiya gleefully announced. "And in honor of Dato's cooking skills, Cook has prepared 'Chicken Tail Surprise.' Hold up your hands."

Such reluctant pilgrims they were! Some could not even muster the strength to move! But those who did reach up received a bowl of sweet nuts and dried fruit.

"But where are the chicken tails?" a confused retreatant asked.

"That's the surprise," laughed Cook standing in the campfire circle. "This is what the chicken probably pecked at to make its tail strong. Hah!"

"And where is the broth?" bantered an elderly pilgrim.

"There is broth if you want it, or something a bit stronger," suggested Ishwa. "We have wine tonight."

"What's special about tonight?" asked a youth.

"Tonight we celebrate blessings you have received. We celebrate even the blessings which we all have ignored or refused, for they still exist and wait for us to accept their presence. We celebrate Life. And we celebrate this Life which is a gift," Ishwa raised his clay cup high for the toast, and then with humor twinkling at the edges of his eyes he warned, "But don't ask for more wine than one cup. If you are still thirsty there is water or broth enough for second helpings!"

Mellow fellowship ended the evening. When there finally was a lull in the talking, Ishwa and Rawiya called for the closing prayer of gratitude and then the pilgrims raised their hands to bless each other; they prayed that the Giver and Receiver accept the blessing. Spirit-sparks softly descended from the scant canopy above like tiny, glittering, falling stars that winked out just out of reach.

After the pilgrims had retired, the three sister moons in their turn gently rose above the horizon. Their combined light filled the night sky and dimmed that from the brilliant plethora of scattered stars backing them. The lunar radiance revealed subtle, persistent movement in the crowns of the gnarled trees encircling the pond. Clinging to the knotted branches and camouflaged against the striated drab wood countless gray, silken cocoons wriggled and writhed in the triple moonlight.

After a sparse banquet of silvered lichen had been consumed the day before, the larvae's brief and single instar had been completed. Then, while the pilgrims reclined around the campfire concentrating on Hidaya's story, the univoltine larvae had spun their pupal sarcophagi. Cradled within the safety of their inner-lined pupal chambers the final metamorphosis of the silver-moth was completed overnight. This sixth night the adult moths split their restraining shrouds of silk. Eclosure abruptly occurred and the wet-furred silver-moths paused to rest clinging to the tough outer parchment-like shell of their cocoons. As they dried they absorbed reflected light from the three sister moons who sailed in mute passage above.

Throughout all this overnight wonder of the silver-moths' emergence, the desert birds merely fluffed their feathers and slept on.

"We may never know the meaning of our lives,
but we hope there is meaning that blesses others.
That hope keeps us breathing, trying, and living
                          Seventh Book of Instruction

CHAPTER 7

❖

DEPARTURES, ARRIVALS, AND DELAYS

By mid-morning the following day the few broad-leafed trees protecting the oasis seemed to have had enough exposure to daylight. They folded their fronds like fans and Bozidara's blinding rays caused the pilgrims below to squint even when standing in shadows. Rawiya was startled by the self-closing movement above, but could not look closer because the glare was painful. She gasped at the heat Bozidara aimed at Hidaya. Their protection at this oasis seemed to be at an end. It was as if drapes had been pulled back and the dimness of a secluded sanctuary room had been dispelled without mercy.

"Time for us to go," Rawiya wryly mumbled to a passing attendant.

"We got the word at dawn," he affirmed. "Most of the supplies will be packed by mid-day, and though it'll be getting to be the hottest part of the day, we will leave then." He called out to another attendant, and hurried off.

Rawiya paused for a moment in frozen concern. Ishwa had not told her they were moving on. She purposefully headed towards Cook's tent for just like a family kitchen, everyone chatted and visited there during the day. Right now, Cook was busy supervising the drying of protein cubes exposed to Bozidara's baking heat. These were small crunchy snacks of grain, beans, and seeds that gave extra energy. Dried fruit balls had already been formed and now were mounded high in enormous bowls made from sturdy fronds scavenged from the oasis.

"'Looks like you are all ready for us to move on," Rawiya idly commented, while reaching for a fruit ball.

"Don't take too many of those now, or we won't have enough for later," cautioned Cook prudently. "Well, we got the word to get ready to go, and so we're doing what needs doing. Any idea what the next place will be like?"

"You know better! Nothing is ever the same. Even if we had planned to go to the same oasis at the same exact month as in the past, it all would be changed. The plants, the animals, everything is always different. Uh – did Ishwa tell you we were moving?"

"No. I only saw him when he walked through here to his first conference. He didn't have time to talk then, and only had time to grab some hot tea and a biscuit. Busy, he was, though, mumbling about injustice and compassion. That was probably about his conference.

"No, roll the mix out like this, and then cut the pieces to shape them into cubes with your fingers. That's it." This last directive was aimed at a new attendant learning how to make protein cubes. Her fingers nimbly nipped pieces off of the protein coils she had skillfully rolled out with the palms of her hands, and then quickly pinched them into cubes. She added these to the stacks already drying. The difference in the preciseness of her last cubes compared to the earlier ones was self-evident.

Cook put her hands on her hips to survey the activity around her. In her own time she relaxed slightly and picked up an enormous mug of cold tea; a thoughtful, puzzled expression clouded her face. "Come to think of it, Ishwa didn't tell us to pack up. But we all knew. We woke up knowing."

The newbie kitchen helper swiped at some stray hairs that kept falling into her eyes. She confirmed Cook's story, but added, "I wanted to stay one more day because it seems so safe and cozy here. Strange," her voice lowered to a whisper of embarrassment. "I didn't want to go so I didn't pack my things. I left my tent to wash up and then went back expecting to clean up the mess. I had left everything thrown all over. When I came back there were some furry little fluff-balls folding my things and stacking them ready to put in my pack. They were so cute and kept chattering at me to stay out of the way. They seemed so "right" to be there, that I just left."

Incredulously, Rawiya asked, "Fluff balls? I haven't seen anything like that here! But you saw them and could understand what they were saying? They spoke to you like we are talking now?"

"No, no, but I understood them just the same. I heard them say that they didn't have as much time as they had thought earlier, so right after lunch we would be leaving."

"But that's the hottest part of the day! Why would we leave then?" shock filled Rawiya's words. To walk across the desert in full daylight would be asking to die.

"Come to think of it," Cook absently said while staring at the mounds of dried fruit balls and calculating if there were enough, "There *were* furry little things next to my ear when I woke up. Imagine forgetting a thing like that! Oh, they were cuddly, though. 'Little hands and tiny feet, and soft little ears. 'All covered in brownish fur and they had big black eyes. They liked their ears played with." She smacked her lips in satisfaction.

"They said they would let us know when we had to do the final pack up. 'seems to me that once they give the word, we'd better be ready to move fast. Is there anything I can get for you?" That was Cook's way to end the conversation.

"No, thank you," Rawiya answered while swiping two more fruit balls. She skipped away from Cook's swatting hand, and towards Ishwa's tent. As she neared she saw that he merely stood by his tent staring inside. Suspicion based on what she had just heard from Cook prevented surprise.

"Mmmm... want a fruit ball?" offered Rawiya while following Ishwa's stunned gaze. "Has this been going on for awhile?" she continued in a monotone voice.

"I - I guess," stuttered Ishwa helplessly blinking unbelievingly at innumerable furry balls rapidly organizing his possessions. Their miniscule hands blurred as they busily packed his things, chittering to each other all the while.

Rawiya was torn between her fascination with the intensive critters invading the tent and apparently the entire campsite, and with the extremely unusual helpless slumping of Ishwa. She watched both speculating. "Have you meditated yet?"

"Huh? No. At dawn I was reviewing my morning conference about justice and compassion.

"Today I want to emphasize that working for justice and celebrating life makes our lifelong journey meaningful and successful. I want them to hear that injustice is not just a personal issue but a cosmic pain, and that Compassion is the true-name of the One who is our strength as we work for justice and celebrate and life.

"If I remember from past conferences, then you will send the pilgrims out to center themselves – to empty themselves – so that they will be filled with the One ready for their constant journey homeward." Ishwa nodded still enraptured by the furballs scurrying around his tent.

"You know they talk, don't you?" Rawiya casually revealed taking a bite from the fruit ball Ishwa had ignored.

"Well, yes, they can talk to themselves in their own way. All animals do," he responded distractedly.

"No. I mean that they can talk to us, and we can understand them."

"What?"

"Listen. Try. Cook said she knew we would be leaving today when they gave the word. They've been informing the attendants and telling them what to do all morning. Fruit ball?" she offered again.

"We're leaving today?" Ishwa reached for the fruit ball in abstracted focus. "Of course we are since they are packing us up." This was another Cham mystery, but talking fur-balls valets? Now he focused his thoughts and actually could make out – in a primitive fashion – what they were saying to each other. Haste seemed to be the main message. *Be ready!*

By lunchtime all the retreatants had perceived that there would be an imminent, hurried departure. They rushed through the meal, donned their travel hats if they hadn't already, and many waited beside their travel beasts even before the attendants had arrived to pack them. But the service-attendants were unnecessary for an enormous squad of fur-ball fuzzies burst explosively from behind the shrubs and furiously climbed the travel beasts, cooperatively filling panniers, hanging bags and other carry-ons with absolutely everything that belonged to the caravan. Then they roughly prodded and poked at the Hidayans until they got over their gawking stupidity and mounted the travel beasts. When everyone and everything was ready, the swarming furries rolled over the sand and dirt erasing all traces of Hidayan occupancy. Only the travel beasts' footprints where they stood now remained intact. And then all the comedic fuzz-balls crouched in unison wherever they were as if a master hand choreographed their pause. But their repose was only momentary.

Polyphonic harmony composed of the purest tones surged upward and towards the awed watchers mounted so high above them. The beauty of the music was tangible, for even though Bozidara glared furiously down at the travelers, the complex harmony washed over them like a polar wave. Icy wetness drenched everyone and everything, coating them with a slick, smooth sheen. They all gasped in shock.

The travel beasts bellowed their protests and stomped angrily. Flakes of snow broke off to melt before reaching the sand. Simultaneously, the Hidayans began experimenting with a new Cham phenomena: a hard layer of ice and frost covered them now, but it felt comfortable both in temperature, and by a confounding icy-plasticity allowing the travelers to move without cracking their new, smooth body armor.

Meanwhile, the contrapuntal chorale rushed forcefully over them, as a frenzied guardian might urgently dash towards a distressed child to pick him up and cradle him in a protective embrace. A powerful, unstoppable crescendo arose, impelling even the stifling air to blast onward propelling grit and debris before it. Hair streamed out like battered flags forgotten in a storm; clothes stretched, ruffled and pasted its frozen folds against frosted skin. The sharp wind buffeted the travelers briskly with unexpected strength before racing like tumultuous, swirling rapids all the while increasing in choral volume until the sound became a dreadfully mindless, deafening noise that shook the depths of Hidaya itself far beneath the dunes.

The hard desert ground shook and dissolved into fluid-flowing sand dunes; and while the dunes shivered like flour sifted through a baker's sieve, rhythmically sliding downward while keeping time to a steady, pounding beat the bushes and smaller vegetation of the oasis were absorbed into the desert's depths.

Travelers bent over now to shield themselves from the wind and grit. Their instinctively closed eyes dared not even squint against the gale; arms and hands grabbed to protect ears from the interminable uproar; robes covered noses and mouths greedy for even a half breath of breathable air. And the endless roar and quake of the desert went on until one by one the travel beasts went down on their knees to sleep in shock through the continuing trauma. One after the other, the travelers slid forward unconsciously slumping over the travel beasts' shaggy shoulders. The defeated mounts with their sleeping riders lay overcome and helpless in the midst of the Cham, eventually oblivious to the sandstorm swirling violently around them.

Rawiya's final thought before she gave in to sleep was, "This is harsh! First the attacking insects injecting us with euphoric serum and now this! The Cham is trying to protect us; but from what? And why do it this way?" And then she slept dreamlessly unaware that all this had taken hours from her life.

Daylight disappeared in a dirty, crimson haze, and the silence of the desert seemed complete. Nothing near the now-prone travelers moved. Hard dirt and sand and partially buried their stilled forms and the fur-ball entourage still looked on calmly and somewhat self-satisfied at their accomplishment.

On the other side of an enormous nearby outcrop comprised of wind-blown sedimentary hoodoos anchored in sand, a posse of vigilantes huddled quietly, for they also had experienced the harsh wind and quake. Though they had not been sheathed in protective flexible ice like the pilgrims, still the upheaval had rendered them unconscious.

When they finally awoke and raised their heads to sharply scan the surrounding dry, hard, scabby land interspersed with whispering sand dunes, there was neither awe nor fear reflecting from their dark eyes.

Gored'na appraised the emerging stars coldly winking at him from the distant dome above. He stretched to assure himself that he was still alive, and then called out, "Eh! Tangi! 'Ya still 'ere?"

A harsh grunt answered him. In the blackness surrounding Gored'na someone cleared his throat and spat dryly. A wheezing cough whistled further to his left, and the sound of rasping, displaced grit advised him of someone else to his right.

"Jabez? 'Ya 'wake?"

"'e's dead."

"Ghanash'am? Ne'igalomea?"

"Over 'ere. The mounts 're either sleeping, dead or 'ave wandered off. We 'af ta walk."

A hissed response greeted this deadly news.

Gored'na again looked up. "'Stars say we're near da refuge closest ta da trail dey strayed from."

"Da travel-mounts could've smelled da water an' led us ta it if you'da hobbled dem."

"Well, I didn't an' t'ey ain't 'ere, so why don'cha smell fer ta water yerself?"

"Yer nexta useless, Tangi."

"Yer da closest ta da unblessed den anyone in 'istory. 'njoy yer life while ya got it. Hidaya'll swallow ya up soon," Tangi cursed back.

Reluctantly they staggered to their feet, slapping fine, gritty particles from their hair and clothing.

"'Sand's in muh mouth," Gored'na complained before spitting out a dirty wad of thick saliva.

Raggedly weary, they stumbled partly up the side of the towering outcrop and grunted their relief to see an oasis so close to them. They could easily reach the oasis by nightfall, and without any discussion they all staggered towards water and refuge. Though minor quakes stopped them twice, the walk was easy.

The Seventh Night:

Rawiya awoke groggily. Soft starlight reflected off of the shiny smoothness of her comfortable covering of flexible ice as if off a prism. The air around her seemed to be all mist and rainbows mixed with shadows and she had to shut her eyes tightly again to orient herself. Eventually she sat up unsteadily gasping for air before ungracefully standing. Sand slid smoothly from her new icy exoskeleton onto the oasis floor, ignoring the folds in her clothing. She blinked and looked downward stupidly as the falling sand created an encircling ridge around her splayed feet. Thinking seemed beyond her abilities at that time, but she vaguely remembered sitting on Cid during an earthquake and a storm. Cid was nowhere near so perhaps he had wandered away.

Hidaya shuddered sharply and Rawiya tumbled back onto her knees. Many tiny hands reached out to hold her up and guide her. They urged her forward, but she was only able to crawl baby-like in her weakness. Squinting in the brightness, Rawiya gasped thinking she was misperceiving. Appearing in and out of the mists an unlikely, shadowy cave in a monumental sand dune ominously loomed before her surrealistically. Rawiya realized that travel beasts, riders, furries, and some now-unseated members of the caravan such as herself were all crawling towards that cavern that logically could not exist. Still, they edged towards that looming maw.

"My knees should be hurting," Rawiya dully reflected to herself. She paused to feel her knees and realized with astonishment that the icy sheen was thicker on her knees and actually cushioned them. "My hands will be bloody if I keep on crawling like this," she feared now disregarding the encouraging pushing of little hands that reached upwards to nudge her onward. Dumbly she followed the feeling to stare down. A growing number of fur-ball beings — not chittering now, but all humming softly in an indiscernible harmonic melody — were bunching up around her to push. Uncomprehending, Rawiya lost the thought of her hands to idly gaze at the furries.

One sharp poke after another ended her dazed lethargy and she began creeping again into darkness ahead.

Rawiya could finally see when the penumbral shading of the sand cave's entrance relieved the iridescent starlight through mists and rainbows, though her understanding remained dreamlike and foggy. She, and the entire caravan, along with the supervising furries, were moving towards the depths of the sub-Hidayan cave. Unexpected rapture made Rawiya gasp when she glanced upwards; enormous phosphorescent moths hovered inches from the sandy walls and ceiling. Their frenetic fluttering wings created miniscule wavering breezes that swept naturally falling sand back towards itself. Unthinkingly, with a reflexive response to the moths' protection from hundreds of tons of sand, Rawiya rasped out, "Thank you." A slight brightening of their phosphorescence was the moth-acknowledgement, but from that flicker Rawiya clearly glimpsed the shallowness *of the cave height and the interminable length of the tunnel that lay before her. They were moving into a tube-passage straight into the desert depths. The weight of the sand should logically push downward to crush them without any chance to run back towards the entrance, and all that kept them safe was the fluttering breezes of these fragile moths!*

Another sharp jolt from Hidaya knocked Rawiya into an ungainly sprawl, and she longingly looked backwards to the starlit cave entrance. But retreat was no longer possible for the quake had loosened the sand at the edge of the cave mouth; the shielding moths hovered and guided the loose entranceway sand that fell evenly in a fine granular shower like a smooth waterfall collapsing and soundlessly closing the entire entrance. Immediately the glowing moths hovered over the sandy wound to keep the encroaching sand away from the lagging pilgrims; Rawiya realized then that she was at the following end of the procession. When the poking furries started pinching her mercilessly, Rawiya crawled forward again in a confused stupor.

The flexible ice cushions surrounding their bodies became thicker as the impressed pilgrims pushed onward and onward hour after hour. The comforting exoskeleton seemed to lighten their body weight somewhat, so that tiredness was minimized, but eventually exhaustion overcame them all.

The furball guides stopped and scurried to gather around each of the Hidayan travelers and eagerly became comfortable pillows to be taken advantage of. Rawiya, just like the pilgrims and attendants around her, curled up surrounded by soft fuzziness, and slept deeply in the dim tunnel light.

Together the travelers drempt a story from the past while four vigilantes stalked them.

Those four vigilantes, Gored'na, Tangi, Ghanash'am, and Ne'igalomea stumbled into the oasis recently vacated by the caravan. Dehydration headaches darkened their moods. Desperation swept away even the roughest sense of civilization. They staggered into closest pool of water causing the disturbed mud to swirl upwards and discolor the purity of the shards of starry light reflected on the pool's surface. But still, the shallow, brownish-gray water was cool to their skin and they gulped it in greedily.

When he had drunk sufficiently, Tangi sat back on his heals looking at the oasis around him and lit by silvered moonlight. There were no small shrubs or plants; there would be little shade from the towering trees when the morning came for their high fronds were folded, probably because they had already had too much light, he thought to himself in disgust. He spat out some of the water before pushing his head back under the cool water to wet his thick, greasy and sweat-sticky hair.

Gored'na was the first to sate himself drinking, and smirked at the rest of his companions over-filling themselves so they would piss it or vomit it all within minutes. He didn't see any berries, fruit, or small animals. This seemed like a barren oasis, and could only be a brief stopping point for them. The Cham Desert did not welcome those whose intent was violent or evil, but neither did it exclude or shun them. The desert absorbed them into its vastness without attacking. If they remained within the desert by choice, or should they allow themselves to be guided by the Cham, transformation would be gifted. However, none of the posse members had a goal to be transformed.

"We missed 'em," Ghanash'am croaked as he squinted around him.

"No foolin' ya idjet. Do ya see any tracks? Spread out an' see where t'ey went."

They searched behind trees and under long-ago broken branches yet could not even find a lizard track. No telltale latrines or signs of dowsed campfires remained in evidence. Neither footsteps around the pool nor tracks leading away from the oasis into the desert beyond revealed any clue of habitation.

"I curse dis place! I know da caravan 'ad ta stop 'ere, but dis damned place shields dem from us. But we'll stay 'ere ta-night even if it don't welcome us. May it be cursed for its un'elpfulness!" Ne'igalomea snarled his disgust and grunted before curling up under a tree and immediately falling asleep. His loud, ragged snores grated roughly through the night. His companions did not bother to light a fire, but merely pulled out chews of jerky, which they gnawed on while sitting in solitary frustration. They did not even feel the camaraderie of shared misery, and ignored each other to focus and fan their discouraged anger into cold intent. They drank more water, relieved themselves without covering their scat, and then fell into their own dark dreams throughout the night.

When the posse awoke at dawn, their travel-mounts were placidly munching tufts of newly grown grass while idly watching and waiting for their riders to take their reins. Surprisingly, the travel mounts seemed refreshed as if they had just left the stable in Viñay. Ne'igalomea stretched and staggered to his feet. The travel mounts looked different to him; their shapes seemed sharper and he couldn't remember when he had last seen each hair on an animal instead of blurred shapes and coloring from increasing nearsightedness. The travel beast's deep umber-colored eyes seemed to hold a peaceful soul staring into his own surprised eyes.

"'ey! Get up!" he cried abruptly as he kicked his companions awake.

"Oomph!"

"What? Damn you!"

"Get up! Let's eat'n go! Now!"

"What's da rush?" grumbled Gored'na with a follow-up curse.

But there was no need for an answer. They all felt an ominous, intense, gut-deep need to leave. This oasis wanted them to move along to somewhere else. Bozidara's morning rays reached them through a steamy mist signaling an imminent change in weather, while transmitting a message that the thin welcome extended to them had worn through and the ragged canopy was rotting before their eyes because of their presence. They mutely filled their canteens from the muddy pond, and left quickly. If they did not find their prey before they reached Cham there would be no bounty to collect.

The Far-Away Story:

Gamba vigorously swatted at his dirty traveling clothes while the busy squire he had spoken to hurried towards a door next to an etched sign stating in two different languages – Pandit and Chi'ma – that this was the office of the Commander of the Hidayan Garrison at Salimah. The squire assumed that the door was closed, and automatically hunched to strenuously bash against it with his shoulder. But the door had been unlatched, and his over-zealous pressure plunged him awkwardly into the room. The astonished squire tumbled into the outpost commander's inner office. His fearful eyes opened widely meeting the commander's calm gaze as if squires were routinely flung onto his office floor.

Both wore the comfortable riding habits of the Hidayan garrison and the only difference was the plain, buttoned flap on the commander's left shoulder. Rank was not a reason to exploit ego with unnecessarily flaunted ribbons, medals or other commendations while on duty, but rather a lonely, humbling leadership in service to others.

The youthful aide jumped to his feet and straightened himself to announce self-consciously and over-loudly, "Lord D'nkrad! Your escort is gathering by the eastern gate."

"Thank you for your efforts," D'nkrad murmured tactfully. "Please wait outside." While he waited for the squire to leave, D'nkrad allowed a momentary smile to brighten his face. He turned to absently glance out the window towards a rising thunderhead he could barely discern near the Bhairava Mountains in the far east. His garrison would travel southwest to Rudra, south to Aichen, and then southeast to his hometown of Adamya. There he would visit family and friends on his personal holiday time, which coincided with the desert, spring blooming – a time which always delighted him to his soul.

A muffled cough let the commander know the messenger-squire had not yet left. He returned his focus to the young recruit whose breathy attendance divulged the unspoken excitement felt at actually speaking with the commander himself. D'nkrad smiled again to himself, amused to be held in awe by anyone. "Wait a few years," he silently counseled the youth. "This is not such an awesome position to behold; it is more like being tied down with numerous sticky webs!"

He allowed himself a moment to pass beyond the wry feeling. How could he chastise anyone when he himself felt awed by the position he held gingerly? There was so much responsibility and balance required, so much tact necessary, and yet others had thought he was quite capable, and so he had trustingly accepted the position of commander to the loosely held together Western Hidayan Province stationed beside the enigmatic town of Salimah. What was this young one's name? Ah, yes!

"You have more to report, Janapriya?"

"Yes, Lord D'nkrad. A supplicant has arrived from Adamya and seeks your counsel before you leave for Aichen." It was easy for the young recruit to perceive D'nkrad's surprise for he watched his commander gather himself obviously before carefully replying.

"What do you think of the supplicant, Janapriya?"

Astonished by this question the young man sucked in his breath sharply, but held his position. After slow minutes of reflection, he answered tentatively, "He seeks someone, for he has three donkeys with him, but only uses one for himself and another for supplies. The third one is so he can return with someone else. And…."

D'nkrad smiled encouragingly, now. The lad was one of the more perceptive aides he had, but was unsure of himself because of his youth and relative inexperience in the field. He still didn't trust his gut instincts.

"…And he is hiding something."

"Like gold and jewels?" the commander questioned sharply.

"No, something that causes him discomfort. He seems to be distressed and very angry about something."

"Then I will see him first, before I leave. That would be kindest for him, rather than let him wait the weeks, perhaps months, that I will need in Aichen and beyond. Besides, 'an unsalved wound is bound to fester if ignored.' Also, tell the escort to relax. We will leave after dusk to travel in the evening cool. I dislike travel when Bozidara bakes me like flatbread."

Janapriya bowed slightly to acknowledge understanding, and left returning short minutes later with the supplicant. D'nkrad signaled the squire to stay.

The big-bellied man had used his waiting time to obviously primp and rid himself of the worst of the road dust. His hair was freshly oiled into submission, and his clothes, the loose robes of the southern settlements, had been shaken, though they still were stained and dusty. Still, even though the man had made an effort to be presentable, the smell of travel – perhaps weeks of it – mixed with the unmistakable, pungent odor of donkey sweat closed the room. Ignoring even the briefest protocol of courtesy, the citizen abruptly went straight to business.

"My name is Gamba. I'm from Adamya in the south, beside Lake Maemi, and near Viñay. Before I went to Salimah directly I thought it best to come here first, to the nearest outpost." His fists clenched in barely withheld rage, Gamba stared defiantly at the commander. No matter what D'nkrad said, whether he supported Gamba or not, he was going to do what he had to do, and his belligerent defiance was openly displayed.

"My wife, Baya, either ran away or was kidnapped and I want her back."

"What has this to do with this garrison, or with Salimah?" D'nkrad dryly asked while moving behind his table-desk and seating himself comfortably. He pointedly did not offer Gamba a chair. If the wife had run off, he already could understand why based on this Hidayan's demeanor. A bully stood before him, an angry bully, and therefore potentially dangerous. A flickered glance at Janapriya assured him that the squire was aware and alert.

"You are closest to Salimah, and I have reason to believe that my wife is hiding there. I want you to help me get her back so I can take her back where she belongs." Gamba was panting now and sweating profusely with passion.

"If she is a Hidayan citizen, as we all are," noted D'nkrad politely, "Then she cannot be forced to return to your obviously happy home. However, if she was kidnapped it is unlikely that Salimah would allow any citizen to remain in such bondage. Salimah is purged of such abominations, I assure you."

"But I know differently," hissed Gamba leaning over the table menacingly and supporting himself on stiffened arms. "I followed her from Adamya across Lake Maemi to Viñay, and then through the mountains. Traveling around all that is difficult for a woman by herself. She needed help. The nearest house my wife would have reached was that of Old T'moyo. Her grandson had crossed Lake Maemi and visited her the night Baya disappeared. When I got there the old woman had cleared out. 'just left without any notice. I went back and talked with the grandson, and he says there may have been someone, a woman, hidden on his boat, but I couldn't get more information out of him."

"And why is that?"

"Why is what?"

"Why couldn't he give you any more information."

"Because he wasn't very cooperative giving me the information from the start, so I had to convince him."

"Meaning you beat the information out of him until he died?" the commander shot back in anxious alarm.

"He didn't die!" Gamba yelled glaring at the commander. "He was in on the kidnapping! Baya wouldn't have left on her own! She wouldn't! Never! It had to be that old woman, T'moyo, and her grandson who grabbed her!"

"Why would they do that? Do you suspect they stole her to be a slave?" D'nkrad tried hard to keep both skepticism and sarcasm from his voice. With conscious caution he continued.

"I know of T'moyo. She is very old, and is much respected. Your charge of kidnapping is serious and unlikely based on her reputation. Perhaps you are mistaken? Maybe your wife visited a relative or friend in need and didn't have time to tell you?"

"No! I know that T'moyo left with a young woman. There are witnesses in Viñay who say they left early one morning at dawn and headed west. Salimah is the most likely place and I demand you help me get her back!"

"What do you propose? Would you expect me to order the garrison to search through Salimah, house by house, for this Baya of yours? If she is as ugly as her name suggests, why would you even want her back? Perhaps being rid of her is a gift."

"She's my wife!" Gamba roared puffing himself out like an adder. "I'll have her back with or without your help!" Gamba defiantly planted himself with his arms crossed and his sturdy legs apart on the stone floor.

Emotionlessly D'nkrad considered his options while carefully maintaining eye contact with Gamba. If he had the scenario correct, a very ugly or deformed wife had either run away or had been kidnapped. More likely she had run away from an abusive husband with the help of Old T'moyo and her grandson, who was now apparently recuperating from a painful assault. His heart grieved for the pain his nephew must be in at this time as he recovered.

If his mother *was* on his way here, one of the main reasons for his up-coming inspection tour was lost. If Gamba had rushed here ahead of Lord D'nkrad's mother and Baya, then there were many reasons for their delay, but none of them included a leisurely sightseer's pace. She probably would be arriving within a day or two if she hadn't arrived already.

With eyebrows drawn concernedly together, D'nkrad asked, "When did this happen?"

"A fortnight ago."

D'nkrad sighed with tight lips. "I know Old T'moyo is not in Salimah. Every visitor checks in, and the garrison receives the listing. She is not there. If she is now on her way, as you believe, her pathway was not direct. She is either visiting here and there, or has met with some endangerment. Let me make inquiries before you enter Salimah tearing it apart." Turning to Janapriya he directed, "Squire, take this gentleperson to the garrison guest quarters. Make sure he is comfortable and has access to whatever he needs while he remains with us."

Gamba was obviously reluctant to leave without more than this vague assurance that the matter would be attended to; but the commander stood and nodded towards the squire dismissively. D'nkrad's shallow bow with palms folded inward before him was courteous, but not deeply honoring to Gamba who noted the disrespect through resentful, slitted eyes. Still, the door had been opened and Gamba's exit was quite clearly expected. It was better to comply right now rather than insult the commander whom he needed, but his true frustrated feelings, despite his disgusted grimace of courtesy and barely nodded head, were expressed his true thoughts.

Pausing before attending to any other issue, D'nkrad's brow wrinkled. His expression darkened in concern. He had been hearing rumors of violence in distant townships. Nothing was verifiable, but there was a nervous, twittering undercurrent within the garrison as well as in Salimah that he had intended to investigate on this tour. Was Gamba's presence here a precursor of that violent contagion spreading to Salimah? Perhaps he would forestall his long-anticipated travels to Aichen and Adamya, especially since one of the main reasons to go there was on her way to him.

"Living each day as well as we can
may be the biggest fear we have; we risk
much in choosing to be alive for who we truly
are is revealed daily to others and to ourselves."
~ Sixth Book of Instruction

CHAPTER 8

❖

PREPARATIONS

B one shaking tremors continued throughout the night while deep, exhausting insecurity wrapped itself around the caravan. The pilgrim caravan slept through one entire night and day while Hidaya shivered spasmodically like a dog shaking water from her sodden fur.

There was no way to perceive the time of day under the shielding dune cave. The tireless flutters of the iridescent moths herding the granular walls and ceiling into submission also provided quivering, dim luminosity; for some this was a trusting comfort that centered and calmed them, and for others it crushed their already shocked minds and hearts deeper into disassociation.

Long hours later, Ishwa opened his eyes to a magnificent display of brilliant, sparkling stars. He was disoriented. Cautiously raising his head to look around, he saw the sleeping hulks of travel beasts and smaller bundles of shadowy travelers radiating around him. He looked above again. Had it been a dream about the tunnel and the furred singers? It had seemed so real, but this scene was only missing the tents to make it a full campsite. There was no oasis sheltering them, so it had not been a dream.

The Eighth Night:

The furball on which Ishwa's head had been resting stirred restlessly, and turned over sleepily. A soft, woofing rustle alerted Ishwa. A singular pilgrim bird hopped onto his knee and looked directly at him imperiously.

"I am honored by your visit, Kind Protector," greeted Ishwa after an emotion filled pause.

"I am honored by your patient faithfulness, Teacher," responded the flyer. "Messengers have finally returned from Viñay and Cham. There is plague, and the elders of Viñay were persuaded that the source of the plague had left with this caravan. The elders sent mercenaries into the desert to kill you."

"Kill me?" Ishwa confusedly questioned.

"To kill you and everyone accompanying you on this trip. Viñay's elders believed that it would be better if everyone on this pilgrimage died in the desert taking the plague with them rather than to arrive at Cham infectious and contagious at the end of the retreat." The birdlet hesitated before adding as explanation, "Those in Viñay were afraid."

"Is the elders' unmerciful response different than killing what they fear? Do we really have the plague among us?"

"The Healing One absorbed any plague viruses when the caravan was inoculated against it at the last oasis, but the plague had not started with someone here. And as you have noticed, all illnesses and physical weaknesses were healed at the same time just to preclude any suspicion of illness."

"The Understanding One is merciful," whispered Ishwa.

"Truly we are blessed," chanted back the twittering speaker.

"What happens now?" queried Ishwa. "We are lost in the Cham, though our novices don't know it. Our service-assistants suspect it, but aren't sure. Will we be hiding until the mercenaries return to Viñay and have given up searching for us?"

"The vigilante posse is close, even now, and they will not turn back for the reward promised them is excessive. The Cham shielded all of you until preparations could be completed adequately. At the next oasis, which their travel beasts have sought out on their own, you will meet up with the four surviving members of the posse so you can embrace them into your circle."

"You want us to accept them as if they are fellow travelers?" Ishwa confirmed aghast at the idea.

"*Your own fear is understandable. How is your response different from theirs of the plague? Is it any different than theirs, even though they are being paid to seek you out?*

"*We can try to separate ourselves from evil. We can push it away, make laws against it, avoid it, and shun it. But such exclusion eventually causes violent retaliation because such actions are inherently non-healing. Think! You know this. There is another pathway to responding to evil.*"

Ishwa's head drooped at the implied reprimand, for he did know the pathway to which his tiny mentor referred. "*You speak of forgiveness and starting over with a clean and humbled heart.*"

"*We don't need any sacrifice, Ishwa. These pilgrims you lead were not part of any sacrifice, though it may have appeared so at the time. Your caravan was inoculated, only. There was no time to advise you beforehand, or to prevent shock among you all. Your anxiety and anger is understandable. You were not told afterwards because too much was being prepared to advise you well.*

"*As for forgiving what we call evil, that is difficult whether it be from others or from within ourselves. We used to acknowledge it with child or animal sacrifices, or with even self-sacrificing actions and denials as if those could manipulate the Knowing One into doing our will. It's like using symbolically superstitious objects to control nature or life when they are harsh and unwanted as they are. It's not that the evil needs to be destroyed, either in fact or symbolically; what needs to die is the need to judge others as valueless when compared with ourselves as well as our need to control everything. We need to accept life as it is, strive to make it better if possible, yet let the One be the One even if there is no understanding or liking of the One's will.*"

"*Won't the posse members kill us anyway because they don't know the truth of the plague's source? And as for embracing them - - healing can be called forth more often than not if the Merciful One is involved. But there are some Hidayans whom evil has overtaken completely. Rehabilitation, refuge, or other mercies – even done lovingly – are perceived by these twisted Hidayans as weaknesses and may incite more of their harmfulness. Only the Healing One, in another time perhaps, can heal their warped souls. In this time we need to be protected! Are you asking for a repetition of what happened to the ten Hidayans we honor by this journey? They died here!*"

"*How they died here is not the same as why they died though both are significant. They are honored because of the choices they made. It was not the One's will that they would die as they did.*"

129

"*The Merciful One could have hidden them as we were hidden. They could have been protected! We were protected once already by the Cham's sand; let the One protect us again! I don't want to die here by treachery, or by blindly trusting that others will only make good and caring choices! And I refuse to lead these pilgrims to their deaths knowingly! It would be as if I had killed them myself!*"

Ignoring this panicked comment, the Protector continued, "Ishwa, I promise you that you will not be leading these people to their deaths. Forgive, Ishwa. Transform the misunderstanding and evil." The flyer's head tilted to let one shiny black eye confront Ishwa straight on, but there was no response except confusion from the overwhelmed guide.

The Teacher looked down in despairing, flustered confusion, and when Ishwa finally looked up, his visitor had left. Only the sleeping figures surrounding him in the darkness relieved the endless vision of grit, scruffy desert shrubs, and mountainous dunes shifting warily in the night chill. A forecasting breeze teased the dune's ridges and crests that blocked out large chunks of the glittering heavens, and began smoothing them into flat hardness. Ishwa centered his tumultuous thoughts to rest and he finally slept. Vividly realistic dreams and nightmares chased themselves through the remaining night.

Gored'na was the first to spy the oasis across a flat expanse of shrub-dotted wasteland. Within a few kilometers of the lush edges of this shelter stretched a wadi whose width testified to a history of voluminous spring rainfall. The wadi crossed the northern Cham like an ancient scar, deeply pitted in places, and clawed in others with erosion. Rose, cream, orange, chocolate, ebony, gray, and buff sedimentary layers rose up impressively, adding their painted, edged pattern to an otherwise bleak location.

Gored'na harshly reined in his travel beast. It bellowed protests and danced agitatedly sideways in pain. When the beast had been controlled, Gored'na pointed with a grunt to the oasis ahead. "Dat's da next stop," he announced flatly.

"'ow'ja know dat?" shot back Tangi, wiping his dripping nose across his stained sleeve, and then licking his dry lips with a smack.

"Shaddup, Tangi, ya good fer nothin' slimer. Dis gotta be da next stop 'cause da spring rains'll be comin' any day now, an' dis here place's got da bes' view and 'ospitality," Gored'na growled back. "Let's git goin'."

"Shaddup, yourself!" Tangi shrieked to Gored'na's retreating back. Ghanash'am, and Ne'igalomea pushed past him dismissively as he fumbled with his tangled reins. His uncoordinated efforts merely caused more knotting.

As they neared, the abundance of this oasis beckoned through shimmering waves of heat. Deep, thick, verdant growth interspersed with barren, waxy tree trunks rose from the desert floor. Shaggy palms, hairy flag trees, silver leafed berry shrubs and other fruit-laden plants grew thickly among tall fan fronds and other shading trees. Scout shrubs and brittle grasses radiated outwards from the edges of the oasis easing one's vision into accepting its presence; richly verdant generosity stretched out and gradually melded into the sturdy desert bush biome.

The mercenaries approached cautiously, finally standing toe-to-toe besides each other surveying what was before them. Several bubbling clear pools of sparkling spring water were easily in sight, and without much trouble the travel beasts tugged their reins from their riders' distracted hands to claim one of the drinking ponds as their own.

The vigilantes tensed using all their senses to perceive safety, danger, or unwelcome, but only pacifically caressing breezes persisted in dancing over them sweetly carrying enticingly perfumed and fruity fragrances while dismissing the harsh desert heat. Unfamiliar and unconditional welcome was the message received so they shambled forward suspiciously and tentatively towards the nearest unclaimed spring.

At the sound of their shuffling gait, the background buzzing and humming of insects paused momentarily and then droned on ignoring the trespassers. Squawking long-beaked spearlings and challenging rainbow parrots silenced other tweets and chirps in the branches above while the screaming heralds announced the posse's arrival. When the spearlings and parrots flew off into the oasis depths to repeat their news, an excited exuberance of cheeps, chitters, trills, and warbles erupted.

Gored'na Ghanash'am Ne'igalomea, and Tangi scowled at each other, and rolled their eyes before falling into the pool to drink and cool off.

A mild chill awakened Rawiya. The coolness and sky above her advertised that she no longer lay underground. "What a gentle morning," thought Rawiya looking at several puffy, shadowy clouds leisurely escaping from a distant bunching on the horizon as Bozidara prepared to peak over Hidaya's curve. These clouds looked substantial enough to cross the Cham Desert without disappearing. The spring rain seemed so close! Within minutes the ochre rays of Bozidara would brighten the heights of the mushrooming, vaporous billows that presently remained silhouetted, like flatly gray rocks without depth. Turning languidly onto her stomach, Rawiya abruptly came nose to nose with Ishwa who apparently had been studying her while she slept.

"G'morning Bright Eyes!"

"Ugh! What –?"

"Get over it. Let me tell you what life is like as of this morning."

"Couldn't it wait?"

"Until…"

"Until I take a break behind that dune."

"You females are alike. You wake up and have to go."

"And you haven't yet, O Great Male?"

"I went earlier, but I'll wait patiently for you. If you don't dawdle I have a protein chew that I'll share. If not, both of them are all mine." Ishwa looked hilariously provocative which got Rawiya giggling and hurriedly stumbling over the sand to the lee side of the dune. Returning in record time she flopped down beside Ishwa claiming her chew. He actually had twin protein sticks that they tore open hungrily and gobbled down before they sat licking their fingers. It took very little time and words for Ishwa to concisely tell Rawiya about his night time visitor, and then they sat in silence looking pensive amidst the still-shadowed sleepers splayed around them.

"So, we go to the next oasis and meet these killers, welcoming them as long lost family?"

"Mmmm…. We'll alert the rest of the camp that we are likely to meet strangers there, and prepare them to be *warmly cautious,* and that's it. We should make it to our next stop tomorrow. We will travel this morning while it is still cool, sleep, and after dinner –"

"'story?" Rawiya checked.

"Yes, and story," Ishwa confirmed.

"And when we arrive tomorrow, if they try to kill us as their bounty requires, then what?"

"We may need to protect ourselves and them from their own selves, and still welcome them into our midst. However, there are multiple protectors surrounding us, and apparently much preparation for this meeting, so action may not be necessary beyond welcoming them."

"No fear?"

"Well, none beyond what is reasonably self-preserving." Somber silence followed.

The ageless troposphere turned a milky hue before transfiguring into successive pastels heralding dawn. Suddenly the dull, flat horizon clouds were surrounded with an edging shawl of blinding gold, and then the depths of the misty swells were highlighted in Bozidara's sudden, revealing rays.

Ishwa helped Rawiya to her feet, and both started singing a morning-song to wake the caravan. They would eat breakfast on the move, as an early start meant an early rest.

*"Life's imperfections either imprison us
or inspire us to live beyond those confining
limitations. One caring person can make
all the difference in how one risks to live
their life."*

~ Searcher's Book of Instruction

CHAPTER 9

❖

SETTLING IN

The Gored'na, Ghanash'am, Ne'igalomea, and Tangi set up camp at the farthest edge of the oasis from which they anticipated the caravan to approach. They camouflaged their lean-tos within the surrounding foliage, and tied their travel beasts inside an overgrown glade to encourage quiet. A tiny, burpling spring conveniently supplied them all with water and there was no reason for the vigilantes to leave their campsite unless they foraged for food, emptied their bladders, or for surveillance.

Creaking leather, light-hearted chatter, and impatiently bellowing beasts announced the mid-morning arrival of the pilgrim's caravan. The watchers had been correct in assessing the direction from which the caravan would approach the oasis, so while remaining hidden, they observed the camp set-up activity, and listened to Ishwa's brief morning presentation. When the pilgrim's were excused and the preparation for the mid-day meal started, the posse met at their own campsite.

"Dey none o' dem look sick ta me," snarled Ne'igalomea.

"Ta me da same," concurred Tangi. "Dey should all be dead by now."

"Dat's not important," retorted Gored'na. "We don' get paid ta judge health. We get paid fer da job."

"Well, we won' kill none o' dem wit' so many o' dem an' jus' us four. Da best is ta pois'n da water," Ghanash'am growled, "an' dey die like dey shudda."

"T'night den. It'll all be over by t'morrow. Who'll do it?" Tangi asked.

"We all will, ya fool!" snapped Ne'igalomea. "We all do it, an' den all get paid, an' if one o' us makes a story fer da law, dey die b'fore dey leave deez sands."

They all looked hard at the others, and with a grunt from Ghanash'am, they turned their backs to each other and retreated to the shade under their lean-tos. Once in awhile one of them would wake up, relieve themselves or go to the spring for a drink.

Bozidara slowly slid across the sky towards the toothed mountains. Meanwhile the flat gray clouds in the east mounted higher and more menacingly.

Rawiya and Ishwa had stayed within view of each other throughout the day. They managed to exchange assured, supportive glances whenever they could; they knew a meeting with the vigilantes would be coming soon, and despite their Cham experiences with the unexpected, they were apprehensive. The midday meal came and went and the afternoon rest had begun when Cook sent an assistant summoning them both.

The cook tent was busy with clean up activities, but Cook stepped out and led Ishwa and Rawiya to nearby shade where they could speak privately. Cook sat down comfortably and waited for the other two to join her, and then stared at each of them like a mother confronting fidgeting children after a vase had been broken.

"All right, you two," Cook started matter of factly, "I've watched the two of you all morning. Something's bothering you more than anything else since we three have been crossing the Cham together. You can keep it to yourselves, or tell me the truth and come clean of it, or wait until it comes down on you." She paused and watched their expressions and slumping postures, and then added carefully, "or wait until it comes down on all of us."

"Do you want to…?" Ishwa asked Rawiya resignedly.

"Yes, but you tell her since you were the one who was told," Rawiya answered shaking her bowed head in defeat. Trying to be stoic, bearing the burden of knowledge had drained her throughout the day. Her shoulders sagged while Ishwa made a gesture of squaring his shoulders before he began. He told Cook, just as he had informed Rawiya of the protector bird's visit, and then sat silently waiting for her response. Cook breathed deeply and closed her eyes as if she was making the effort to meditate.

"We need to live as we believe, and believe as we live," she finally stated. "We live this crossing together. How are you planning to unite us? And I mean it. No more of this on-your-own-so-we-won't-panic crap."

"I think we should meet together…"

"In small groups…"

"Assistants first, and then…"

"And then pilgrims."

"And then pilgrims. But never all together at once."

"It's too overwhelming and impersonal."

"We start waking up the assistants now, then," summarized Cook. "Let's start and us three meet with them so we can get the information straight, and then each get a group to talk with separately."

"No," Rawiya interjected thoughtfully. "You were right. We live this crossing together. We can start with a small group, and keep them together and add the next group, and repeat the information, until everyone knows over and over what we are facing, and that we do it together."

"That's going to take a lot of time, maybe more than we have," said Ishwa.

"How about we meet with one group, get a feel for how they respond, and ask them how we should proceed?"

"Agreed."

"Agreed."

"Let me get the first group from the cook staff first," said Cook. "I know them the best."

Group after group met throughout the day sometimes in small clusters discussing the future visitors, and sometimes meeting with

Ishwa for a conference. Today he focused on loneliness, solitude, and the importance of community. One formed community in different ways to feel meaning and belonging Ishwa taught; loneliness need not be a state to be perceived as suffering, though isolation could be painful if unwanted. Solitude could be peace-filled. However, a balance needed to be achieved for each individual, and the pilgrims were encouraged to re-evaluate their lives and social needs.

By the time Bozidara's ochre rim caressed the distant horizon, the assistants and novices were already waiting for that moment of silence that interrupted the oasis chirps, and chatter, and before dusky darkness revealed pinpoint diamond lights above. They waited for the silence when the One walked Hidaya, and when the planet breathed in and then exhaled gently, the sounds began again, and the evening proceeded like all the earlier ones had: meeting at the campfire, supper, story, blessing, and then sleep.

Gored'na Ghanash'am Ne'igalomea, and Tangi awoke abruptly when the evening silence startled them into wary consciousness for until now they had been unaware of the silence. Then the normal, natural sounds started again along with the ordinary sounds of Hidayans talking, laughing, and gathering for a meal. For a while the vigilantes suspiciously squatted back to back with knives drawn ready for an attack. When they were assaulted by the savory aromas of supper permeating the oasis they salivated uncontrollably. They individually wavered in their intent to poison the spring from which the caravan got its water; the fragrance of herbs, braised tubers, and other delights made their stomachs grumble. They were frustrated knowing that for them, unless they revealed themselves at the campfire, their supper would be stale, dry jerky from their packs washed down with clear spring water.

Anger filled them, jealous rage that they weren't included in the feast, so it wasn't difficult to deliberately steal through the foliage intent upon reaching the pool wherein they each emptied various powders and liquids. On their way back to their shelter they heard the conversation level of the pilgrims dwindle into silence, and froze where they were mid-step. A clear, warmly inviting voice filled the silence with a story-telling rhythm. They crept to the edge of the campfire light and sat down camouflaged by shadows. The pilgrims' attention was focused on a woman alive with the history she told. Her rich, deep, melodic voice, graceful brown hands, dark eyes, an accenting head nods all moved and mesmerized the listeners.

The Ninth Night

Life is never perfect even in the Cham Desert where blessings and healings overflow. All around Hidaya we seek perfection and peace. Yet there is no possible way that we Hidayans can cure all the illnesses, woundings, abuses, and crimes that harm us. We pray for the strength of the One, while questions of, "Why is life like this?" nibble at our heels. Eventually many of us find personal peace in small communities, and find rest by laying our overburdened selves in the lap of the Compassionate One who is our strength.

Nettles of worry filled Salimah. A handful of merchants and fleeing families had arrived from other townships with distressing reports of guards and governing-authorized vigilantes imprisoning, torturing and killing Searchers mercilessly. Citizens who protested received the same treatment. When several of these stories were pieced together, there was an obvious pattern, like that of slowly, predictably falling toy blocks. It was apparent that agitated mobs were drawn like mercury drops clinging and melding into each other, gathering and then oozing into other townships, and unleashing their violence on any Searchers they could discover.

It was not just having this information causing Commander D'nkrad's face to darken with anger and worry. Right before him his mother, T'moyo, and Gamba's wife, Baya-Emina, sat companionably on his only piece of decent furniture, while D'nkrad himself now claimed a low hassock. Their guide, A'kil, and Lord Che'ikh, who were both Searchers, sat on the hard floorboards next to Dato, a child roughly eight years. They all were travel-grimed, but relaxed as their journey to refuge had finally ended.

"Why?" D'nkrad asked T'moyo in exasperation. "What have you done?"

"No laws were broken, son. Emina chose to leave an unfortunate marriage and Dato is old enough to choose a different life. They both have that right. And I chose to meet you here so as you make your regional sweep I can accompany you back to our home." She sounded so calm and logical that for a moment D'nkrad was convinced of her naiveté. But her words were too soothing, too simple. Blast her!

"Do you know that Hidayans from other cities have been cajoled away by people just like you! Your life, all your lives are in danger! Did you think that no one would notice when people were missing, even relatively unimportant people? Did you think everyone would accept disappearances without speculation? This is so damning! And you brought them here, and probably others, too!" His mother nodded confirmation casually.

D'nkrad ranted on, "Even as my aide ushered you in and while you made yourselves cozy he told me that there are confirmed sightings of armed ruffians rampaging through the countryside looking for their allegedly missing citizens and their accused Searcher-kidnappers. The townships want an end to the kidnappings and want to take care of these stolen citizens by repatriating them to their hometowns. So now, within an hour of your arrival we are preparing to be attacked. We can either evacuate the city, fight off this rabble of reactionaries, or —"

"They would have come up with any reason to fight, my son. This is only an excuse. If they truly had valued the Hidayan citizens they are seeking, they would have treated them as persons of worth and value while they were still in their midst. It's control and power they are aggressively protecting regardless of anyone's rights. They truly believe that they are righteous, but it follows the historical records of Hidaya. Even with unlimited blessings, selfish fears and grudges blind us to our own reactions, and we try to control life itself. And so, here we are."

"What do you want me to do? How can I help you *and* protect Salimah? What do you expect of me?" D'nkrad pushed his hand through his hair in frustrated exasperation.

"Well, I did not come to cause you or anyone else hardship. None of us knew of these dangerous changes."

"You have heard that Searchers are being killed?" questioned Che'ikh more closely.

"Yes, Searcher." Commander D'nkrad's voice lowered in distress. "Just as in the experiences you've described to me, Searchers everywhere are being tracked and hunted like conejos. Many have been killed.

"I don't know if other Searchers beside you have come to Salimah, but farmers leaving the city a week ago told a strange tale of a mythical glass beetle carrying strangers across the Cham Desert almost to the gates of Salimah. I don't have any more information about that because the strangers entered the town and apparently are staying with family because they have not been seen since. But even in this tale the strangers were supposed Searchers escaping from vigilantes."

"Do you know for sure if they were Searchers?" A'kil asked.

"All I know is that to the farmers the riders of the glass beetle looked exhausted and dirty from travel and were wearing filthy Searcher garb. Most of the farmers' attention was focused on this mythological gigantic glass beetle that carried them here."

"It musta' been real big!" exclaimed Dato. "It woulda hafta' be big ta carry ev'n one Hidayan an' yer sayin' der were more!"

"That's why I don't credit their story," D'nkrad commented wryly. "Only late night tales around campfires tell of giant insects and beasts protecting Hidayans. The farmers' report sounds more like the hero-legends and epic songs bards entertain us with. And yet –"

"And yet in spite of the ridicule these farmers might earn from making up so bizarre a story, they told it anyway. Perhaps there might be some truth in their words," Grandmother T'moyo suggested quietly.

"Whether that is true or not, or even if they *were* Searchers brought here to safety, we need to find refuge here, now, for all of us. Emina and Dato need safety and recovery. And we all need food and rest. How can we enter Salimah without being observed by Gamba or others?" Che'ikh shrewdly questioned.

Weariness edged his words, and commander D'nkrad noted that Che'ikh's hands shook slightly. D'nkrad thoughtfully questioned himself while he pondered possible choices, "What happened to these people? What happened to his mother?" He cleared his voice abruptly to end his musing.

"There is a roundabout way to enter Salimah, but it would be much easier to bring you into the city inside of a supply wagon. One is scheduled to enter Salimah this evening, so you would not be noticed entering. Once inside, you must find the haven you seek in Salimah's depths. I will not know anything about this if questioned, and only my aide knows of you. He will help you into the wagons now and before Bozidara sets you will find refuge. Let me call him now."

Janapriya was summoned and apprised of the situation briefly without an in-depth explanation to ease his curiosity. A hidden side door allowed the travelers to exit the commander's office, and as D'nkrad had predicted, they found refuge in Salimah before nightfall.

Oblivious to their arrival, Gamba also slipped into Salimah, too impatient to wait at the garrison. He quietly checked into an inn near the city's main gate and began a vigil to surprise his errant wife, Baya. He left briefly to speak in the gate's shadows with a tall Hidayan merchant, and then Gamba rubbed his hands together in satisfaction. He returned to his inn with determination to stay awake all night watching.

Late the next morning Gamba emerged from the inn on his way to breakfast. His sleep-crusted eyes widened when he saw the swirling rainbow of robes, and his mouth almost watered as he greedily wandered among the street venders selling crafts of such high quality that he coveted them not for their use or beauty, but because no one back in Adamaya would have anything even close to the quality of these crafts and textiles. He was too near with his money to buy any baubles, however. He bought a meat pie from one of the early street venders and wandered through the market eating as he walked.

An abrupt uproar drew him back towards the gate. Turning on his heel he saw farmers, country families with screaming infants, and terrified children running into the market place from the city gate. Behind them burst a thundering clamor.

Shouted orders to halt were lost in the tumult. The mobbed invading ruffians following the panicked citizens charged into Salimah, angrily overturned booths and wares, breaking everything impeding their own progress. No longer were they looking for specific people; they brutishly sought the thrill of conquest and the rush of power when citizens fearfully fled from them. The sense of power and defiant strength was intoxicating. Once they had lived ordinary lives with occasional moments of attention and praise, but as part of this vengeful band, adrenalin and importance flowed unchecked through their veins until they were addicted.

Those citizens in the upper stories of the buildings who were able to see over the walls encircling Salimah, saw billowing black smoke and angry flames rising from the southern corner of the garrison compound. Tattered mercenaries swarmed around the walls while the garrison fought a singular battle. Alarms were given and the people of Salimah moved with purpose.

Because Salimah was a refuge city, long-planned preparations included hidden rooms within the thick walls and stairwells led to concealed, connected cellars where refugees could escape undetected through tunneled passageways far into the forests beyond Salimah's gates. It was because of this forethought that the vigilantes eventually captured relatively few citizens.

But the inner city also housed neophytes at various stages of recovery. They had to be evacuated and protected for many could not yet protect themselves. Searchers and those staffing this retreat stronghold rallied. The invaders realized that this section of Salimah held something important when the first organized resistance to their takeover abruptly forestalled them. As more mercenaries flowed into Salimah they were directed to attack this inner sanctuary and to breach the defenses. That became their main objective.

For all they knew, treasure lay within the inner city, and they were outraged to be denied access anywhere. They could not scale the inner walls easily, and all attempts to enter were rebuffed expediently, so their righteous resentment at denial exploded into unrestrained action; walls, entryways, and sturdy doors all splintered, shattered, and collapsed into rubble through endless assaults. Imminent total conquest of Salimah would be accomplished by nightfall.

Deep within the refuge Lady Ansh'mati's room once again welcomed Angharad who had this time brought a friend. Kamalei had brought a packaged gift of bant berry tarts with her, but she abandoned them in a wooden bowl still in their wrapping when she was offered tea with warm, sugared-cinnamon bread. She marveled at the box in the corner that produced a flame used to heat the tea water. Angharad had told her of this convenience, but to see it was still astonishing. Even though Lady Ansh'mati's voice and gestures were smooth and gracefully calm, both Kamalei and Angharad sensed a tenseness and distress in the room. Ansh'mati's dreading anticipation was difficult to conceal.

Hurrying feet and a precipitous knock on the door surprised them, but the three had no chance to move before the door was flung open. Angharad and Kamalei gasped, but Lady Ansh'mati only straightened her back and raised her hands as if blessing the messenger.

"They are here! The ones who kill Searchers! Everyone must leave Salimah now! Every citizen of Salimah that the renegades have found has been killed! No one is spared! We have to leave. Now!" The messenger bent over gasping for air.

"But there are so many who cannot escape! Grandmother T'moyo arrived last night. She is not capable of out-running anyone. And the other elders and younger children can't escape so quickly!"

"We must try," The messenger managed to breath out. "The older boys and girls are carrying the younger children. The elders and those in the infirmaries are being ferried on tunnel barges. We blocked the irrigation waters from the fields days ago when we first heard of the brigands coming closer. By now the underground channels are filled and the barges are already afloat and loading those who cannot walk. And we all must leave *now*!"

An enormous shout of triumph echoed through the hallways advising everyone that the inner sanctuary had been breached and those who hadn't escaped would find merciless death soon. Ansh'mati unhesitatingly jumped up and pushed a crimson pillow aside. A trap door lay hidden underneath. She deftly swung it open and saw the over-crowded passageway below swarming with fleeing people. A few glanced up at her into the light of the room but their individually fearful faces were immediately lost as the intent mob forcefully pushed them along. It would be difficult and nearly impossible to inject oneself into such a rushing river of people.

"This is impossible!" Ansh'mati shouted. "There must be another escape."

"All tunnels lead to the fields and forests beyond."

A crash of stone and that of tearing, splintering wood told them how close the invaders were. They were moving quickly and either escape or death was minutes away.

"The tunnel into the Cham Desert!" the messenger exclaimed. "It's the only way now!" They all looked at each other in surprise and then orders were given.

"Angharad, you and Kamalei must take the Cham tunnel. We will stay behind and resist these fighters to give you time. Don't argue. We have a better chance of survival without you, and you have a better chance if we stay behind. Go! Here!"

The trap door was quickly closed and re-hidden while a small cabinet beside the stove was pushed aside and a ragged, rough crawly hole between the walls was revealed. Kamalei grabbed the tart package before she and Angharad hastily stuffed themselves into the darkness. Behind them the cabinet was shoved and scraped back into place. Already a fight of resistance was heard just beyond the hallway corner, and all the Searchers dashed forward to join in.

No citizens of Salimah had chosen the escape route into the Cham Desert, so Kamalei and Angharad crawled for what seemed hours in total blackness alone. At one point a small slide tumbled them to a lower level, but the tunnel remained cramped, musty, and dark. At times in tiredness they cried softly as they moved whispering encouragement only when necessary for they didn't know what sounds could be heard on the other sides of the walls between which they traveled. They prudently stopped when furniture or crockery crashed on the other side of the walls, and several times they heard painful sounds and shrieks immediately silenced. Terror and hope vied inside of them.

Eventually exhausted they just stopped to eat some of the bant berry tarts, and then slept. When they woke, there was no way to determine how long they had slept, so they set out again. They hadn't gone very far before a short slide dumped them into a large, roomy space hollowed from packed dirt and rock. Flickering globes of dim light automatically became operational triggered by their movement.

They were in a small supply room with bundles of dried meat and tubers ready for the taking. A sunken, hollowed floor space in a dark corner held a crude defecation hole. At the opposite side of the room a rough clay cup was placed near quick-dripping water from a pipe emerging from the earthen wall. There were bundles of supplies neatly piled everywhere for this cache had been regularly attended to.

Angharad and Kamalei alternately relieved themselves and slaked their thirst before examining the bundles stacked everywhere. Desert clothes, sandals, canteens, dried food and basic medical supplies had been stashed here.

They froze in terror as a sliding sound from across the room heralded the arrival of others. An elderly female, a young boy, and perhaps the boy's mother slid down the ramp. Much bulkier shapes rapidly followed them. These next refugees were dressed in desert garb; they immediately began riffling through the supplies with experience, ignoring the others who looked on. They found bedrolls and small cooking utensils. There was even a small star-cooker that used the light from Bozidara. A primitive, lightweight, water condenser was stacked beside the other chosen supplies.

"We have to leave soon," whispered the one introduced as Z'van. Angharad recognized him as Lord Z'van and was comforted, though she did not reveal his recognized identity to the others. He continued, "Our only hope as perhaps the last citizens alive within Salimah is over the desert. We can make it across to safety, but if we are discovered and caught out in the desert, the anger these attackers have for us is mortal."

"If we stay here," explained A'khil unnecessarily, "We are all dead."

"Damn *dat* plan!" muttered Dato angrily.

"What about the garrison? Can't they protect us?" Che'ikh questioned.

Old T'moyo answered, "They are outside of Salimah, but are unable to enter yet. I know the commander, and know that he is trying to help us, but many of the guardians were lost when the garrison was attacked. Commander D'nkrad lives, though, and is well." There was a brief smile as the old woman shared this information without revealing her relationship to the commander. "I know we must leave. I wish we had had more time to recover from our own journey to Salimah, but that is not possible now."

"We have several hours before it will be dark enough to leave across the desert. They won't be expecting this."

"What if they see us leaving?"

"Then some of us will become a distraction so that they will not look for you or the others."

"Did many citizens of Salimah survive and live?" Emina asked fearfully.

"Most lived. Almost all citizens of Salimah were saved, but there might isolated groups still sheltered inside the city unable to get to an escape tunnel, though I doubt that. Let's get rest. And pray to the Merciful One for help." But Emina's thoughts were on all those years of prayer to one god or another goddess and she hadn't been saved then. What was different about the Compassionate One? How was trusting one god different from another? Was prayer any different than a wishful hope? She fell asleep with bitter, jaded, angry and confused thoughts of abandonment and betrayal.

"I hope your thoughts are more peaceful than that tonight. We know that all prayers are answered by the One, though often not as we Hidayans would want that answer to be. In this oasis we have food, water, and all that we need. There is no need to fret over the resources richly gifted to us by this place and the Compassionate One. There is no need to doubt the presence and response to prayer of the One."

A groan accompanied by several whining protests that the story should continue was lost when Ishwa loudly noted that rain was due either tomorrow or the day after. They shivered with excitement. With hands raised they all participated in the closing prayer and blessing. Then, after silently watching until the last of the spirit sparks had dissipated, the pilgrims burst into animated conversation about the coming of the rain as they left the campfire, took a smudge light from the attendant's tray, and prepared for bed. Soon the sounds of tired people quieted with regular breathing and occasional snores. The Cham's nighttime darkness gradually covered them all like a spark studded velvet blanket tucked in around them carefully.

Gored'na, Ghanash'am, Ne'igalomea, and Tangi had used the noisy pilgrims' chatter as they left the campfire as cover to slip back to their encampment without notice.

"Dey be dead t'morrow," Tangi muttered. "An we won't 'ave heared da rest o' da story."

"Shaddup! Dey be dead by breakfast an' our job be over, an' we can leave dis 'orrible damned desert," Gored'na snarled.

"It ain't dat bad 'ere," Ghanash'am commented as he settled himself into his branch cushioned bed inside his lean-to. "Ev'n I 'ave heared da story, but I ain't never tire o' hearing it again. Too bad dey got so close ta seeing da desert flowers, but won't never."

"Eh? Where's Ne'igalomea?"

As if on cue for a stage play Ne'igalomea answered, "'ere I am. I went ta see if'n sumptin' was left in da cook tent. 'ere's some meat pies."

Ne'igalomea was rushed and was glad he had eaten some of the pies on the way back to camp. There were no thanks given neither for the pies nor for Ne'igalomea's effort to snag something for them all.

Later they returned to their lean-to beds; after a long silence Tangi whispered to anyone still awake, "Dis place ain't so bad after all."

"Life is all risk: risk to discover oneself, risk to make choices, risk committing to a person or ideal, or risk accepting life itself. The only safe path without risk or danger is to not live as fully as possible and regret that forever

~ *Searcher's Meditation Guide*

CHAPTER 10

❖

SECOND ESCAPE

The Western mountains were hidden under bunched grey and white clouds the next morning. Though a few stray clouds elegantly sailed across the desert throughout the day as if they were snobbish advance scouts for their clan lagging behind on the horizon, the sky remained mostly clear. Both the weather and the mood within the camp were tense with expectancy of change.

Ishwa reviewed yesterday's lesson before beginning a new conference, and then began today's conference.

"With our thoughts we create our world." At that moment Gored'na, Ghanash'am, Ne'igalomea, and Tangi emerged from the oasis foliage and sat quietly behind the retreatants. They had expected to find all of the caravan inhabitants to be dead from the poisoned water, but such was not the reality. They had checked the water first before joining the conference and had discovered that stately Spiked Frill-Flowers grew along one side of the pond now. Usually Spiked Frill-Flowers were white and lacy convoluted clusters of delicate tissue, but here they had taken on the yellowish hue that was familiar to the vigilantes for it was identical to that of the poison they had added to the water the prior evening. Evidently the Spiked Frill-Flowers had grown up and had purified the drinking water overnight; they had taken on the telltale coloration of the poison.

Now, the wary vigilantes joined the pilgrims and listened to Ishwa's teachings while they observed. Ishwa chose to continue speaking without causing a sensation of attention, but the pilgrims and attendants were acutely aware of the newcomers. For this time they had been prepared.

When the conference ended, Ishwa and Rawiya casually approached the four rough Hidayans and welcomed them. The mid-day meal was served early so everyone could welcome their new companions who explained their appearance as stragglers from another caravan who had elected to stay behind to witness the desert's up-coming blooming rather than rush ahead to Cham.

Although it was blatantly apparent that this was untrue, the story was not challenged. The crude speech and manners of the four Hidayans was not commented upon and they were included in all activities, including the evening meal.

The Tenth Night

What we perceive may be real or not, but it is real enough to the one who perceives. If someone calls us hurtful names when we are young, we may perceive the others' judgment as valid and live with that as our truth. Our life journey includes ridding ourselves of the false images and judgments burdening us; the ones that continue to harm us and hold us back from a better life. Some choices, however, are not made between one good possibility and another equally good possibility, but rather between one we'd rather avoid and another we'd also prefer to avoid. Tonight we face many of those harsh choices with those who traveled this path through the Cham many years ago.

Long before Aroha, Taeko, and Satya, the sister-moons of Hidaya, had risen the remnant residents of Salimah, the nine hidden ones, packed up and departed Salimah. Darkness cloaked the nine travelers as they emerged from a dirt encrusted crawly hole hidden behind dead brush. Care was taken to roll the bushes away quietly without breaking twigs – the sound might be heard by random guards patrolling the wall. The nine stealthily crept into the desert shadows.

The night's darkness deepened so greatly that the gentle starlight above could not relieve the blackness. Then Aroha, the first of the sister-moons, appeared above the horizon giving nighttime Hidayan terrain a pale blue cast. Two figures barely visible in Aroha's muted light walked Salimah's parapets slowly, deep in studied conversation.

"Mayor Alameth, there is nothing here. Salimah is just a town with a restoration spa. There is no one here of significance, no important trade or service that would single it out as notable. Perhaps the information we were given was incorrect – just like all the other false facts about other towns and farms we were given.

Yet, we cannot leave this pimple on Hidaya's backside because Hidayan troops surround Salimah and demand our surrender." He paused in abject frustration before continuing. "There are no citizens left alive to find here, and we can't discover where they disappeared to. I know there has to be a way out of this cursed ruin, but to find that way out we'll have to go room by room looking for hidden spaces or tunnels."

A gruff voice scraped out, "We may have to do just that not only to find the citizens of Salimah, but perhaps also to find a way out of this damned hole for ourselves. Sometimes I think I hear something, like someone moving around, and then maybe it is mice or some other little animals."

"There are very few animals left in Salimah, Mayor. The farmers can't come into the market with their produce even if they wanted to – or if they could get past the garrison; and the cows, sheep, and fowl were slaughtered as we traveled through the farmlands, so we have only whatever foodstuffs and supplies that are already here. Any animals we are finding are being killed and cooked. Mice, rats, and bugs may be the only animals left in this town as a source of meat. We may be starved out of here."

"Well, there is no need to rush to emergency attitudes," blustered the mayor. "There are enough greens and fruits to last for a while, and we've found wells and cisterns throughout Salimah so we have water – unless the mangy riff-raff following us has fouled it stupidly. It's just – it's just as you have already perceived - that we are trapped here, and eventually the food will be gone and we will be forced to surrender."

"It's just a matter of time then. Do the others know this?"

"I'm sure they are starting to realize that. They see so much food still in the fields and in the orchards, but most of our following haven't figured out that what is outside the walls is staying outside the walls because the Hidayan guards keep us inside and the food outside. They are a dense lot.

"And then there is the desert on this other side of Salimah." The mayor's plump, red hand gestured expansively at the wasteland over the city walls. Both looked bleakly upon the apparent barrenness of the Cham Desert that seemed to share their bitterness. They rested their weary thoughts in that way for a lengthy time with no desire to rush back to their disillusioned followers.

They watched as Taeko peeked above the horizon and sailed gracefully after her sister, Aroha, in the night sky. She softened the blue hued reflected light trailing after Aroha to Hidaya's night surface, and added a purifying tint that demystified some of the darker shadows. Abruptly Mayor Alameth caught his breath in surprise and hissed, "Look at that! It seems as if the Cham desert goes on forever with only those bushes, rocks, and useless wasteland sand, but what is that over there? It looks like..."

"What *is* that?" the mayor's aide echoed narrowing his younger, sharper eyes.

"That - it looks – it looks like tracks going into the desert. It's like a pathway with several people following one after the other. At least that's what it looks like from here. I'll bet that's how some of these sneaky fellows got out of Salimah. Do they really think we would let them report what has happened here at Salimah and name us as responsible? If they arrest us for our parts here, they would eventually investigate the other townships, and – damned. We are trapped and damned! Fools!

"First these rebels steal property and people and think it would go on forever! This "spa" is nothing more than a nest of deceit. And that so-called Hidayan garrison covered this snake pit unlawfully protecting these seditious rebels! They have no right to protect any Hidayan, nor have they any right to enter any other townships from now on. We will stop their injustices against us decent people.

"But until we are in a better position to punish them, we must hurry to save ourselves," reasoned the Mayor rapidly. "Those tracks show that there is a secret exit from here. We must move quickly because if a morning wind rises and sweeps away those tracks, we won't be able to follow. I'll just bet they were counting on that morning wind to erase their tracks."

"Mayor Alameth, we know already there is a gate leading into the desert! But that gate is probably guarded by the garrison by now!"

"Clever fellows! Salimah is beginning to appear more and more like a miserable rat's warren with crawly holes and escape routs everywhere – Quiet!" he harshly growled abruptly. He pattered silently along looking over the desert side of the parapet with his advisor trailing behind until he backtracked the trail leading into the desert right back to where stopped dead amidst thorny brambles and various detris butting against the city's solid stone wall.

"We've found it! There's their blasted exit," he whispered excitedly while pointing to the thorned clutter which successfully discouraged close examination. "Aha! There aren't any guards around at this angle of the wall to see or even suspect anything unusual! Even *they* don't know about this secret entrance into the desert. We have a chance!" Exhilarated anticipation and relief energized the mayor who was now hopping from foot to foot and grinding one fist into the palm of his other hand as he thought quickly.

"This will be our way to get out of Salimah without being caught. We'll follow their tracks, and eventually find those who made them. We *will* find them, and kill them, but not before they have shown us the way across the Cham to safety. Their traitorous bones will find rest out there, on the other side of the desert in sight of their salvation, but not closer.

"Go quickly now with the best ones we have. Search the rooms! Move every piece of furniture and lift every rug looking for trap doors or hidden doorways; but narrow the search to this side of Salimah nearest to the desert! Hurry! We must leave before the morning wind traps us without a path."

The aide pivoted with practiced expertise, hunched into a scurried run, but turned quickly back, weathering the scowling, exasperated condemnation on the Mayor's face. "Mayor Alameth, what about that perfumed bumpkin, Gamba. We didn't find his ugly wife, but without his information it would have been difficult getting into Salimah. We made promises to him. He will slow us down if we take him with us. What should we do about him? Kill him or bring him along?"

"Ah, you're right! He is a loose end that must be dealt with now. He *was* useful, but I don't trust anyone who betrays his own family. Salimah is basically abandoned, so while we search for the hidden exit into the desert, divert his attention and let him take whatever he wants and is able to carry back to Adayama where he comes from. He, actually, can go right out the front city gates as he was also visiting the garrison, and they will give him safe passage home with a couple of our people as escorts part way back to Adayama."

"Part way back, sir?"

"Yes. If he is as greedy as I think he is, he will take more than his miserable wife was worth. The escorts can take their share from him when they leave him. There should be more than enough to satisfy their own needs. If he protests, his loss is meaningless."

"Ah, Mayor Alameth! You are truly a devious power!"

"Thank you. Now hurry!"

The garrison fire had been contained with difficulty, and the burnt out corner could easily be rebuilt. The smoking logs were an acrid annoyance already being attended to. There had been some hand-to-hand fighting, and Commander D'nkrad visited the wounded no matter whether they were from his garrison, Salimah, or elsewhere. He noted that the rebel farmers, mayors, and citizens of other townships, unlike his guards and the citizens of Salimah, were not as used to earnest hand-to-hand combat, and their horrendous wounds testified to their unbelievable inexperience and ignorance of basic personal defense.

"Janapriya, some of these are just lads barely out of grade school," D'nkrad murmured to his aide. "So young!"

"Yes, though some look like grandfathers over there," Janapriya whispered back pointing to a group of shock-weary elders. "And all so foolish as to follow a crazy rumor! Commander, many of these youths will be seriously scarred and maimed for life, and for what? They conquered a village and scattered its people because of greed and rumors. They could have stayed home and done that to themselves! Beyond shame, this is disgusting! The elders should have known better!"

"Calm yourself, Janapriya. It is a disgusting shame to be sure, but Salimah *was* a key city for the Omniscient One. And don't look so blasted confusedly at me!

"Salimah was just what its name said: it was a refuge. Gamba was right. Old T'moyo and many others traveled here, as well as to other refuge cities with the forsaken, unprotected, unwanted, lost ones of Hidaya. Searchers brought slaves and beggars, indentured prostitutes and small-time thugs, and so many, many others left out of the abundant blessings of Hidaya, and were willing to find a better life learning the loving way of the One. The searchers from Salimah didn't steal people, but they provided means so that those who wanted a life without abuse and oppressive burdens, or a reformed life focused on forgiveness, hope, and healing could find that here if they chose. And most did find that here or in other refuge cities around Hidaya. For the first time, those collected by the Searchers found reasons to live, hope that gave meaning to their breath, and the freedom to choose how they wanted to live a joyful, meaningful life. There are many in Salimah whose first experiences with self-respect and friendship were here."

The commander paused with a bitter twisting of his lips before continuing. "However, by nature, our species often greedily wants power over others to make up for what they perceive is lacking in their own lives. They can't find integrity, honor, and control in their own characters, so they need to get it from others, by force or manipulation – whatever it takes. If they succeed then uncontrolled greed and absolute power are addicted to themselves. Together they become a perverted lust that destroys both those humbled and shamefully victimized by oppression, as well as filling those who help enforce the oppression with a tenuous power of their own that destroys them also because they are allowing and using the perverted power to continue. All of these addicts rely on those whom they hobble with hopeless misery and merciless subjugation to feel better, always righteously justifying themselves as near-deity nobility, god-ordained leaders, or more intelligent and enlightened than anyone else.

"No, Janapriya, this was much more than a mere village. Salimah *was* one of the hopes of Hidaya that gave meaning to many lives. Perhaps it was an idealistic pipedream, but it was one that offered real hope, welcome, and loving blessings to everyone. Perhaps someday it will again be a symbol of that hope fulfilled if it is the will of the Living One." Janapriya was astonished by his commander's open confession and explanation. Now so many oddities of Salimah and the placid, confidently contented temperament of the city were explained. Janapriya's face showed consecutive changes from befuddled surprise, to full comprehension, and then awe-filled understanding of the situation for all of Hidaya. He inhaled slowly and stood taller; he paused before exhaling and looked around, but, when he looked on the wounded now, a new light filled his eyes. The angry shock and rush to judgment revenge was no longer sparking and snapping impatiently in sharp glances; instead dawning compassion filled his eyes with a calm strength, and he looked slowly and quietly at each wounded person. D'nkrad noted the change silently, and continued through the infirmary talking with the wounded.

Later that morning, D'nkrad eased into his office chair and lowered his head to rest on his crossed arms. A deep, anguished sigh escaped from his heart.

"Commander?" Janapriya questioned with hesitating concern. "Can I get you something?"

D'nkrad raised his head to peer up at his squire, but immediately closed his eyes as he roughly rubbed his forehead. "Janapriya, I need you to do something for me."

"Yes, sir!" Janapriya came to a tired attention. Already this day was overlong.

"Janapriya...," again D'nkrad sighed, and then straightened with resolution. "I need you to give me until nightfall before you report my desertion to the junior officers."

"Wha'! But, sir! No!"

"Yes, Janapriya," D'nkrad continued tranquilly now as his plan formed. "Perhaps you have already suspected, but T'moyo is my mother, and I cannot allow her to be trapped in Salimah, though I doubt if that is where she is right now."

"I followed your orders, sir! I delivered her and the others into Salimah, which is now surrounded. There is no way out. Surely even if these ruffians gathered the innocent citizens as hostages, she – she is old and elders are respected. Surely she is with other captured citizens and unharmed!"

"Not true. Here is the situation. When you and the rest of the guards enter Salimah you will all eventually find escape tunnels leading to the northern forests. Bring food and other supplies to them and help them relocate to other cities for Salimah, as a township, will not be rebuilt for many years, I fear. Salimah and this garrison will be busy caring for the welfare of the surviving citizens here and in other nearby townships.

"My mother, T'moyo, could not travel quickly enough to safely traverse the tunnels to the forests, so I know that she is either dead, trapped, or has eluded the rebels another way. I believe it is this last possibility that probably has saved her."

"Commander," Janapriya interrupted, "I don't doubt your word about these escape tunnels, though none of us were aware of them. But since you are confident that she is alive we will find her and she will be safe. There is no reason for you to desert. We will find her; and if she is not in the tunnels or forests, or held captive as a respected elder, there is nowhere else she can go. Desertion, Sir! That is – is an unnecessary drastic response!" Panic edged Janapriya's words.

"Listen Janapriya. No, listen! Refuge cities are safe because of many preparations. T'moyo may be dead or alive, but she is clever enough to find a way to protect herself and her charges. And there is one other way out of Salimah, though it is a desperate one. She would take that choice, especially if there were others with her. That is why I must resign this commission and follow her into exile. She and any others unable to leave by the forest tunnels will have gone into the Cham Desert to escape."

"The Cham! Commander! Even if there *are* escape tunnels to the north and perhaps into the Cham, there is always the chance that someone carried her to safety. Perhaps –"

"No. Somehow I know where she is, and I will follow her."

"Where do you think she is? And – sir? How do you know these things?"

"I know because even though I am an officer for Hidayan guardians, I am also a Searcher. I am one of those who speak for those who cannot speak for themselves, and protect the defenseless ones. Right now, my mother is one of those defenseless ones, and I believe that if she lives she has escaped into the Cham."

"Sir! You are a Searcher! Ah, but that explains so many things! But be realistic! Your mother is as good as dead for as old a woman as she is she cannot possibly endure and survive any journey across the Cham! Besides, she just arrived from a tiresome journey that apparently took her days longer because of her age. Sir, this plan to desert you commission is foolhardy! You can do more good by staying here."

"Perhaps you are right for your instincts are usually true. Nevertheless, I must go."

"The garrison will go with you and help to protect her!"

"The garrison will be here and then in the northern forests assisting the refugees," D'nkrad flatly stated. "Will you give me the time I need?"

Janapriya slumped speechlessly, dumb before the full implications of this request. "Can I go –"

"No."

"What if –"

"You will not be blamed or charged with any fault. If you agree, I will write my direct order to you absolving you of responsibility and blame. But you must agree or not."

"Sir? I... yes! For you I will risk anything!"

"Do not risk anything or everything ever, Janapriya, unless you are offering yourself to the Compassionate One. Only then is such a gift as great as that understandable." D'nkrad stretched out his hand for a farewell gesture, but changed his mind midway and stepped forward to connect his right fist squarely with the squire's jaw. Janapriya fell heavily, and D'nkrad quickly bound and gagged him. "Sorry, young one," D'nkrad apologized to the unconscious boy. "On second thought there really is no time to write a letter of explanation, and this way you won't need one. Only you will know the truth, though, and you will have the choice to tell or not to tell it. May you be wise."

D'nkrad tore off his uniform and replaced it with desert robes and sandals. He snatched a heavily laden knapsack waiting in the same corridor he had used to lead T'moyo and the others out of the garrison without being seen. Once outside with his head swathed and hooded, turmoil and chaos still distracted everyone's attention from one more citizen. D'nkrad took his time as he reconnoitered the situation within the garrison; and after rubbing charcoal and dirt over his clothes and face, he joined a small group of shocked citizens waiting for evening.

Gored'na, Ghanash'am, Ne'igalomea, and Tangi listened raptly to the story just as the others around them.

Twilight shadows stretched beyond the many small campfires around which huddled straggler citizens and stranded farmers. They half-heartedly ate the food provided by the Hidayan guards, and lethargically drank the water provided, but were disinclined to talk. Intense guards surrounding Salimah were oppressively near and intimidating. The garrison loomed quietly nearby in the gloaming until a loud uproar caused them all to stretch their necks to resolve the clamor from the garrison. Shouting, scurrying, triple-speed searches from room to room brought more shouts and cries. Messengers ran towards the guards encircling Salimah, and shouted questions were relayed around the parapets. The huddling citizens overheard that the commander was missing, and as already distressed people they speculated on what had happened. Perhaps the commander had been killed or seriously injured; perhaps the attacking rebels had captured him. They glanced at each other by now emotionally over-exhausted and hunkered down lower unsure of which rumor to believe.

After awhile a nervous, middle-aged widow rose, explaining, "I have to go." She wandered off into the darkness to relieve herself.

"I might as well go, now, also," muttered a tall, limping Hidayan. He hobbled hurriedly away from the firelight in the opposite direction.

Soon, the widow returned and reclaimed her place in the circle. The limping Hidayan never returned, and was soon forgotten by the others in their distracted shock.

One by one Aroha, Taeko, and Satya, the sister-moons of Hidaya, slid gracefully above the horizon. First Aroha dimly lit the Hidayan nightscape with pale, silver blue gentleness, bringing out faint, wistful shadows. Taeko soon followed with an ivory coolness brightening the silent landscape. Satya took her time, as if reluctant to wake up, and her irregular shape was silhouetted against the star-studded blackness beyond when she did glide into sight.

Seldom did moon watchers wait for Satya's clumsy form, preferring the smoother, rounder, more regular forms of Aroha and Taeko to gaze upon. All three moons had once been one satellite moon orbiting around Hidaya until that moon had shielded Hidaya from the impact of a rogue comet and had been divided. Still, poems could be written about Satya's pastel loveliness, but she reminded Hidayans of that centuries old natural disaster more so than her two sister-moons and so ignoring or belittling her eased the apprehension and helplessness Hidayans felt in her hunching presence.

Satya was not concerned with Hidayan perceptions, however, and she persisted in following her sisters' endless orbits like an awkward toddler trying to be like her adored older sisters. Her unbalanced shape reflected Bozidara's distant light from innumerable awkward angles, and the resultant shadows and reflected light she cast down upon Hidaya was sometimes the golden light of Bozidara, or more often a wistful gathering of pastel hues mysteriously blending into an ineffable loveliness. When the moonlight of the three sisters blended together, soft pastel warmth flooded the nighttime surface of Hidaya as if an artist's hand gently played with the light and shadows to create tremulous phenomena.

Tonight the Cham Desert was illuminated with a muted, sad, lavender hue that matched the feelings of nine resolute escapees from Salimah. They could do nothing about the tracks they were leaving in their wake, and hoped that the morning breeze would erase them by the time Bozidara hefted its bulky weight into the skies. They had made good time for already-exhausted travelers.

The Searchers guided the others, taking turns leading through the thorny bramble bushes and fragrant herb shrubs, and by their united collaboration it was apparent that the Searchers all knew the Cham well. A pale greenish light emanating from the front of their night vests allowed them to see in front of themselves without being seen from the rear. After the third turn over of leadership, they all took a rest. Hunkering down in a shallow gully, they drank water and chewed on jerky rations. For a while there was only weary silence; but after relieving themselves they whispered and chatted among themselves.

"Z'van, how are you holding up?" "Do you believe we made it far enough away by now?" "T'moyo let me rub your feet. I saw you stumble back there." "Is there enough water to drink right now?"

Lord Z'van wiped his sweaty forehead on his sleeve. "Until we are out of this desert, we are not safe. I'm really not sure, though, how far we have come for what seems like hundreds of meters of trekking tonight may only be a few, and we can't keep up this pace forever. That's just not realistic. Our tiredness skews our perceptions of how far we have come. Che'ikh, just in case, would you take this branch and brush away as many tracks as you can bearing in mind you must return to rest and brush away your own returning footprints? It's just a precaution."

"But a wise one," Che'ikh agreed grabbing the branch and jogging back along the trail a-ways.

"I agree with both thoughts," whispered Ansh'mati. "The sister moons have traveled almost half way across the sky, and we must start finding a daytime shelter, or risk moving during the day when we can be seen should anyone be following us."

"I don' see 'ow t'ey coulda followed us if ta mornin' wind wipes off all our tracks," added Dato.

"Preparation pays off, but there is always the danger that the morning breeze will arrive too late to hide the evidence of our departure, and then there will be killers looking for us to keep us from reporting what has happened at Salimah. They would not want us to live to witness against them."

"Hsht! Listen!"

"That's only Che'ikh returning, but rather too soon I think."

A solitary Hidayan runner rustling through the herb shrubs almost passed them by, while they froze in silent terror. Then he stopped, leaving the fragrance of the musky desert herbs wafting in the air. They could feel the runner's intense effort to listen for their breath, for their heartbeat, for their location.

"Mother! Are you near? It is D'nkrad!"

T'moyo stood unsteadily. "Son? What are you doing here?"

He rushed to her side and then squatted down close to the hard ground, pulling her down with him. "The sister moons were too honest, and illuminated your tracks just enough for the rebel watch to see and identify it as an escape. They are following, but at a much slower rate than you as it took them awhile to find the desert exit, and then they are not in as good of shape as all of you." Taking his mother's hands in his, D'nkrad looked into her tear-filled eyes and whispered, "I also saw your footprints and could not let you go out here alone. I could not bear that. I deserted, but as garrison commander I know where we can go from here to find safety during the day. I have that memorized right down to the footfall."

"Won't they punish you for deserting?" asked Emina fearfully. "Won't they punish us all more severely if you've led them to us?" Panic edged her words and her voice cracked. "What if they find *your* tracks and we'll all be caught and punished? What if –"

D'nkrad started to explain that for parts of the way he had dragged branches behind him to erase as many track as he could, but he was interrupted by his mother. "Enough!" silenced T'moyo. She signaled to Ansh'mati who gathered Emina into her arms to calm her trembling fright.

Che'ikh returned and stood menacingly over them all. He stared intently at D'nkrad and then relaxed, nodding slowly. As he sat on the ground he marveled, "You know where the desert caches are, Searcher! 'Good disguise. Even after meeting you and talking with you I did not know. You hold our secrets well."

"Thank you, but we must go now. There isn't sufficient time otherwise to reach the shelter if we don't leave now. We are all followed."

Angharad rose to comply and stretched her self. Turning at the waist to work out a kink in her back, she looked back from where they had come and promptly dropped to the ground. "Down! Now!" she ordered, and the survivors immediately obeyed.

Their faces pushed into the dirt, and they waited. Emina wet herself in fear. Dato tried to spit out dirt stuck to his tongue and was tired of wasting valuable time when he heard stealthy rustling in the desert behind them. Suddenly a scratchy voice spoke.

"Damn them! I thought we were finally right behind them, but I cannot see their tracks any more. They either learned to fly or erased them again!"

"What do you want to do now, Mayor? We could spread out again looking for their trail again."

"No, let's not do that. The situation right now is that we have gotten out of Salimah past the guards. We are safe for a while, but soon the guards will become curious when they don't see us walking around the city. We have maybe a day or at least part of this morning before they realize that we have escaped.'

"Then we must find the ones we are following before the ones who follow *us* actually find us. To kill these witnesses means that there is no real proof that we were the ones attacking Salimah."

"They're not going to believe that we were just out here in the desert for our health!"

"You're right, but they can't prove that we weren't. The law is on our side because they must prove that we were the ones inside of Salimah. Only the last defenders would have seen our faces and those are the ones we must kill for our own sakes."

"If we cannot find them −?"

"Then our reason for being here is thin, but still defensible. If it comes to that, we can march back towards Salimah and meet the tracking garrison. We can tell them that we crossed the Cham because we wanted to help them. We left our own cities to be on their side. How can they disprove that as we would be marching towards them as saviors, not running like cowards?"

"Which we are, Mayor. At least, I am a coward. I don't want to die fighting trapped in a city I dislike and have no interest in, or die of thirst in this desert! I don't want anyone to hold these past few weeks against me to haunt me even until I am old, should I be so lucky to grow old! I don't want any of these running dogs to meet me at the doorway to my own house sometime in the future, and call me out for what I'm already ashamed of!"

"You mangy beast! You *be* a coward then, but I will hunt these dogs down and let their blood wet the desert! I am not ashamed for having defended my people and my property! They had no right stealing our citizens, even low dirt-dwellers as the ones missing! They had no right, and they will be taught that with their lives! Now, get away from me if you can't help me track them anymore!"

"No one can help. There are no more tracks. We have been stopped until the morning, and perhaps then all of us will see each other at the same time so we can all kill and be killed at the same time!"

"Quiet!" The sound of a loud scuffle and fight was near, and the ten refugees feared that the fighters would come so close as to fall right on top of them. But the brawl ended with a crackling sound of breaking bone and an anguished moan.

"Like I said, you are useless." A metallic swishing sound divided the air and ended with a sighing cry, and then momentary silence engulfed them all. No one from either group moved for a while, and the Mayor spoke.

"Leave him here to divert the garrison from our path."

"Lord Mayor, sir, if we are following those who escaped from Salimah and have tracked them this far, won't we have to keep going in the same direction as we are going to find them again? Even though the few bits of track we were able to find seemed to head off in different directions, it actually seems to be leading in one direction, as if they were on a sailboat tacking into the wind back and forth to get to one specific harbor. If we turn away from this overall direction so the garrison won't find us, then we may lose those we want."

"All true, lad. But I found a Searcher's map on that youth trying to change out of those green robes they are fond of wearing. He tore the map out of my hands and destroyed it right before I killed him. But I saw the map for long enough. There is an emergency cache of supplies nearby, and a hidden shelter large enough to hide us all long enough to lose the garrison. But we must hurry. Follow me to safety!"

The stumbling mob of rebels rallied and rushed after the Lord Mayor leading them more westward than south. The dust they kicked up choked those who waited in the gully, and only when dirt and sound were stilled and stifled did they sit up.

"Well!" A'khil exclaimed. "I guess they can have that old shelter if they've really got their hearts set on having it. We can find something better."

"So there!" added Old T'moyo with a forced chuckle. "This is both good and bad news."

"How can you laugh when our only hope is being snatched away? We can't just cross the Cham out in the open like this! What's wrong with you?" Emina was gasping and sobbing in terror now, and all could see than no mere hug-and-hush would help until she had cried out her heart's pain.

"Her tears of grief had to come sometime," explained T'moyo. "Now is as good of time as any other."

"But what *shall* we do now?" Angharad asked timidly.

"We shall stay together," answered Kamalei grasping Angharad's hand firmly.

"And we will find our way out of the Cham together," Lord Z'van added solemnly.

"Well, if we are going to stay together, then we should decide *where* we will go together," D'nkrad observed. "Salimah is behind us to the north. The garrison will be looking for the rebels, and if we go back towards the garrison there will be protection."

"There will be protection for most of us," corrected Che'ikh. "You deserted, and will be answerable for that. Even if there is absolution, it will take years of your life to go through those resolution processes. You risked much to be with us."

"Well, it is still an option, and we will all find safety by going north. Even I will be safe, though probably court marshaled. But let's decide on a plan now.

"To the direct south is more of the Cham Desert, but if we veer slightly to the southeast we will find the lakeside community of Viñay, which my mother and I are quite familiar with, and to which we can swiftly guide you all. But it is a long, dangerous walk across an unforgiving desert. We may not make it to Viñay."

"From one bat choice ta a bat'r one," mumbled Dato. He pressed his lips together after intercepting a tear-filled glare from Emina. He noted, though, that she was breathing deeply and calming herself as she listened.

"We could go southwest, generally in the direction the rebels went, and by passing them further south we could head for the village of Cham. That is an even longer trek across the desert, and one which none of us will probably complete singly or all together as the rebels might cut us off; but even if they don't cut us off we don't have adequate supplies or stamina to persevere in that direction unless there is another cache between here and there that I don't know about."

"Dato was right," Angharad whispered to Kamalei. "The choices get worse as they go on."

"We could turn immediately west and aim for Aichen, which two of you are familiar with, and to which you could swiftly guide us. That is the closest of our choices."

"They would kill us on sight," Ansh'mati advised hopelessly.

"They would not welcome even a neighbor of many years knowing that only a few days ago they themselves killed my family. If we all went to Aichen together, we would all die there together for sure."

"Is there another choice?" Kamalei asked hopefully.

Old T'moyo shook her head as if to clear it from cobwebs. "Yes, there are two more choices. We could stay where we are right now, and die within a day or two, or we could wander in circles throughout the Cham, and still die within a day or two. We must choose between three very despairing choices."

"I knows sumtings how to live in bat places," Dato slipped in. "Mebbe we could use 'em and make it outta 'ere alive."

"Looks to me that we actually have two choices to make," summarized Searcher A'khil, sidestepping Dato's contribution. "What do you think, Lady?"

"I see what you mean," agreed Ansh'mati. "We must vote if we will go our separate ways, as in the case if we should vote to return to

Salimah to meet the garrison at D'nkrad's loss; or we stay together and throw our lives together wherever we vote to aim for."

"Just as I see it, also," agreed Lord A'khil. "Let's think for a few minutes and then vote."

"We don't have a lot of time to think," observed Angharad. "The sister moons are moving swiftly now that they see their home beyond the mountains drawing closer."

"And so we will vote now."

"Let us choose to live then as we believe, and believe as we choose to live." Lord Z'van added drawing from ancient proverbs.

At the end of the first vote, Emina surprised everyone by voting they stay together, which made that choice unanimous. And for the second, they agreed to travel west towards Aichen, but only as far as the Foothill River. Then they would travel south along the river until they arrived at Cham. For now, however, they dug in nearer to the taller desert plants to find some protection, and then lay still exhausted. Whatever sleep they managed to wring out of the desert night was in brief, anxious turns.

Rawiya could feel the atmospheric tension around them as rain and the flowering of the desert neared. Though many pilgrims were tired, their excitement that possibly tomorrow would be wondrous kept them awake. Gently, almost as a caress, Rawiya concluded the evening. "I ask the Compassionate One that your dreams are more peaceful than theirs were years ago when the Ten were hunted." Tonight all hands except those of the newcomers were raised in blessing. The vigilantes were visibly startled by the spirit sparks, which they had never seen before. They chose to return to their own hidden campsite rather than to join that of the caravan.

*"To be patient with others is difficult, but
more so with yourself. With patience you will
not lose courage facing your faults. Eventually
you will mend those faults beginning each day
with renewed vigor and purpose."*
~ *Tenth Book of Instruction*

CHAPTER 11

❖

HOPE TO THE
BEGINNING

Weighted, sultry air greeted the caravan in the early morning. The gray and white clouds that had climbed and mounded atop one another over the Western mountains now dashed across the desert in an unrestrained race. They pushed and jostled each other blocking most of the pre-dawn light from Bozidara. It was obvious, even now, that should any of Bodizara's golden rays penetrate the thickening blanket of clouds, that light would be brief.

Rawiya, Ishwa, and Cook stood in the dim dawn light watching the wildly, scudding clouds.

"We need to quickly break camp this morning and go on to a better viewing oasis," adjudged Rawiya.

"What about our extra guests?" questioned Cook in a worried voice. "We don't want to look as if we are breaking camp and sneaking out just to get away from them and force their hands to violence,"

"I suggest we break camp with a lot of noise and exuberance," Ishwa suggested. "After all, we are going to only two more oases, and the one we are going to this morning will bring us to the best viewing of the blooming of the Cham. Our excitement will wake and invite those four out of hiding to join us. If we do it noisily they cannot accuse us of sneaking off. They must not suspect that we know who they are yet!"

"I agree," Rawiya nodded. "This must seem normal, yet have the light mood of a holiday. After all, we have come through so much to see and feel this beauty, we should celebrate."

Cook was scowling though. "They will kill us."

"We will be protected."

"But –" and then Cook's eyes strayed upwards to the branches above where the desert birds roosted. They were fluttering back and forth nervously.

"We will be protected," Ishwa repeated.

"All will be well," added Rawiya. Cook sighed and turned back into the cook tent.

Scarcely had she turned than the birdlets began loudly cheeping and twittering so much so that it was impossible for anyone to remain asleep. The attendants passed the word that camp would be struck immediately and a dry breakfast would be taken on the travel beasts. There was some grumbling, but when the pilgrims realized how close the rain clouds were to letting loose their heavy burden excitement energized them all.

In record time belongings were packed, and the loud noisy departure did as Ishwa, Rawiya, and Cook had wanted. Gored'na, Ghanash'am, Ne'igalomea, and Tangi haphazardly struck their secret campsite and joined the departing caravan. They were astonished that breakfast foods were shared with them, but they munched on the dry protein squares and drank from the re-filled water skins just like the pilgrims they had hunted were doing; they joined the caravan, but lagged behind squinting suspiciously at the pilgrims ahead.

Their traveling companions, however, felt protected from harm for the desert birds flittered and swooped beside them as if encouraging them to move on. With the playful birds diving and darting around them and calling to one another, and with the hope of arriving just in time to set up camp to view the desert change, there was no room for tense, negative apprehension. Attendants constantly checked on the pilgrims' welfare and free chatter made for a noisy parade to their oasis destination.

The vigilantes were distrustful of the attendants' attentions even though they were aware that they were not being singled out for special attentions.

"I say we shoulda killed 'em back der," gestured Ne'igalomea.

"We tried da poison in da water an' it di'n't work!" shouted Gored'na angrily. "Somet'ing was wrong wit' it so it di'n't work!"

"Or mebbe it jus' wasn't put in da water because one of yous got another deal goin' an' da rest of us will git notting out of dis damned job!"

"An' mebbe ya jus' might git dead fer sayin' dat before we git where we're goin' t'day!" The threat in Tangi's eyes was deadly.

"Dat poison was put in da water. Ya know dat! It's dis cursed desert dat changed it into nottin'. Ya heard da stories before how dese caravans don' git lost an' no one dies because of da desert. It's in da sand!"

"Dat's jus' stories dey tells da children! An' ya believe dat slop, ya disgustin' bastard!"

"Nah, it's true! It is da desert! It's da deal made by da ten holy ones dey follow. Dey called for a sign o' hope an' gave der lives. Da desert won't accept any more death or blood; it only heals." Gored'na looked down and repeated himself, "It only heals."

"I heard tell dat people go in an' come out wit' da same scars an' sicknesses so how come dis group which is supposed ta carry plague has no fevers, sores, or bruises? It's as if dey wuz all cured an' are protected. I'll bet if I tried ta kill dat skinny kid right in front of us either I'd miss — an' I never do miss — or my knife would go right t'rough 'im."

"Ya wanna try it?" urged Tangi. "Go ahead an' let's kill dem off one by one an' git dis over wit'. I'm creeped out wit' dis whole deal."

Ghanash'am had had enough of all of everything. He didn't want to have to follow the caravan to another oasis; he didn't want to be part of the caravan; he was disgusted with the stupid storytelling and make-believe myths about the Cham. Without a word he flung out his blade that would have easily buried itself in the base of the boy's skull had not a birdlet swooped between the boy and the knife deflecting it so that it harmlessly buried itself in the desert dirt instead. The bird's flight was unsteady after that, but it continued on with its companions.

"Damn dat bird! May it die in pain!" Ghanash'am cursed between gritted teeth.

"It's not da bird! It's da desert! Can't ya see it's da desert dat's protecting dem?" Gored'na was now shouting so much that the last pilgrims quieted and looked back fearfully before urging their travel beasts to speed up so they could travel with others ahead of them. That left the vigilantes even more isolated and left behind. "I will kill dem somehow before we leave dis desert," vowed Gored'na darkly.

The next oasis spread out expansively near a breath-taking, precipitous cliff abruptly rising out of the Cham Desert. Protective, broad-leafed nurse trees flourished prolifically and swayed with fluttering leaves in the pre-storm wind. Smaller trees with delicate fern-like leaves waved more frantically since their trunks were thinner and more flexible against the wind's force; they folded their fronds close to their stems for strength. Silvered or roughly barked trunks of other patient and sturdy desert trees stretched and shook themselves like dogs as the gusts of wind became more urgent and intense.

Flurr bushes with long, grey, leaf strands straggling to the ground like overgrown beards clustered here and there, while thickets of twisted bant berry bushes vied with more diverse and verdant foliage. Narrow pathways were woven between the vegetation suggesting that animals inhabited this oasis. The desert birds ignored the swaying tree branches above and swooped low to shelter themselves amongst the lowest shrubs with the thickest leaf covering. The oasis spread itself over the crest of the bluff and partway down its gradually sloping back like a blanket covering a bed.

Near the edge of that verdant, inclined coverlet a wide, flattened tract amongst the bushes and trees formed a natural campground where the pilgrims set up a cozy camp. The mid-day meal was necessarily of a convenience type of variously flavored sticks of vegetable and protein varieties, which allowed everyone to eat while securing their tents with greater care over and under thick-fibered tarps that added additional protection against the imminent rain. Ishwa ordered the caravan attendants to break out additional tarps and tents that would expand the cook tent allowing everyone to be sheltered while they ate the evening meal.

Further down the bluff where it was unprotected by abundant foliage, ancient sedimentary rock scoured for eons by harsh grit-laden winds the desert, dotted with hardy succulents, cacti, and sparsely leafed thorn bushes stretched in all directions, only stopped by the coastal mountains to the west and the Bahairava Mountains to the North and East. Quickly moving shadows of light and dark caused by the rapidly moving clouds above changed the terrain moment by moment.

The vigilantes were forced by circumstance to set up their tents within the campground with the other travelers. At first they sullenly hung back idly watching the pilgrims scurrying about until they reluctantly realized that their help would ensure that they had a hot evening meal and protection from the coming storm. They hunched their backs with barely-contained hostility and joined the others with the physical set up while their minds whirled with conflicted thoughts.

They were frustrated by the pilgrims themselves who ignored their rough appearance and dialect and welcomed them as if they had started out in Viñay with them and had become comrades. And then again it seemed as if they would have to resort to brutality to dispatch the members of the caravan in order to collect their bounty. None of the vigilantes would be adverse to such a solution to their dilemma, but it would take more physical effort and planning to do so so no one would be left alive to hide in the dense vegetation.

They were currently confounded, but bided their time as well as they could while observing their quarry close up. Gored'na seemed to be the most hurried to get the job done. He seethed with barely hidden rage observing that Ghanash'am, Ne'igalomea, and Tangi seemed to hesitate now that they had found their target. While he shouldered a tent support for the enlarged cook tent an ingenious idea became rooted in his mind that he could treat his companions the same way as the pilgrims and then collect the bounty without sharing.

When Ishwa passed nearby, Gored'na casually asked what was planned for the remainder of the journey. Ishwa honestly told him the plans: they would weather the first spring storm in the desert, and maybe others if necessary. From the escarpment they would observe the flowering of the Cham in all its magnificence, and when they had rested scantly one day further in this particular oasis, they would travel on to one more oasis slightly northwest of their present location. The final stop would be the city of Cham which was their final destination.

Gored'na mulled over this information and surreptitiously repacked all his gear when the opportunity came.

Meanwhile, Ne'igalomea and Tangi worked side by side while the camp was being set up. They suspiciously joined the attendants caring for the travel beasts, but idly chatted with them. When the animals had been covered by a rough lean-to structure and fed, then the attendants went on to other tasks, but Ne'igalomea and Tangi lingered.

"Dees people are dif'rent. It's not jus' dat dey are protected by da desert, it's somet'ing else."

"I feels dat too. Mebbe it's cuz dey are rich an' can pay fer dis trip."

"Dey better not ask me ta pay fer it!"

"Naw! Lissen! We both t'inks da same. Dey be diff'rent. I don' t'ink dat dey have da fever dat kills. But if we don' kill dem den we don' get no money.

"We be killin' dem for no reason 'cept for da money."

"We done it before."

"But – mebbe I gittin' soft or old – but somehow I feel wrong 'bout dis. I like how dey treat me, like I count. I matter 'ere."

"But it's only 'ere in da Cham. It won' last."

"But what if it did? What if we didn' go back ta bein' ourselves an'… an'…an' mebbe tried ta git somet'ing outta dis so-called 'retreat?'"

"What're ya t'inkin' of?"

"Well, mebbe we could jus' try out livin' like dese folks while we're 'ere, an' see how it is. If we don' like it we jus' kill dem all like we planned. If not – mebbe we could sorta fit in wit' dem and mebbe –"

"Do ya hear what yer sayin'? We'd be turnin' down da money an' be broke agin. An' what do ya t'ink we'd be doing instead of bein' what we are? Have ya thought o' dat?"

"I'm jus' t'inkin'."

"Well, keep yer thoughts in yer own empty head an' keep dem outta mine!"

Ghanash'am joined the "fetching detail." He went for water for the cook tent and then fetched water for the travel beasts. When he was sent out into the oasis to see if there was any fresh fruit – though that was unlikely before the rain – he wandered through the oasis on the narrow paths. Rough as he was he recognized that the paths were cared for rather than merely tracks used by herds or game animals.

As he meandered aimlessly realizing that there was no ready-to-harvest fruit, and unwilling to dig for edible roots, he suddenly realized that he was hearing soft whispers wherever he strolled. He stopped to focus his attention on the whispered words.

"You are a good person!"

"You are valued and worthy of love!"

"You are a worthy and important person!"

"Who are ya?" Ghanash'am shouted in frustration and fear. "Damn ya! Who are ya?" But the voices continued murmuring without answering him:

"You are a good person!"

"You are valued and worthy of love!"

"You are a worthy and important person!"

Ghanash'am gnashed his teeth and swatted at the bushes hoping to scare whomever was speaking into jumping up. But no one did, and the whispering continued:

"You are a good person!"

"You are valued and worthy of love!"

"You are a worthy and important person!"

Now Ghanash'am was curious and terrified. Was the oasis haunted and trying to trick him? Getting on his hands and knees he searched under the vegetation near the path. Small, square-headed locusts were clustered under most of the bushes and did not jump away when they were discovered. They just stared at Ghanash'am.

Angrily he got up and stomped off to another section of the oasis. But even here he heard voices, this time of a different sort – somewhat high pitched.

"You can make different choices."

"You can have a different life."

"You can be happy if you leave hurt and anger behind you."

Ghanash'am screamed at the voices, "I'm not angry! An' I made my choices a long time ago. Dey can't be changed after all dese years! Shut up! Shut up!" But when the voices persisted he stopped again in angry panic to search out their source. He found the same kind of square-headed locusts grouped under some bushes, but there were skinny, grey caterpillars clinging to the stems of dried grasses both of which seemed to look right at him intelligently.

"Are ya da ones talkin' ta me?" Ghanash'am shouted frantically, desperately. Then, he watched horrified as the bugs and insects actually moved their mouth parts. The box-headed locusts spoke to him:

"You are a good person!"

"You are valued and worthy of love!"

"You are a worthy and important person!"

The caterpillars wriggled and mouthed:

"You can make different choices."

"You can have a different life."

"You can be happy if you leave hurt and anger behind you."

"Yer jus' stupid, dumb bugs! Ya don' know nottin'!" In a moment he was stomping on all the foliage he could in an effort to squash the speakers. Then he was darting through the oasis in full retreat back to camp where he promptly hid in his tent sweating heavily in the sultry air. He stayed there shivering until dinner was called and Tangi came to check on him. Together they walked to the cook tent just as the first heavy drops of rain started. Ghanash'am could still hear voices talking to him beyond the patter of the rain. An uncharacteristic terror filled him and made him more silent than ever. He ate the delicious soup Cook had prepared and the freshly baked bread without tasting either. After awhile he became used to the voices that became part of the natural sounds around him.

The Eleventh Night

"Our journey is almost complete. We have been learning about our inner being and that we need to forgive others and ourselves for not being perfect. Only where there is forgiveness can peace and love flourish. There needs to be some humility to reach this point, and we have experienced quite a bit of that on this

pilgrimage. It is not always like this. But perhaps you have already realized that life is about relationships. We find our value in relationship to others, and that gives us our meaning and reason to exist. We have traveled separately into the Cham Desert, but are here together because we became a caring community. We may not be as protected as we are outside of the Cham, but the lessons we have learned here are still valid. These are the lessons learned by the ten noble ones we have shadowed on this retreat."

That first night, after the Searchers and followers had voted to travel west towards a definite destination they trekked rapidly energized by the hope ahead and the danger behind them. By their second day in the desert it seemed as if they would make the Foothill River more quickly than they had hoped. They hiked more easily and confidently knowing how close they were to the Foothill River, and contentedly stopped to rest and find daytime shelter while the morning star still shone brightly in the night sky. Yet, there was still anxiety that would not disappear until they had finally left the desert and had found a definite refuge. It was that persistent anxiety that kept them in a guarded mode so that only taking brief naps felt comfortable. That is precisely what saved them once again.

The garrison had lost the rebels' trail, and had sent detachments in several directions. One of those southern-traveling scouting detachments from Salimah stopped to check their position and progress in the pre-dawn night. While the Hidayan officers conferred and the guards chatted and petted their hairy desert mounts companionably, the nearby darker shadows under sparse vegetation silently and gradually flattened out.

The listeners scarcely breathed because they were so close to the officers, and they were able to hear the officers' final decision before the detachment hastily trotted forward to create a thinly spread blockade to the foothills.

"How much water do we have?" D'nkrad quietly asked as he dispiritedly sat up.

"I have bottom covered."

"Almost gone."

"A couple of deep swallows."

Nods all around confirmed similar low water supplies.

D'nkrad sighed before beginning, "We have a basic water condensation unit, but it will not serve all of us adequately at this time. Our best survival plan is to meet up with that detachment. Even with the wide spacing of the scouts it would be difficult to pass by them. We aren't their enemies. We can all survive with the garrison's help."

"That won't −" Angharad was cut off abruptly by Dato.

"No! We choosed! We go t'get'er an' make it t'get'er!"

"Dato, that plan may no longer be our best chance," counseled A'khil. "D'nkrad may be facing some disciplinary action, but he will survive, as we all will if we meet up with that detachment. Our supplies are almost gone; the only other alternative to finding the garrison is changing our direction and risking the death of all of us."

"That is so," Kamalei added. "But so many friends I have known were left behind to allow others to be safe or to avoid punishment; tonight I am no longer willing that one person be sacrificed for the rest of us. I just don't want to see that again."

"It would be best to do it one more time, child," D'nkrad encouraged. "Next time can be different, but not tonight."

"No! No-no-no-no-no!" sobbed Dato. "Ta ones lef' b'hind may find it needed or noble, but I know − *I KNOW* − what dat feels like ta watch ot'ers go on. Dat part feels good 'cuz dey are safe, but t'ere's always ta second part dat's always done by yerself an' feels bat.

"I − I won' − I won' 'ave someone else do what I knows feels 'orrible. Not fer me! Da good part is what makes sense 'ere," he said pointing to his head. "But t'is part," Dato cried pointing to his heart, "T'is part hurts an' is alone! Not fer me! I won' 'ave someone else feel dat hurt fer me!"

"I won't either," whispered Kamalei. "Maybe it's being out here in the desert again with nothing to keep me alive, but this time you are here with me. You are more than friends. You mean more to me than any family could. I would rather die here than let one of us be harmed for just my sake."

"Wouldn't you give yourself up so that the rest of us could live?" probed Lord Z'van. "If you would be the one left behind or who would be handed over to the garrison for treason, like D'nkrad here, knowing that by doing so we would all be safe, wouldn't you do it?"

"Yes."

"But *I* wouldn't accept that!" cried Angharad in great distress. "You're my friend! If you stay behind I won't go on without you!"

Old T'moyo was torn and shattered at the possible loss of her son more than she was concerned about her own self. Yet her long years led her to observe the others' reactions, which she could summarize even as her heart ached.

"It seems that if we go back to Salimah and the garrison, most of us are safe, but not all. If we go in any other direction, unless something radically changes, we will probably die. The one logical decision would be to save as many of ourselves as possible; if we all are dead no good can be gained by that in this life. And yet, you all seem to be unreasonably fighting to stay together knowing how impossibly desperate that choice is. This makes no sense."

"No," Emina slowly agreed. "When I left my husband, every one of those people in the village risked their lives for me – just me. They knew how angry he could be and what he could do to hurt them, but they did it anyway."

"Your death wouldn't honor their bravery," responded D'nkrad.

"I don't know how to explain this, but something within me has been getting bigger, like a quiet place that I haven't known before. If I did know it, it's been so long since I've felt that quietness, that I forgot it years ago. But I feel it now. As illogical and crazy as I know I sound – for I sound crazy and unreasonable even to myself – it's important that we stay together no matter what.

"I know that it doesn't make sense. I know that! But I also know that we must stay together if we are to do something more than just save our own lives. Something greater than ourselves is being asked of us. Something greater than our selves will be created out of our unity."

Che'ikh had been hunched over himself since the detachment had left. His face expressed cycles of anger, despair, and morose stubbornness in turn, but he had been intensely listening throughout the discussion. As Emina spoke, his face cleared with peace and resolution.

"I agree with Emina. It seems hopeless, but somehow I know she is right. I have lost everything except myself and you, my friends and companions here. There are so many emotions tumbling within myself and none of them are resolved; but what Emina said – what she said for me is true also. There has been a peaceful space growing inside of my heart especially when I think of us being together no matter what happens." He waved his hand to briefly forestall interruptions. "I know this makes no rational sense. All of us Searchers have been trained to make hard, logical decisions, and this choice goes against every bit of that training and experience. For you I would sacrifice myself so that you would all live. But I deeply know right now, like Emina, that we must stay together."

"You are crazy!" hissed D'nkrad. "This is nonsense! We will all go now to find that detachment and live! No more of this useless, crazy idiocy!" He started to rise and stumbled as Old T'moyo seized his hand.

"Son –"

"No, I want *you* to live!" D'nkrad pleaded taking his mother's hands in his own and looking deeply into her troubled eyes with his own distressed and weeping ones.

"Son, it *is* idiocy, but I agree with it. My heart also knows this is right. And even my brain knows it, though I don't know why. The peace they speak of, I feel it also."

"But –"

"Hush! Let us vote."

"We will find the garrison detachment and live," voted D'nkrad choking with emotion.

Ansh'mati shook her head saying, "I can't believe myself, but I know with my whole being that going towards Viñay is what is best. Z'van?"

He mopped his forehead with his sleeve leaving a dirty smear upon his wide brow. "We would be walking without adequate supplies into the desert. If we do this… ah!" He pointed upwards.

With all eyes looking above, they saw a gentle gathering of an opaquely, luminous cloud that softly pulsated as it expanded over their heads like protective tenting. It was a wonder to behold.

"We are not discussing this alone, apparently," commented T'moyo dryly. "Z'van? What is your vote?"

"That we go east. Angharad?"

"East towards Viñay."

"East."

"You know my vote. East."

"And mine. East."

"East."

"You are insane! All of you! We will all die together without need!"

"'Possibly, my son. But this is what we choose to do because of our heads and our hearts. What about you? Since we are going to do this with or without you, what does your head and heart say really now?"

D'nkrad was in excruciating emotional pain and conflict though he tried to be stoic. Still, tears of confused frustration streamed down his ruddy cheeks, and he was given long minutes to choose while the predawn sky visibly lightened. There was still time to jump up and call back the slow moving detachment.

When he spoke his words were enunciated slowly and clearly, "I also know that it is important that we continue on. But it doesn't make sense, but it's right. I do not understand why I choose this, but I will go east with you towards Viñay knowing we will probably not survive much longer."

The ten Searchers and postulants rested throughout most of the day. There was no anxiety of being discovered nor was there fear of possible death. They all slept deeply, fitfully, and exhaustedly.

Meanwhile, two rebel scouts who had been ordered by Mayor Alameth to backtrack from their secret Searcher cache to reconnoiter the situation, had found the refugee's tracks. They followed the desert tracks of those whom they were searching for with great joviality. Creeping closer they observed the ten sleepers. The refugees were not even aware they had been discovered they slept so deeply.

The scouts could have finished them off at that moment without resistance, but instead they clumsily and noisily scrambled away in their excitement, choosing to get reinforcements rather than bring in some prisoners while losing others escaping. The scouts had maimed and killed many citizens of all ages wherever their leaders had taken them, but there was something overwhelmingly unsettling about killing the children and Searchers as they slept peacefully, though they looked exhausted; and the scouts refused to accept that abomination as their own chosen personal responsibility. The ten did not even turn over from the sounds of scrabbling escape of the scouts so unconscious and exhausted they were in their dreams.

Dusk. Almost no water left, and even with the condenser in use, it was not enough for more than a few gulps, and that would have to suffice for them all. After rising the ten weary, shadowy figures stumbled eastward in a ragged, scraggly line, guiding themselves by the stars. A soft almost indiscernible luminosity guided footsteps without their awareness as they trudged doggedly on until reaching the crest of a minor outcrop.

The Cham Desert stretched away from them in all directions, dotted and blemished with innumerable scrubby plants and bushes, all painted in flat, gray shadow-shades. Beyond the Cham to the west, south, and east were low foothills; to the north, past a brief banking of foothills, were the hulking Bahairava Mountains blocking out an immensely irregular swath of stars from the horizon.

"Look there," directed Che'ikh, pointing towards the west and the north with a sweeping hand. Campfires glowed like brilliant flowers. These were the Hidayan guardians searching the desert for the escaped renegades who had attacked Salimah. Apparently unaware of the ten refugees who were the prey of those rebels and who were trapped between the two groups, the Salimah squadrons believed that they were merely tracking the insurrectionists in order to make them accountable for the bloodshed, terror, and destruction they had caused.

A distant, muffled shout went up from one of the guards' campsites. Apparently the silhouettes of the ten on the mound were discernable enough to be spotted by one of the sharp-eyed squadron lookouts, or maybe it was the green glows from the vests the ten wore, thoughtlessly forgetting that anyone or anything they faced could see the phosphorescent glow that helped them trek through the night. Smaller flowerets of light bloomed as the squadron members lit torches and ran into the desert towards the same outcrop upon which the ten refuges gathered. From one campsite to another more and more torches lit up the desert as the Hidayan guards surged forwards towards the outcrop. However, it would take several hours still for the guardians to reach that outcrop.

"Lady Ansh'mati!" whispered Angharad urgently pointing now in a different direction.

"I don't see anything," she whispered back.

"Ahhh!" Kamalei, A'khil and Dato sharply inhaled together perceiving what Angharad had seen. From the far southeast the desert in starlight writhed with movement. "That would be the rebels," A'khil stated emotionlessly. "How they found us is a mystery."

"Perhaps they have seen the squadron fires and are on their way to attack first before daylight," Lord Z'van suggested.

"Perhaps," affirmed T'moyo, "But even if that is true, they are all coming towards us as if we were a beacon to follow. Both are on an interception course towards each other, and with us in the middle; we are trapped between them."

"There is no place to go!" wailed Emina. "We are in the middle and are lost!"

"Let's not stand up here in the open, then as targets," suggested Old T'moyo pointing simultaneously at the green glow of her vest. "Let's go down and out of sight."

Slipping and wearily falling down the southern side of the mound, they reached a temporary shelter.

"This is it," judged Kamalei sourly. "There is no place to go, except death. Perhaps we chose wrongly."

"I don' t'ink so," breathed Dato. He and Lord Z'van exchanged meaningful glances.

"There is one other place we can go, besides death," Z'van explained. "We can go to life." The others just stared uncomprehendingly at him willing that he explain more.

"Kamalei, what you say may be true. We may die here if the garrison cannot reach us before the rebels and they won't be able to protect us. We will be killed then, and though justice will prevail when the rebels are arrested for all the destruction and deaths they have responsibility for – including our own – life on Hidaya will go on as it always has. Our lives and deaths will have affected a finite number of other Hidayans directly, and many unknown lives indirectly.

"But what if we turned our lives into something more? What if we gave a blessing to Hidaya with our final breaths instead of just another death, another groan of agony and terror?"

"What are you talking about?" questioned Emina disparagingly. But Z'van interrupted.

"We are waiting here for either the rebels or the garrison guards to find us. There will be a struggle and some will be hurt. Unquestionably, if the rebels arrive first, we will be brutally killed outright because if we live our witness will reveal their identities. They would be captured as participants in the killings of Searchers and terrorizing of the various townships. If the Hidayan guards arrive first they will subdue us roughly, but not cruelly or savagely. Their arrival will protect us."

"They will be uncompromising, but they will not intentionally kill us!" D'nkrad exclaimed decisively in agreement.

"No, but expect unpleasantly stern treatment since we ran from them as well as from the rebels. We won't be trusted."

The Hidayan guards and the rebels meanwhile pressed on, simultaneously converging towards the same outcropping. Being better trained and alert, the guards perceived movement beyond the outcrop and suppressed their torchlight. They fanned out attempting to surround the larger group they perceived coming towards them beyond the outcrop.

The insurgents stealthily crawled forward keeping as low as possible to the desert ground so as not to be seen; their only thought was to assassinate the Searchers and children who might identify them from Salimah. Because they did not raise their heads to survey the desert, they were ignorant of the garrison swiftly hemming them in.

"We will not survive this night, my son," Old T'moyo bluntly whispered. "Your life has honored the One, and I am proud of you." D'nkrad embraced her and murmured lovingly into her ear.

Meanwhile, Angharad and A'khil had carefully surveyed the desert and then ducked down to report, "The squadrons are moving quickly towards us, but they are farther away than those who come from the southeast. Those others are moving slowly, but they are closer than the guards. It will take them less than 2 hours to arrive here."

They unconsciously huddled closer to each other. There was no place to blend into the desert terrain or otherwise disguise themselves. Faint, distant scraping sounds now could be heard intermittently from the southeast as well as the crackling of bushes from the north and west. Nocturnal animals added deep, deliberate silence to the desert, and both groups' approach could now be clearly heard.

Dato nervously fidgeted and then asked, "D'we jus' sit 'ere waitin' ta die den?"

Che'ikh tentatively asked, "Z'van, what you said before... what if we chose to bless Hidaya rather than merely die? I mean, we probably will be cut down and killed like... like my family. That was bloody and horrible, and that is all I see for us in the next hours. I can prepare to meet them, but I just thought – what did *you* mean by that?"

"It's nonsense! We will just add our cries to those throughout Hidaya's history," Emina bitterly rejoined. "People have been massacred and slaughtered before. People always die from war, disease, old age, accidents, or other causes. They all cried out! Now we will add our screams and groans to those of our ancestors. It cannot be stopped."

"What d'ya mean, Che'ikh?" Dato asked persistently.

"It's just that... Emina was right both now and this morning," Che'ikh explained. "We will add our pain and fear to the history of Hidaya if we leave it as it is. Pain, anger, and fear floats around us like air because of our circumstances now. The hatred of the rebels hunting us down also joins our situation. If you look at the reality we are living right now it is as if the balancing scales of life are heavily and unfairly weighted to just one side, stacked so that there can only be one catastrophic outcome for us – pain and death. And just as the air, dirt, and energy around us are recycled in time, what we anticipate to happen here - the current fear, pain, terror, anger and hatred will mix into the history and atmosphere of this world. We will add our own pains and deaths to the weighted cosmic scales, allowing the hatred and anger of the rebels, and the hopeless despair of the garrison to join us in weighting and pushing down one side of life. And that side will be breathed in and will affect every living and non-living thing here throughout Hidaya now and in the future."

Kamalei's brow wrinkled. "What 'side' are you talking about? What is about to happen to us within an hour or two is certain. There is no other outcome or reality possible! We are trapped. Would you have us do something else at the moment of our deaths? Or – or are you suggesting we pray for a miracle from the One? Ha! There are more stories of innocent people praying vainly for that than there are stories of miraculous interventions!"

"Kamalei is right," added Angharad. "There are historical stories of pilgrims traveling to holy places seeking miraculous interventions in their pain-filled lives, and stories of martyrs who went to their deaths singing and forgiving, and there are stories of heroes fighting to their deaths to save others. There are stories of whole townships fleeing invaders and begging for mercy, yet being raped, tortured and massacred despite their beliefs and faith.

"Are you asking us to hope for a different outcome – perhaps a miraculous one? Is that what you want? Or are you asking us to pretend that we aren't afraid of what is going to happen, and rejoice at its coming? Agh! This makes no sense! I don't want to sing at my own death," sobbed Kamalei. "I can forgive, but not sing it!"

"I am not sure of what you are saying either," persisted Lady Ansh'mati. "What do you mean?

"You talk about 'balancing scales of life' and how our lives, emotions, actions become part of the painful history and atmosphere of Hidaya," Ansh'mati said swirling her hand above her head. "But you also tell us that this history is recycled throughout time to join the weight of the one side of the scale – if it exists. What do you want to happen here instead if your 'philosophical' diversion is worth continuing? Do you have a defensive plan or trick to hide us in plain sight? We have no weapons for a violent defense – as if that were a choice. Or are you merely wasting our time so that the hours pass more quickly and we are distracted from –" Ansh'mati could not go on.

Dato scooted closer to Lady Ansh'mati so that his face was almost nose-to-nose with hers. He spoke almost in a whisper, but the others still could hear him. "Che'ikh an' Z'van, dey was tellin' me sometin' o' dis b'fore. It can be diff'rnt. He," and Dato nodded toward Che'ikh, "He didn' git ta tell ya 'bout da otter side of da scale. Dey be blessin's on da otter side."

Angharad leaned forward. "Unless it is broken there is another side to a scale, if such a life scale exists. What are you saying is on that side?"

It was Z'van who answered. "We focus on the things we dread – the worst things that can happen. In our case, here, it seems that the worst will happen to us – torture, maiming, and painful death. What we dread and fear to happen is a real possibility for us. Our hope of escaping across the Cham to safety has been cut off by both fact and choice, and most of our alternatives have been taken from us."

"You want us to pray for the Merciful One to intervene and cover us with a blanket that will make us invisible?" Emina's tone was bitterly sarcastic. "Are our prayers going to balance out the scale? Huh?" She sneered in disgust.

"Prayers are always answered, Emina, but maybe not in the way we want. But I know with my whole being that they are answered," Z'van continued.

"What I want us to do – besides those prayers – is for us to look at the other side of what we are calling the 'scale of life.' There is no real, actual scale sitting on a shelf somewhere. But look! Life is not all one sided. There are good things that happen, good people around us. Look! Even here as we face something awful I am thankful to be blessed with such good people near me. I wish you were safe, and that we had made it across the Cham, but you are a here, and –"

Old T'moyo stepped in to continue the thoughts. "We either focus on the fearful things or the blessings. If we die here filled with fear and there is hatred and anger around us, then the one side is heavier. If we die here filled with something other than fear and anger, then the blessing side of Hidaya's scale is weighted. And that blessing side is what will become part of Hidaya that gets recycled.

"Let me explain it this way: if you went to school you learned about rock cycles. Some rocks come from volcanoes, some are lying on top of each other like folded towels flattened on top of each other, and there are other rocks mushed together under other rocks into hardness. And as time passes, one kind of rock might be melted by lava and become something else, or the flattened rocks might be pushed so far down to the bottom of the pile that they became the mushed-to-hardness kind of rocks. They all change places in the cycle eventually."

T'moyo's voice lowered and slowed so that her points would be made to the others straining to hear and understand, and thus were completely focused. "Z'van, Dato, and Che'ikh are trying to say that our feelings and intentions are recycled like Hidaya's rocks. If we leave them as they are – as all of us are feeling now, afraid and dreading what is to come – they stay as they are and the face of Hidaya remains as it is.

"But if we allow our feelings and perceptions to change – and even I am having difficulty changing my attitude to this kind of end of my life as I never thought it would be like this – but if I, **we** move past the negative then there is change. Good change. And that changed perception becomes a blessing to Hidaya. It strengthens and attracts more of its same substance to itself so that there is more and more, and the blessing side of the scale becomes heavier and more abundant than anything on the other side. They want us to perceive this ending differently so that it becomes a blessing to Hidaya. They want these blessings to outnumber the dreadful things."

"Ya mean, like, da angry people seem ta hang 'round otter angry people, an' dose dat laugh a lot hang 'round otters who enjoy everyt'ing, an' what we feel an' how we see life becomes a curse or a blessin'?"

"Is it like that?" A'khil asked. "I think I am starting to understand."

"Well, it is something like that –"

"So, how do you propose that our deaths bless Hidaya?" Angharad asked Che'ikh.

"I want to focus on the other side. I don't want us to ignore what is real, but I want us to try to balance the intentions around us so that there is less twisted Hidayan history around us."

"I still don't understand," whispered Emina in dejected frustration. "All I can think of is asking the One for a miracle. Asking for something that is the opposite of fear, pain, anger, and hatred. That's all I can think of."

"If that is what you choose, your prayers will be heard," Lord Z'van quietly responded.

Kamalei reasoned slowly out loud, "They are heard, but not granted always. I always wondered, 'Why?' or 'Why not my prayers?'"

"That has confounded many of us," added Lady Ansh'mati.

"What would you have us do in our last moments?" Angharad asked shaking with the desert chill and with fear. Z'van silently reached over and placed his poncho around her shoulders.

"He wants us to ask for a miracle so we can die disappointed. He is just wasting our last moments with hopeless stupidity!"

"No, Emina," Che'ikh quietly explained trying to put his own jumbled thoughts together as he spoke. "I want us to ask the One to bless Hidaya and possibly change our historical personality as Hidayans so that the spirit of Hidayans who bless are greater than the spirits that harm. I want to create a refuge of blessing here on Hidaya that overcomes any tendencies to inflict emotional, physical or spiritual damage.

"We tried with our refuge cities to create safe places where healing can happen; and there once were refuge cities in the past that were known and honored briefly. But eventually the sanctuaries were violated. We Searchers formed un-named refuge cities that were known only to those who lived in them, or searched for those in need of sanctuary and a second chance at life in a different way. I want us to re-create that 'refuge of healing' here, right here and now, but without walls or roofs. I want a 'refuge of healing' that reaches beyond without limits."

Old T'moyo had been listening carefully, and quietly spoke. "We have created a family amongst us, a community if you will, even if it is not as large as Salimah. But it is here. And somehow even now, anticipating what will happen in a short while, I feel... I feel happy. I feel relaxed and I'm not worried. I'm with you, all of you. My dread of what I anticipate is not as great as what I feel now. My life has a meaning – to add to the blessings of this world."

"Yes, and more," Lord Z'van grinned. "Each of our lives has its own history and we ourselves know they have been marked by shame, fear, oppression, and other harms. When we've held onto that instead of being aware of the goodness around us, we were thinking it was part of the very atmosphere of Hidaya because it was what we breathed in day in and day out.

"We Searchers and others wanted to create a place of healing for ourselves, and a place beyond because of our heart-felt need to care for others so they also would be healed. We started with what was in our hearts, and we created the refuge cities. We proved that we could reach beyond our own personal good to create healing places on Hidaya. We wanted even with our last breaths to bless Hidaya with healing – total healing – once and for all. The refuge cities were a start."

"Ya want'd a mir'cle. A big un!" exclaimed Dato.

"Yes," Angharad agreed. "You wanted a miracle to make all of us Hidayans different than we are. Now you want the One to make us different so that we aren't passing on the same hurts, feuds, or abuse into the present and the future. We don't want to breathe and live the same old hurtful things without compassion!"

"This will be just a tiny effort," T'moyo slowly said. "But with **my** last breath I don't want a miracle from the Merciful One. I don't want to die, but I don't want to be so miraculously special I wouldn't be able to share it with others! It would separate me from others; I would be alone.

"But being here together, with you, for me **this** is a miracle that doesn't separate me from anyone. We are just here together because we care. Somehow we care, and that goes beyond just this place and moment." Old T'moyo's eyes were shining with waiting tears.

"If that is true –" began A'khil.

"Tonight we are going to be one more group of people killed by power madness, insanity, self-righteous fundamentalists, and weak, fearful followers. I don't want to die with their warped, poisonous intentions filling my lungs. I don't want to die waiting with hopeless thoughts. I want to even up the intentions on the side of hope, mercy, healing, and compassion," D'nkrad's voice was emphatic and determined.

"It would be a gifting of ourselves to the will of the One who wants only good," A'khil summarized slowly. "It would be both acceptance of reality as it is here, but also gifting ourselves beyond this time and space."

There was silence as they all contemplated the expansive thoughts they had been discussing. And then came more tentative doubts.

Angharad shivered slightly as she said, "Others have done that before. Would our acceptance and submission be anything different? We might be honored for our bravery, but Hidayan history would probably continue without disruption. To expect something else seems futile - hopeless."

"Perhaps. I just know that I want us to make the gesture – a hopeful effort to heal Hidaya. Maybe it's just another effort like uncountable others, but still… the Merciful One will make it good enough. We are enough."

The enormity of the discussion overwhelmed them again, and then Dato repeated his question, "So da we jus' sit 'ere waitin' ta die den?" He was answered with relieved, good-natured laughter.

The rain steadily pattered against the overhead tarp and seemed to be louder when Rawiya stopped speaking.

"Could we stay up longer and hear the rest of the story?" asked a youth. "Please?" he added with a wheedling tone.

"Tomorrow will be an important one for all of you," answered Rawiya. The desert blooming will begin and continue on; but we can't stay here at this campsite –"

"Nor stay even here in this tent," added Ishwa with a chuckle. "It's bedtime for all of us!"

All hands were raised in blessing. Ne'igalomea and Tangi almost joined in, but caught themselves in time. Gored'na scowled and Ghanash'am seemed distracted. They were all surprised as the spirit sparks rose from the lamps scattered throughout the tent, and then all ran for their own tents trying not to get too wet.

"If we want to change life
we must make a living gesture."
~ Second Book of Instruction

CHAPTER 12

❖

LAST DAYS

The storm continued through the night and throughout most of the next day. Lightening illuminated the majestic nurse trees tossing their broad leaves high with the windy gusts like wild stallion's manes and then bowing them down under the steady rain.

Card games, strategy games, and similar pass-times occupied many pilgrims while attendants casually finished tasks and then joined the relaxed groups in the cook tent. Ishwa and Rawiya quietly conferenced with various pilgrims. Cook kept her attendants busy making snacks, treats and other surprises so that there was never a break when someone felt they had to wait for breakfast or lunch. There was a general break for rest in the afternoon, and most travelers returned to their tents to nap.

Gored'na took advantage of the afternoon naptime to gather his belongings and steal an extra tent along with a map of the scheduled stops of the caravan.

He tried to saddle one of the travel beasts, but it shook him off after sniffing him and realizing that Gored'na was not his rider. After several such rejections he found his own mount. Despite the balking of his travel beast that was unwilling to leave the lean-to shelter for the harsh rain and wind, he managed to ride down the smooth back of the bluff and head towards the next oasis stop. It was a miserable trip, and the extra exertion he had to maintain so that the travel beast would not turn around exhausted him.

There was little Gored'na could see when he finally did reach the scheduled oasis as the rain pounded so roughly that it seemed as if a netting of opaque curtains surrounded him. He quickly unsaddled the travel beast and found shelter within a cluster of wuff trees. Their shelved bark dovetailed and wove itself together to form a rough but comfortable roof through which most rain was discouraged to penetrate. He found a protein snack in his pack and held his cup out so the rain could fill it. After he had drunk enough water to satisfy himself, and left his shelter briefly to relieve himself, Gored'na curled up in the comfortable wuff tree cave and fell asleep. The travel beast waited obediently until dawn, and then slowly turned toward the direction from which he had traveled. Trudging slowly and deliberately the travel beast unerringly returned to the caravan and to the lean-to stable. Attendants that morning noted that his fur was overly wet as the other travel beasts had been sheltered under tarps.

Gored'na woke as the bright, warm rays of Bozidara welcomed him. The storm clouds were leaving temporarily, and the wet leaves of the foliage reflected bright daylight. He stretched and then left his shelter to relieve himself before exploring the oasis.

It was abundant with copious varieties of fruits and starchy roots. The first part of the day Gored'na only had to walk around and stretch out his hand and there would be something to eat. Juices ran out of his mouth and onto his already-dirty tunic leaving a sticky stain that widened as the day continued. It was a small oasis in comparison to the one on the bluff, but here there were berries and fruits newly ripened because of the rain they had received. Gored'na did not question the presence of the fruits, which normally would take longer to grow and ripen. He could not find any animals or insects though he could hear them under the lower bushes shuffling about; he could hear the squeaks, squawks, and chirps of other animals, but was unable to see even a glimpse of one. He assumed that his travel beast was sleeping quietly hidden by the dense foliage.

In the afternoon Gored'na started to build traps, which would kill the pilgrims when they arrived. Spears, trenches filled with sharp sticks, and vines became trip wires that released deadly swatting branches or sacks filled with maiming rocks. They were in place by evening. Then, Gored'na waited.

The caravan would probably not arrive for a day or so because the retreatants would be enjoying the desert blooms, but he could be patient. He did not perceive that the travel beast had gone until evening. But that did not matter because he would have a herd of travel beasts to choose from after he had earned his bounty. He would make sure that he did not have to share that bounty with his other comrades. With that gleeful thought he went to sleep on the first night.

When he woke the next morning, Bozidara welcomed him instead of stormy weather. Gored'na started his day by jumping fully clothed into the main pool of fresh water. Thus refreshed and roughly cleaned he sought out breakfast. Nuts, and fruits of all kinds offered themselves to him again. He checked his traps, scanned the horizon that oddly in the distance swarmed with heavy gray clouds while he waited in pleasant, but not uncomfortable warmth.

Day after day he waited in vain. It was only after the first week that he suspected the worst: the caravan would not be coming to this oasis.

"No worries," Gored'na muttered to himself. "I'll meet dem at da next oasis, or go back ta dat bluff an' track dem down." He left at sunset traveling straight towards his destination as the stars and moons affirmed. By dawn he spotted another oasis. It was small with bounteous bunches of long, yellow edible pods, yellow-red globes of sweet, juicy fruits, bant berry and ollum berry thickets, and a pool of fresh water. There was a cluster of wuff trees whose woven bark shelving formed a shelter that looked familiar. Somehow he had returned to the oasis he had started from.

Gored'na checked his traps and found that they had rotted or had been filled in so that none of his effort existed.

He set out again the next morning to leave the oasis, but found himself back where he had started again. And again he tried. After numerous unsuccessful departure efforts, Gored'na realized that the desert had adopted him – or imprisoned him – and there was no way he could physically escape. His anger and frustration became unending rage. He tore at, cut, and maimed the trees and bushes; he fouled the fresh water and destroyed everything he could. And the next morning the oasis would be healed and would welcome him with overflowing goodness and consolation.

In furious desperation Gored'na turned his rage and hatred upon himself; but even as he cut at himself violently the oasis reached out in healing; vapors from the abundant flowers sedated Gored'na into a cushioning stupor while spores from the nurse trees engulfed and embraced him with healing.

When Gored'na finally awoke his fatal wounds had been healed.

It took many such self-attacks of fury and hatred over many months before Gored'na calmed enough to listen to the life of the oasis and fully hear it. Alone with himself he let his hatred and unending anger control his life and fight itself, for there was nothing outside of himself to fight. Only when hatred turned on itself could it be defeated; until then it sought and fed on outside fuels like a viral contagion.

And finally the fighting was over. Gored'na woke from one of his many suicide attempts and sat up; his hatred was spent. Before him on the ground a tiny dust lizard stared at him thoughtfully. Slowly Gored'na reached out to touch the reptile. It tolerated a brief touch before creeping onto his hand, where it resumed staring at Gored'na.

Was this one of the dust lizards that had been tortured and torn apart by Gored'na on some earlier day and subsequently healed by the oasis? Or was this a new dust lizard that hadn't been maimed multiple times like the others? Gored'na looked at the tiny creature perched on his hand and with a tired whisper of realization and wonder whispered to the dust lizard and the oasis itself, "I'm sorry."

Time is irrelevant in the Cham Desert. Days and years may be unaccounted for, but eventually a caravan of retreatants traveled to Gored'na's oasis. He welcomed the pilgrims carefully and joined their campfires in the evening. On the day of the caravan's departure he was offered a travel beast and a place in the caravan's circle; Gored'na declined to leave, but offered welcome to any retreatants who wanted to stay, or should another group of travelers and pilgrims come to his oasis, Gored'na offered hospitality. As he watched this first caravan of many disappear into the Cham's wavering haze, Gored'na realized how peaceful his heart had become.

Meanwhile, the pilgrims awoke after the second day of start-and-stop stormy rain and sunshine to discover a dripping, but clean, refreshed world around them. There was delight everywhere. Rain would come again, but not today.

Tiny desert toads dug themselves out of their holes and burped mating calls back and forth. Elfin insects with iridescent wings emerged from the dirt where they had pupated until awakened by water. They whirred through the oasis playfully while other insects fluttered about after their escape from hidden cocoons.

The pilgrims could almost see the fruit budding and growing on the branches of the trees. Cook scattered her helpers throughout the oasis so that the morning table was heavily laden with bright new fruits and edible flowers.

The morning workshop was obligatory for all the travelers. They walked to the edge of the cliff and looked out over the desert.

The Cham Desert was magnificent. Flowers of all colors already swept over the rough dirt so that it seemed as if a thick carpet of impossibly lovely colors flourished to the far horizons. With the storm clouds of this first spring rain rushing off to the east, the variegated hues and movement astonished all of the pilgrims and the attendants.

"Excuse me," inquired one of the young women.

"Yes," Rawiya answered with some distraction for she was fascinated with the beauty spread out before her that seemed to change moment by moment with the quickly passing shadows of clouds.

"That insect you spoke of in the story that carried the Searchers to Salimah…"

"Yes?" prompted Rawiya.

"How could that have happened? I mean, glass beetles are never that large."

"Ah! On Hidaya the glass beetles are usually small, and in most of the oases you will find them reasonably small. But the Cham Desert used to be the site of chemical experimentation in long ago times. Once in awhile you will find a mutation. Actually, every year we find several mutations, and —"

Ishwa, who had been listening interjected, "There," he pointed. "Look there." It was difficult to see anything unusual from the outlook.

The Cham blushed with vitalized life. Shadows came and went as the clouds streaked off in the sky alternately darkening and lightening the rainbow hued flora bursting moment by moment from the desert floor. Rawiya and the retreatant followed where Ishwa pointed. They all focused on one motion above the floral display. Then there were two active and erratic forms dancing above the Cham together. It was astounding.

Two globules of light hovered over the flora involved in some kind of courtship flight.

"Why did the scientists do that?" the young woman asked incredulously. "What good could they accomplish by manipulating nature like that?"

"I think they did it because they could," Ishwa responded. "It wasn't an issue of right or wrong morality, nor was it an issue of what danger or good would be the consequence. They did it because they could, and the giant glass beetle is now part of Hidayan life forms."

"But then it was not the will of the One," the woman concluded with a furrowed brow.

"Perhaps not," Ishwa thoughtfully commented. "But even if it was not done by the will of the One, good is created out of what is. For the story of our history, the truth is that a giant glass beetle was called forth by the presence of water no matter how minute an amount that was. And the good that was served by that creature's existence was to save the Searchers so they could be delivered to Salimah safely."

"Ah! So good can be created out of accidents and mistakes."

"Mmm," both Rawiya and Ishwa responded. It was both of their experiences that the harshest realities could eventually bring forth good with the presence of the One. Otherwise the hurt, abuse, anger, and pain were passed on to others. The One was the Compassionate, Healing One.

After lunch the oasis was explored in detail. Buds were quickly forming and fronds were sprouting. There would be other spring storms, but the first ones that brought life-giving rain eased the strain of the desert plants which had been living off of their own reserves for so long! They soaked in the water as if they were sponges, and the wet goodness awoke the first fruits that had been yearning to be born. The parent plants anticipated the rainy storm and nudged the buds into readiness to receive what was needed and necessary for their species to continue.

By mid-afternoon it was apparent that Gored'na was no longer with the caravan. Tangi, Ghanash'am, and Ne'igalomea stared at the brilliant desert floor silently at a distance from the pilgrims.

"Where d'ya t'ink he is?"

"Knowing him, he's trying ta git da money fer himself an' leavin' us outta it."

"Bastard! Dat's what he'd be doin'"

"Whatta we do now?" Tangi asked after a long pause.

"Whatta ya wanna do?"

"What's der ta do? If we kill 'em we may not git paid cuz Gored'na will take da credit! Whatta we do now?" echoed Ne'igalomea.

"Hold up!" Ghanash'am warned. Ishwa was approaching them.

"Let's talk," Ishwa simply said and led them to some large rocks on which they could sit.

"Whatta ya want?" snarled Ghanash'am.

"Your friend, Gored'na is no longer with us," Ishwa stated forthrightly. "You are new to the caravan and have become part of us. But now, as we near Cham township, you are facing hard decisions. Perhaps you know that."

The others stared down at the ground or sullenly stared at Ishwa for he seemed to have perceived their thoughts.

"You are invited to continue on with us to Cham where you can leave us or join us for the return trip to Viñay, or you can remain here and we will pick you up on our return trip. Or, then again you can go off on your own traveling separately from us. But," concluded Ishwa, "You are welcome to stay with us in whatever manner you choose."

There was heavy silence and anger.

"Why would ya let us stay wit' ya? Do ya know why we met up wit' ya?"

"I believe you were trying to catch up with us for some reason, but perhaps the reason you did so is no longer worth the effort. Whatever that reason is, you are welcome to join us."

"We heard ya carried da plague," Tangi burst out as an accusation.

"As you can see, we are all healthy. Had we carried the plague you would have already been exposed and be fevered and suffering from diarrhea by now which is the first symptom."

The three vigilantes looked at each other confirming their own health by checking with their comrades.

"Are any of you ill?" questioned Ishwa.

"Naw." Tangi answered while the other two shook their heads.

"Can we really stay here?" Ghanash'am asked in a monotone. Tangi and Ne'igalomea stared at him in confused surprise. "Cuz I wanna stay 'ere 'til ya come back. Der's somet'ing I wanna do 'ere."

"What's dat?" Ne'igalomea snorted. "Ya can pee anywhere! Ya don't need a bunch-a flowers fer dat!"

"Yeah!" Tangi added with a mocking tone. "Ya belong wit' us. If we leave yull be off by yerself 'til someone comes 'ere, an' we're not sure if dis guy will come back fer ya."

"I give you my word and promise that this caravan will return here. We will not forget you. I understand if the oases in the Cham call people's names because the One is the real one calling you and asks you to listen." Ishwa looked Ghanash'am in the eye for a long moment and then repeated, "We will return for you." Then Ishwa turned to Tangi and Ne'igalomea.

"What are your plans?"

Tangi and Ne'igalaomea were unsure of their plans, but they finally decided to stay with the caravan and return to Viñay with it. Then Ishwa formally welcomed them all and offered them long desert tunics to replace their long-worn leather clothing. The three accepted though planning to hold onto their own gear. As they all followed Ishwa to the supply tent, they quietly muttered between themselves.

"Why'd ya really choose ta stay 'ere?"

"I – I heard voices talkin' ta me 'ere. I wanna know why dey are talkin' ta me like dat. What about ya? Why're ya gonna travel wit' dese people? Why aren't ya gonna finish da job?"

"Gored'na will probably claim da bounty an' we'll get nottin'"

"Yeah. Dis is startin' ta look like too much work fer nottin'." And by then it was settled. The desert robes made the vigilantes officially part of the caravan. Truly, they could be lying and be still planning to kill the travelers, but Ishwa would make it as difficult as possible without making his efforts overly obvious.

Dinner was a sumptuous feast that did Cook proud now that there were uncountable gifts of food from the oasis. Her mumbled response to any compliment that night was, "Give me the right foods, and I can do anything."

The Twelfth Night:

Once again pilgrims surrounded the campfire. The enlarged cook tent tarp was still up in case an unexpected storm should arise. The rain had washed any dust particles from the air and the stars brilliantly glimmered and winked down at them. The three moons of Hidaya began their journey across the heavens, and there seemed to be peace everywhere. And so Rawiya began the telling without preamble.

The ten refugees relaxed against the outcrop or lay prone in the dirt, making a rough circle for conversation.   A quiet accepting attitude underlay all their words, and now they were in a frivolous mood.

"They will remember you, Ansh'mati, for your adept stealing! You may be a Lady, but how you can steal trays and trays of cookies from the kitchen without being caught by those sharp-eyed cooks is beyond me. 'Cookie Thief' should be the epitaph on your death marker."

"But those cookies were good, and I liked them! Don't pick on her for that!" Che'ikh laughed.

"Oho! You have a defender, Ansh'mati, so tell us what epitaph will be on *his* marker!"

"He will be called, "Skerl Cheeks" because he could stuff in more of those stolen cookies in one sitting than I could ever steal! Che'ikh, just your head full of cookies would weigh more than any one of our moons. You never lost a crumb!"

"Ah, it's a hidden talent!"

"It's a crummy talent! Ha! And not so hidden since we could all see where the cookies had gone, you greedy, fat-cheeked friend."

"Eh, now, wut 'bout me?"

"Oh, I'll tell you that!"

"Not ya! Ya don' like me!"

"Actually I do. We will write, "Master Chicken Chef" on your stone because you are the only one I know who can come up with a million ways to cook chicken."

"And a million words to describe those million ways. How about calling him something like, "Chattering Chicken Child?""

"Ooh! I'll git even wit' ya fer dat. "Ya can be called, "She Who Deafens Donkeys!" Ya used ta grumble so much da donkeys stopp't lis'nen ta ya."

"I'm glad that I've changed that much that you said, 'ya used ta.' I... I hope I *have* changed a bit," Emina sniffled.

"I'd call her 'Silent Runner.' Do you remember the night you got out of the boat and ran up the beach to hide near my house? My grandson and I were laughing so hard because if that was your sneaking up walk, people could have heard you on the other side of Hidaya. Ach! You made so much noise on all that gravel. Ah ha, ha!" Old T'moyo's wrinkled eyes twinkled with mischief.

"On your behalf, Emina," D'nkrad interposed, "I would name my mother, 'Troublemaker' because she never has been a typical mother or grandmother. 'Always doing something unexpected and different, and you are always causing me trouble! And to honor your age, I'd add 'Old Troublemaker' to that since most of the world knows you as Old T'moyo."

T'moyo nodded nobly to all the others, but looked sternly at D'nkrad. "You forget that I am your mother and have all sorts of stories I could share about you that wouldn't do your reputation any good anywhere. I could call you, 'Milk Breath,' or 'Slouching Sovereign,' in deference to your status as Commander, but that might be embarrassing. I should stick to something simple, like – hmmm...."

"I can't think of anything funny to call you," Angharad said looking warmly at Z'van. "When I woke up you were calling my name, the one I have now. You listened to me even though I could barely speak and was so afraid I couldn't move. You gave me a home, a place to belong with friends to trust. I was never shamed for what I shared with you;

for the first time I could trust someone and know you were worthy of that trust, and that I was worth listening to."

"You gifted me with your trust," Z'van responded. "But I will call you something."

"Another name!" Angharad laughed. "This one is good enough for me."

"But tonight we all should be called something else," Lord Z'van teased with his head cocked thoughtfully to one side. "You should be called, 'Big-Eared Mouse,' for we found you at the door listening, and since then you've listened and actually heard everything and grown from your heart."

"Hmmm... 'Big Ears,' Kamalei giggled. "I've got it! We will call you, Angharad, 'Bat Child,' and you, Lord Z'van, you won't get off without a name if *we* are to be stuck with one. You can be called, 'Laughing Water,' because your words brought life to our Bat, here."

"Ya sure dat ya don' wanna call him 'Mud Hole' fer da same reason?" smirked Dato. "An' don' t'ink we f'got 'bout yer namin', C'mmander."

"We shall call my son, 'Hairy Travel Beast," because he is a good companion wherever we go."

"Hairy?" exclaimed D'nkrad in mock distress.

"Then Kamalei should be called, 'Lizard Friend,' because she is always nearby, and a small desert companion for us."

"I'm not that small, Bat Child!" Kamalei protested laughing with the rest. "But what about A'khil? We haven't named him yet."

"That's true," affirmed T'moyo, the Old Troublemaker, with an expression that fit her naming. "While we traveled to Salimah you were usually at the back of the group. Let's call you the "Wagging Tail."

"Well, that's better than what you could be naming me. Let's see now – let's see who's here." And they shouted out their names gleeful with delight at their renaming:

"I am Wagging Tale – A'khil!"

"I can't decide, so I'll be Laughing Mud Hole Water Z'van!"

"I'll be myself, Old Troublemaker – T'moyo."

"Ah – this renaming is unfair, but I am Cookie Thief Ansh'mati.

"And I," putting her fingers behind her ears to wiggle them, "am Bat Child Angharad."

"Skerl Cheeks Che'ikh, here."

"Lizard Friend Kamalei."

"I like da sound'a Chattering Chicken Child Dato more t'en Chicken Chef."

"Hairy Travel Beast D'nkrad is my choice over anything the Old Troublemaker over there chooses."

"And I'm changing mine slightly to She Who Deafened Donkeys Emina because I don't do that anymore."

"And so we are renamed."

"We are renamed."

"But," hesitantly added Angharad, "Each name ends the same? We are still Beloved?"

"If even us Searchers went back to our first renaming, what caused us to become Searchers to rename and remind others of who they were from the beginning, beloved, than you are right. We are all Beloved," Lord Z'van explained.

"Look up," Lady Ansh'mati quietly interposed.

Above them and about them was a mist that reminded them of the chill surrounding them. Far above them were fluffs of gray clouds edged in white by the reflected light of the three sister moons. The gauzy clouds floated freely towards the Bahairava Mountains where they would line up like ragged lace trying to pass beyond and continue their voyages across the skies. Only when the Cham Desert was blanketed with heavy clouds that burst into an everlasting downpour, only then would the Bahairava Mountains allow any remaining clouds lightened enough by their release to travel beyond their spiked peaks to the rainshadow desert lands beyond. When the daystar, Bozidara, shone on the Cham after the cloudbursts ended, the Cham would no longer be a desert, but a jeweled garden of multicolored delights as once-a-year flowers bloomed brilliantly.

Lord Z'van solemnly interrupted their thoughts. "It is time for the blessing."

The outcrop rose up before the swarming rebels crawling on hands and knees like deformed animals; it blocked their view across the desert to the pinpricks of light gathering right in front of them, and already cutting them off from retreat. Had one of them even raised his head he would have been able to alert his companions, though it was too late now to effectively change the outcome.

They stealthily paused, and then edged closer to the mound. How strange that mound appeared now that they were so close to it; it reared up shallowly, shadowed and still under a mostly star-mantled night. Stars and moons softly illuminated a gently rising vapor that wafted over the desert, hovering formlessly before them in the chilled night air. Lonely puffs of clouds sailed above through the darkness having broken away from a larger foaming mass of clouds billowing beyond and over the western horizon. The spring rains were due.

The rebel scouts tensely peered through the rising mist impatiently seeking any telltale movement or sound. Those behind them finally gave in to their impatience. One by one many of the rebels stood from their crouching and squatting positions to get a better look. One individual after another stood and stared about them mute and aghast.

From the north and west the Hidayan guards had run swiftly. They had sped around and through the Cham's bushes and dried grasses, and over the uneven ground lit by their torches. When the garrison saw the standing rebels they mistook the actions of the insurrectionists to be capitulation and submission.

The advance garrison guards boldly skirted the mound, while their strategically surrounding comrades pulled their encircling trap tight. A few of the rebels spasmodically, violently twitched as if thinking to use their weapons in a panic-driven frenzy of blood; but realizing their true situation they did neither attack nor defend themselves. Instead they stepped forward tentatively to witness clearly what their wavering torches revealed. They stood mesmerized by the scene playing out before them, committing it to memory for it was something they would remember and retell for the remainder of their lives.

Ten bent and shivering figures huddled closely together in the lee of the mound. One was clearly a child, but the others were bare-youths and elders. The Hidayan guards uneasily murmured among themselves when they recognized D'nkrad. Shimmering light pulsed around the silhouetted figures. Each had one hand flat upon the desert floor and the other hand rested upon the shoulder of the person next to them.

They knelt on one knee, and looked as if they were blessing both the ground and each other. Certainly they were in prayer.

The forward rebels twitched in desire to bloody these very refugees knowing that it was useless. They stood tense and nervously stiff so that the Hidayan guards could not discern what they would do next.

But nothing happened for long silent moments. The rebels watched the guards and the ten bent forms while the guards watch the rebels and the refugees. And then as if a play had ended the ten Hidayans raised their heads and shook themselves smiling at each other. Their prayer was ended and they were still alive! With their lives and anticipated deaths they had blessed Hidaya and all that lived on her.

They hadn't even looked beyond themselves, however, to see their audiences when they started to slump forward. The guards rushed forward to give assistance, but it came to late. The ten lay like a litter of puppies upon each other in endless sleep.

They could have awakened from their blessing reverie and walked out of the Cham Desert with the others. They could have been massacred despite the presence of the Hidayan guards. They could have been enveloped in the pulsing light that gently faded before their gaze, but instead they fell asleep exhausted and at peace. The Cham Desert, and Hidaya itself gently absorbed their life energies and compassionate blessings.

Later, the Hidayan garrison supervised the rebels who dug graves and laid the ten there side by side. They named the place Allambee – a quiet resting place – and left. However, they could never find Allambee again. Caravans traveled east and west and back again. South and north and back again, and still Allambee wasn't located as if the desert itself had trundled them within itself hidden through the ages until it decided to reveal its secrets.

At first the caravans contained pilgrims trying to find proof or relics of the ten who blessed Hidaya; but then the exotic blessings actually began and the caravans became retreat journeys. Counselors, guides and storytellers joined them, and the retreatants didn't end their retreat upon arriving in Cham or Viñay. Their retreats of blessing were just beginnings.

And so we are here, now. Tomorrow we will start at dawn and arrive our last oasis and then Cham before the following evening. As with every evening remember, take no food into your tents, and light the smudge candles at your tent entrance. The teacher will ask now for blessings of peace and protection as you sleep. We leave early tomorrow morning."

"But, Storyteller! Is this all?"

"Shouldn't it be more?"

Ishwa's hands, already raised for blessing, lowered to face the incredulous eyes of those around him in the fire circle.

"What would you have us do? It is time now for you to continue the blessings you have recognized here as a pilgrim, and to bless Hidaya with your presence as best you can."

"But shouldn't we stay here longer to watch the Cham blossom more than just what we have seen? Shouldn't we be able to stay here longer?"

"It will never be more lovely than what you have already seen," explained Rawiya. "Your hearts are at peace after this journey, and the beauty within you is ready to be shared. You are the blessings of the ten. The beauty you see around you is in yourselves."

"You are the blessings," repeated Ishwa. "You always were." There were some unbelieving murmurings at this announcement.

"But tomorrow at the other oasis will be our last night together, Storyteller. If you end your story tonight what will you tell tomorrow?"

"Tomorrow you will tell your own stories around the campfire." And then for one more time on this journey Ishwa raised his hands in blessing, and made his request of the unnamed holy ones and the Compassionate One for blessing on those around him. The gathering also raised their hands in blessing, saw the spirit-sparks condense above them and then fall gracefully into the dimming firelight.

One by one the retreatants silently left the campfire. The drowsy birds above, the large-eared mice scurrying out of deserted tents, and the motionless dust lizards listening at the edge of the campfire noted their departure.

Tonight's ending was difficult to accept, and from the camp fire the pilgrims gradually, reluctantly moved away for one last long lingering look at the beauty around them shimmering in the moonlight of the three sisters.

Rawiya and Ishwa were left standing with Tangi, Ghanash'am, and Ne'igalomea who defiantly hesitated to return to their tents.

"Did ya mean watcha said? It's over?" Ghanash'am asked gruffly.

"Yes," answered Rawiya. "Our journey is almost complete."

"But —" began Tangi.

"You haven't been paid your fee by your masters this time," commented Ishwa with a knowing nod at each of the vigilantes. "But still, you have been blessed with other opportunities and many different choices than those you have made in the past. There will be other Hidayans available to help you make those choices and changes."

"Those who traveled with us as pilgrims have recognized that they are blessings to themselves and others," Rawiya added. "When you allow yourself to think about different possibilities changes happen." Rawiya looked at the travelers ranged around the desert beyond the campfire and commented, "It's difficult to change what you believe about yourself and others if there are negatives involved. But if there is just one possibility of seeing good in the lives of oneself and others then there are blessings of compassion and hope."

Tangi, Ghanash'am, and Ne'igalomea postured angrily in silence.

Finally Tangi barked out, "Even us? Ya know who we are an' why we're 'ere. How can what ya say be even close ta truth?" asked Tangi gesturing to himself and his two comrades.

"You have been hidden blessings that is true," answered Ishwa drolly. "While you were with us, however, you allowed the Cham to surround you and communicate with your souls. The Presence of the One will now be able to guide you." Noting their shaking heads of disbelief and life-long learned rebellion Ishwa continued, "Yes, you also are blessings. You just didn't know it, and didn't believe it. Perhaps now...."

"I don' believe dat," snorted Ne'igalomea defiantly.

"But if dat was possible -" began Ghanash'am haltingly.

"Let's begin this way," answered Rawiya. She and Ishwa raised their hands to alternatively hover over Tangi, Ne'igalomea, and Ghanash'am's heads. Moving their hands in unison in the air above them Ishwa and Rawiya encircled the air with the Blessing of Mercy. The sign pulsed softly with light and remained intact while the second blessing — the one of Belonging and Acceptance — was begun. Those signs glowed gently and persistently above them all.

"There remains only one more gifting for you," explained Ishwa. "You have the choice to accept or reject a new name. The changing won't be easy, but it will be possible." *Ishwa then whispered quietly into each person's ear his new name. The former vigilantes looked sheepishly at each other and with some confusion.*

"Why did I hafta git a new name?" questioned Ghanash'am.

"Your new names each mean, 'Beloved,'" responded Rawiya. "You can now perceive yourself beloved, welcomed, and in the arms of the Merciful One, for that is what you are, and always were."

"Don' tell anybody yet," muttered Tangi. "It don' sound strong ta be called dat." And they all wandered off with their own thoughts.

Bozidara glided over the western horizon the following morning gilding the piled clouds in the west as well as those billows hiding the Bahairava Mountains in their thick mists with golden brilliance before they spilled over the Cham with more storms. The air was clean, sweet, and moving with a freshening light breeze that would grow stronger as the storms neared.

Rawiya awoke hearing persistent twittering near her ear, and opened her eyes to face several dust lizards and an iridescent mock scorpion. They seemed impatient as they stomped their fragile feet on her pillow or plucked at the cloth with their pincers.

"I guess you want me up," sighed Rawiya. There was one last twittering and gurgled exchange and the dust lizards scuttled away. However, the haughty mock scorpion stared at Rawiya and remained while she dressed. Since it was the last day of travel to another oasis Rawiya had thought to wear one of her dustiest desert robes, but the mock scorpion kept plucking at another, less soiled robe. When she carelessly tried to tie up her dark hair into a shapeless, but out-of-the-way bun, the mock scorpion wickedly snapped the hair band with its sharp pincers so she would have to be more attentive of her appearance the second try.

Finally, grumpy with extra efforts, Rawiya rushed off to the cook tent for a cup of hot tea. Already many of the attendants were up and readying the travel beasts for departure. Retreatants relaxedly emerged from their tents to slowly dress, eat, and enjoy their morning without hurrying.

Not wishing conversation with anyone no matter how pleasant Rawiya wandered off into the oasis by herself. Everyone seemed preoccupied with their own preparations so she was not missed. She idly kicked at rocks or clumps of dirt in frustration.

Almost ready to violently shove a frond out of her way Rawiya was suddenly stopped by a desert bird sitting on that frond stem at eye level. Rawiya and the birdlet just stared at each other for long moments.

"I greet you, Protector," Rawiya reluctantly conceded.

"I greet you also, Storyteller. You found no answer to your difficulties on this journey," the brown bird stated flatly.

"Not really," affirmed Rawiya. "I found no peace. I still will have to make a hard decision."

"No. Your loved one was ready to meet you at Cham, but instead will meet you at the last oasis today," informed the bird. "He has discovered that living with you as you are is better than not having you at all.

"He made his own choice, Storyteller. I only tell you now so you will not suffer unnecessarily throughout this final day. I will see you again in this desert again, though we will meet differently than we do now. But we will surely meet again. Perhaps the next time you will have a soul-companion with you to draw into communion."

"He is there in Cham now?" Rawiya asked breathlessly.

"He will be at the city gates now depart for the same oasis you travel to today. He will be there to greet you when you arrive. Perhaps it will be easier to accept taking extra time to look so pretty this morning."

Rawiya grunted sarcastically remembering the mock scorpion's insistence that she start taking care with her dressing. That exchange revealed that others knew she was awaited by someone significant later in the day. The birdlet turned his head to one side so its eye could see her clearly, shook itself, and then flitted into the leafy canopy.

"Well," breathed Rawiya with relief and pleasure, aware now that she had been holding her breath. "Maybe I can find one or two treats for Cid. He did well this trip and deserves them."

Names and Meanings

Achan – Harsh, besmirched; a city

A'kil – Wise one who lives; a guide

Amunet – Hidden one; a city

Adamya – Formidable; a city

Allambee – A quiet resting place; desert locale where heroes died after blessing Hidaya

Angharad – Beloved; a refugee

Anwyl – Beloved; a refugee

Aroha – Love, mercy; one of the three Hidayan sister moons

Bahairava – Fear inspiring; a mountain range

Bozidara – Divine gift; a star around which Hidaya orbits

Cham – Warm hot; a city and a desert

Chi'ma – Gift from God; the universal language of Hidaya

Dato – Beloved; formerly *Bankim,* crooked half one; a refugee

Dhakiya – Smart; an egg seller

Emina – Beloved; formerly *Baya*, ugly looking; formerly *Bahia*, lovely, happy one; a refugee

Gamba – Water tortous; the husband of Emina

Ghanash'am – Dark as a cloud; a vigilante

Gored'na – Storm cloud; a vigilante

Hidaya – Gift; a planet orbiting the star Bozidara

Ishwa – Spiritual teacher; the retreat guide leader

Jabez – Sorrowful pain; a vigilante

Janapriya – Beloved; a young officer under Lord D'nkrad

Kamalei – Beloved; a refugee

Lady Ae'sha – She who lives; a Searcher and counselor

Lady Ansh'mati – Wise; glorious; a Searcher and counselor

Lord C'dmon – Wise warrior; a Searcher and counselor

Lord D'nkrad – Wise counselor; the commandant of the Hidayan guards at Salimah; a Searcher

Lord H'shmand – Wise one; a Searcher and counselor

Lord K'van – Hidden by God; a Searcher and counselor

Lord Z'van – Filled with wisdom; a Searcher and guardian counselor

Maemi – Ten thousand blessings; one of the three Hidayan sister moons

Nebjosa – Fearless; a city

Ne'igalomea – Unforgettable pain; a vigilante

Pandit – Scholar; a regional dialect

Rawiya – Storyteller; the retreat guide

Rudra – Remover of pain; a city

Salimah – Whole, to be safe; a refuge city

Satya – Truth; one of the three Hidayan sister moons

Sudasi – Good servant; indentured servants

Tangi – Crying with great sadness; a vigilante

Tevita – Beloved; a refugee

T'moyo – Wise person; retired Searcher, guide and counselor; the mother of Lord D'nkrad

Viñay – Leading, guidance, modesty, humility; a city

Acknowledgments

I want to thank Tim Fitch from AuthorHouse for his constant prodding, check-ins, and design direction. I also want to thank Lester Diaz for patiently guiding me through the technology; and thanks to Hilary Kanyi who kept asking me to think beyond skimpy expectations, as well as allowing me to rattle on when she called with enthusiastic plans and options for me to consider.

My sister, Carol Ann Nellen, who proofed <u>Desert Refuge</u> with me, critiqued without mercy, and made important suggestions deserves great thanks. She, my husband, John, my daughter, Mary, and my mother, Veronica Nellen, read and constantly encouraged me, including urging me to get the darn thing done whenever I slacked off.

I want to thank the St. James parish community in Davis, California for their prayers, personal encouragement, and supportive ministries when my family's health was seriously challenged before and during the time that <u>Desert Refuge</u> was being written. I truly believe that those constant prayers were (and are being) answered, and know that the warm, caring presence of this community has kept all of my family going despite seemingly overwhelming challenges.

And finally, I want to acknowledge and thank the doctors and nurses at Woodland Healthcare and Memorial Hospital, Mercy Hospitals, and Sierra Hematology & Oncology who have kept me as healthy as possible these past few years. Especial thanks to Dr. Mark Ewens, Dr. Seth Robinson, Dr. John Kailath, Terry Passmora, R.N. and Marla Master, R.N. They have managed quite a few compassionate miracles for the Murphy family. Without them this book would not have been completed.

There are more good people around us than we will ever be aware of. I have been blessed to know so many of them, and doubly blessed to be able to know some as friends; for that I am deeply grateful.